In Plain Sight...

The Committee

By

L. R. Staples

In Plain Sight . . . The Committee

Cover Art Designed by David Craycroft

Staples, L.R.
    337p. 0ill. cm.
    In Plain Sight . . . The Committee
    ISBN: 978-0-578-12001-0

Printed in the United States of America by Clearview
Press Inc.

Dedication Page

This book is dedicated to my first and forever love, Pat. Oh, to have met her a million years ago.

Also to my three daughters, Shell, Kim, Jen—wonderful people all.

Finally, I also dedicate this work to my inspiration of more than 50 years, my teacher, Madeline Marcum, who once told me, 'One day, you'll write the Great American Novel.' I think of those words often as I sometimes sit, staring at a blank screen, waiting for the next page to spring forth from my fingers.

Thank you, Mrs. Marcum.

Cast of Characters

Throughout the book Arthur M. Jacobson, Executive Director of 'The Committee', refers to Presidents by coded names, or nicknames. We have listed them here for your convenience, with rationale for each of said names.

Franklin Delano Roosevelt . . . . The Chair
Mr. Roosevelt contracted polio and was left with an infirmity that was kept from the public as much as possible—privately confined to a wheelchair, hence,' The Chair'.

Harry S. Truman . . . . The Hat
Mr. Truman, partner of a Haberdashery Shop, which sold men's ware, hence 'The Hat.'

Dwight D. Eisenhower . . . . The Eagle
Mr. Eisenhower, commander of the Allied Forces during D Day and a four star General during WWII, hence his nickname, 'The Eagle'.

John Fitzgerald Kennedy . . . . The Kid
Mr. Kennedy was the youngest president ever elected, hence his name, 'The Kid'.

Lyndon Baines Johnson . . . . The Texan
Mr. Johnson, it is well known, hailed from Texas, hence his name, 'The Texan'.

Ronald Wilson Reagan . . . . The Actor
Mr. Reagan, an actor of some renown for many years, hence his moniker, 'The Actor'.

William Jefferson Clinton . . . . The Redneck
Mr. Clinton hailed from Arkansas—which is no reason to give him an insulting moniker, yet, Mr. Jacobson did just that in dubbing him, 'The Redneck'.

The rest of the characters in the book are easily placed, so no explanation is necessary.

The currents of time . . .

flow endlessly into the future, creating a series of events defined by humans as history. In the short term this information is written by those who remain transiently in power—so the accuracy of these interpretations can be at odds with the accepted reality of history.

As time goes by, historians will write about the dark and sometimes-treacherous activities, which have taken place over the past century. Versions of these happenings will be retold until the accounts yield a glimpse, which is plausible as well as interesting enough to be accepted as reality. Sooner or later the unvarnished truths of the actions of world leaders and governments throughout the twentieth century will come into focus. Various versions of the past, with its heroes and its demons will then emerge, and depending on the writer's perspective and understanding of what occurred, will come into view as the truth.

The irony of the search for this ever-changing absolute truth is, very few will ever be privy to reality—and those who are may not understand.

Prologue

Boston, Massachusetts - May 1915

The little boy sat at the top of the stairs listening to the chaos. Though he was just shy of four years old he could understand the loud and disjointed debate. They met like this often, smoking their cigars and drinking from the beautiful crystal glasses. He enjoyed the excitement.

Just as the huge grandfather clock in the elegant foyer declared the half hour, the loudest man proclaimed, "This means war, Prescott! By almighty God, if he doesn't take those scoundrels to task for this, they'll have his head. Those Hun bastards may have killed hundreds of Americans." The man wheezed and coughed his exasperation. The other men articulately grunted their agreement.

The boy understood and heard his father quiet the man and take control.

"All in good time, John. I know Woodrow, he won't stand for this." As usual, he was the most composed and rational man of the group—and they all listened when he spoke.

The boy knew even though it was late, his father would indulge him. He walked down the stairs and into the room. One by one, the men grew quiet.

His father looked stern, but it seemed to the boy a bluff. "Do you know what time it is, young man?"

The boy looked back and studied the grand clock, causing the men to laugh.

"Yes, father, its 12:32 a.m."

The men stopped laughing and looked to the father, who shook his head and smiled down at the little boy.

"Arthur, you are truly *my* son." Prescott Jacobson smiled.

1

The nature of his work required meticulous planning, moreover, many late nights. Day jobs were generally dangerous and could end up badly. He was not well known to the police, the F.B.I. or Interpol, because he was simply too good. His carefully chosen targets always ended up dead, while he personally, simply did not exist. One fundamental element in his planning was no two kills ever appeared to be similar. He used great imagination in his preparation. Through the years he had employed car accidents, drug overdoses and heart attacks, as well as a host of untraceable bacterial or viral infections. There are, he mused, many ways to die after all.

A former Navy Seal, Eric Suskind worked out three or four hours a day, always careful to avoid bulking his body. He was determined to look average and his conditioning was perfect.

At six foot one, one hundred eighty five pounds, he was fairly nondescript, allowing him to add bulk with his 'heavy suit,' or shed five pounds while wearing elevator shoes in order to allow him to appear rail thin. His face offered no distinguishing features except for a previously broken nose. Those women who glanced his way found his looks ruggedly attractive.

Eric was always available for communication and seldom refused an assignment. He had the uncanny ability to blend into any surroundings. While in Chicago he would wear tailored blue pin stripe suits—in San Francisco, black leather. Someone once described intelligence to Eric as, "the ability to adapt to one's environment." His adaptability was a testament to his brilliance.

Women tried in vain to interest Eric, but they held little fascination for him. He was extraordinarily careful and selective in relationships, especially women. When he sought female companionship for sexual purposes, he would use discreet services, careful to use a plausible cover story and wear a wedding band. This discouraged women who might become interested in him. In the end women found him cold and calculating. It was he realized, for the better.

The *assassin* seldom used guns unless the client or special circumstance called for it. Although he was an accomplished marksman, his physical skills were such that he could kill silently with his hands. He felt that only amateurs and thugs used guns. The art of the kill was his master, the science of the kill, his enjoyment.

His passion for detail was obsessive. He researched his clients conscientiously. Moreover, he never questioned the rationale for the job. He had no particular political allegiance or ideology. This was simply a business, and quite lucrative.

Eric's clients used a simple method to initiate a "job." The coded message reached him through a scrambled telephone line. Assignments were called "financial opportunities." All monies involved in the transactions were referred to as stocks and options. Eric's response was always succinct, essential in the event a message was intercepted: *Yes, I would like to exercise my option. Please enter my request immediately. I will forward $3,000,000 by wire transfer with the remaining balance to be paid within one week.*

The carefully coded message yielded two pieces of information. The fee for services rendered would be six million dollars, and the reference to a week signaled his estimate for the completion of the job. The dollar amount reflected Eric's assessment of the relative risk of the job.

A friendly Caribbean banker held eight of his accounts. Eric owned certificates of deposit, as well as accounts that paid simple interest. Usually, he converted the payments into stock shares within thirty days. He always invested in Blue Chips, in the exact amount he was paid for services rendered.

Over the years, Eric had found it necessary to change bankers only once. His contact in Zurich had died in a house fire, coincidentally just three days after the contact. The man had, unfortunately for him, come face to face with Eric as he was placing stock certificates in his safety deposit box. The death was never questioned nor investigated. Eric was the best.

One simple fact helped Eric remain anonymous: the worst eyewitness in the world is a human being. No one who met and recognized him ever lived to tell about it—no one until now—Arthur M. Jacobson. Over the past several years, they had done business together, but neither man knew the other. Many times the client, Arthur Jacobson had never before been the victim—until tonight.

A typically pretentious cocktail party at the Senator's house had been perfectly suited to Eric's purpose—a house filled with hired help, handsome waiters and waitresses, a full staff of strangers delivering food and beverage to the hungry and thirsty. Eric's plan perfectly suited his victim.

The assassin would administer a lethal dose in a glass of champagne, then wait and watch. The fast acting drug would cause nausea and abdominal distress. This particular plan called for the old man to excuse himself, go home and quietly have a stroke.

Those who witnessed the event would talk about how Arthur had left early, complaining of everything from a severe headache to chest pains. In Arthur's case, most epitaphs would begin with, "Well, at his age . . ."

Arthur's life was saved by an oddity. That is, at least an oddity in Washington D. C. He did not drink. To be social he would simply place a glass to his lips and pretend. No one had ever noticed.

The drug Eric had chosen was extraordinarily potent, just one sip and the job would be done. However, with Arthur there was barely a sip. Even so, he felt immediate distress, stomach cramps, nausea accompanied by an alarmingly high pulse.

Cocktail parties made for perfect cover. Groups of two guests formed three or four, then six. A group of six people was conversationally unmanageable, so the first two or three, having heard all there was to hear would wander off in search of fresh blood and gossip. No one noticed as Arthur backed away from the Senator's rambling discourse.

Tonight, Eric was dressed as a waiter. He carefully avoided eye contact with everyone, even though tonight he had chosen blue contact lenses to match his blonde hairpiece. He also adopted a lisp and a slight southern drawl. The mission was almost ended, when for the briefest of moments he lost sight of his prey in the mass of bodies.

Random luck had placed Arthur only a few feet

from the foyer. As he felt the drug course through his body, he immediately understood what was happening to him, and went into an instinctive survival mode. Once in the front hallway, he hit the door hard, almost falling headlong onto the front porch, still unnoticed. His security was nowhere in sight.

Arthur righted himself, struggling to maintain his consciousness. His pulse raced, beads of perspiration rolled down his face, dripping silently onto his custom tailored coat. His labored breathing came in short anxious gasps.

Eric lost his target only briefly. He sized up the situation, knew Arthur's only escape was the foyer, so he flew out the back doors and through the kitchen.

He questioned the speed of Arthur's reaction to the drug, and as usual his instincts were right. Arthur's advanced age, when coupled with his *yet undiagnosed diabetic condition*, conspired to rush the events into a spectacle on the Senator's front porch. Arthur was moments from extremis, and only the superhuman effort of a man such as *he* could delay the effects.

Eric swore silently to himself. He had calculated the dosage with precision and he knew he couldn't have been *so* far off.

Moments from a blackout, Arthur grasped the railing and clung to it fiercely.

As the night lost its color, he felt someone gently lift and support him from behind. Although barely conscious, he could hear the man's voice.

"Are you all right, sir?" the man drawled. "Are you all right? You look kinda woozy."

Eric carefully gripped the old man's wrist in order to calculate his pulse. *My god*, he thought, *it's already 180 plus*. At this accelerated rate, Arthur would be dead in minutes, right here on the Senator's front porch.

Eric's mind raced. The Westin was only two blocks away, and offered a secluded entrance on the north side. Arthur turned to face the man who was helping him and looked squarely into his eyes.

His last thought was *contact lenses*.

2

Present Day
Washington, D.C. George Washington Medical Center
Room 671
4:23 a.m.

As the old man regained consciousness, his thoughts were twilight slow, gray and unimaginative. He tried to move his right hand, but nothing happened. Intrigued, he moved his left hand over to his right, and tapped it. It felt numb. The hand, maybe the whole arm, he realized, was deadened. To him, it felt like clay, and even seemed cold to the touch. He vaguely thought this to be much the same sensation as Novocain. He laid back and tried to focus on his surroundings.

The smells in the room were of alcohol and disinfectant. The sheets, he realized, were much too rough for him to be those of his own bed at home. He could hear muffled, busy noises just outside the doorway. With jumbled, unsure thoughts, he began to realize he was in a sterile hospital environment.

The oxygen tubes that snaked into his prominent nose restricted his breathing. The background sounds offered intermittent beeps and chirps of monitors.

Within this confusion, he thought, "I'm alone," realizing this would not do. Someone should always be with him. Otherwise he might say things, which should not be said. He wondered if he had been delirious. He wondered if he had spoken while in such a state. Then fear, an emotion almost unknown to him crept in to his consciousness. A slight frown creased his leathery forehead.

So this . . . is how everyone else feels . . .

3

White House 4:48a.m.

The Secret Service agent moved with care in the silence of the Presidential suite. He was the only agent on the White House staff allowed inside the sleeping quarters of the First Lady and her husband.

The President was a poor sleeper who prized his infrequent rest. The staff, under strict orders, kept the bedroom blacked out. The darkness helped.

The agent was wary; not wishing to awaken his boss, but was following orders to do so.

As was the protocol for such an event, he stood at the foot of the large antique poster bed on the President's side. His hands rested on the beautiful carved wood.

"Mr. President." The agent spoke in a hushed voice.

The Chief Executive stirred and put his finger to his lips to silence the agent. The intruder picked up the heavy Terri cloth robe that hung over an ornate rocker located beside the bed. As the President stood the agent slipped it over his right arm, his back, and onto his shoulders. They walked to the adjoining sitting room closing the door with care as they left.

At the corner of the room sat the President's continual shadow, Lt. Colonel Martin L. Cherkon, one of the many black bagmen who carried nuclear launch codes. The case, handcuffed to the soldier, sat by his chair with quiet menace, a failsafe for the seemingly innocuous cards that a select few carried.

"Good morning, Chick," the president offered. As the president entered the room, the man picked up the bag, and stood at attention.

"No, no relax, Chick. Unless there's something I don't know, it's a little early . . ." but he stopped in mid-sentence, noticing with surprise that his breakfast was already in place. A large carafe of coffee freshly squeezed orange juice and Belgian Waffles. The tray was adorned with a beautiful assortment of fresh fruit, and garnished with four freshly cut gardenias, the First Couple's favorite.

He looked back at Chick, then to the agent. The President's face was puffy, but he looked well for a man working on less than four hours sleep.

"What is it Trey? What gets us up two hours early?"

"Sorry to wake you Sir . . ." he began, but the President simply waived him off.

"Sir, Mr. Jacobson is missing."

It was a simple statement but the implications of it would change the face of the most powerful government on the planet over the next twenty-four hours.

White House Oval Office 5:39 a.m.

The President stood with his back to the hand- picked men who headed up the most prestigious of his appointments—certainly the most strategic and clandestine. He was unmoving and staring into the pre-dawn darkness at the Rose Garden. As his breath fogged the cold glass, he looked at the reflection of his two visitors—truly two of the top minds in Washington for several decades—now the Directors of the CIA and FBI. He was frustrated to realize, despite their vast talents, they were of little use at this moment

"Any thoughts on where Jacobson is?" he asked, not bothering to turn.

Before speaking, the FBI Director glanced at his colleague with a rueful expression.

"We've got nothing yet, Mr. President—not a clue but he's got to surface soon." The President noted the tension in the man's voice.

"If he's still alive, or not in someone's custody. You may have forgotten to add this," he was sarcastic, but in control.

The President then exhaled, leaving the men to sit and stare.

The CIA Director rallied to his comrade. "Mr. President, this is vintage Arthur—a *Grey Ghost*. He'll show up—always does. Besides, this is domestic, and I'm not sure . . ."

The president interrupted. "We don't know what it is, yet."

The President turned and walked to his high back, red leather chair, and stood, hands on its back without speaking. The men watched as he reached for his coffee, his fourth of the day. His hand trembled; they noticed.

He pulled the chair forward and sat on the crisp leather. The chair exhaled loudly. To them it sounded very much like a presidential sigh.

The tan, well-dressed former governor leaned forward and placed his hands on his knees. He glared at his men, speaking to them in a calm clear voice. "We have a very old man—what, eighty, ninety; I guess he simply walked away, was abducted, whatever . . . while enjoying some pretty tight security; it was only a cocktail party after all. Arthur's people were there, yes?" he questioned. His naturally ruddy complexion darkened. No one moved.

"What about them? One at the front door, one at the back—what, nobody saw anything?"

Both men shook their heads, almost in unison.

"We questioned them—one minute he was in a crowd near the front door—the next, gone."

"He's been in Washington for, since the '30's, and in all that time, and correct me if I'm wrong on this, we've never, uh, *misplaced* him before."

"Mr. President, you know he's reclusive. He can become a ghost and then reappear." The words were true, but they fell flat. A pregnant pause permeated the room.

Both men shuffled in their chairs, inching for a position that would be more comfortable. Though the President had been their friend for years, they were still cowed in his presence in this particular venue—abiding by strict protocol—always addressing him as Mr. President while inside the Oval Office.

"That's true," he said nervously tapping his teeth with his fingernails. "I know . . . but he's never gone missing for what, almost six hours now." The President's angst was obvious but he seemed able to gather his emotion. "Both of you get your people together on this." He glanced at his C. I. A. Director. "Domestic or otherwise, we've got to find him and pretty damn quick. I need a report on Arthur's movements, calls, contacts—everything over the past twenty four hours."

"It's gonna be tough, Mr. President. He doesn't keep daily records anyone knows about, and his aid is like a damn sphinx—no doubt on Arthur's orders," said the FBI Director.

"The phone logs may help a bit," the president chided.

Standing, he looked warily at them and folded his arms across his chest. He turned his back to them, his typical dismissal—while again looking out the Oval Office window. His mind was drifting away to dark thoughts of Arthur.

"Jesus Christ on a pony . . . if the old bastard's not alone, I hope to fuck he's dead . . ."

4

George Washington Medical Center Room 671
6:50 a.m.

The old man stared at his feet beneath the sheets. He had just started to pull out of the deepest recesses of his murky thoughts. His head ached and the cold grip of numbness had stilled the right side of his frail old body.

Aware of the abundance of medical equipment, he realized his every bodily function was being monitored. As he reached up his hand found a large head wrap.

My God, he thought, *did I have some kind of surgery? Did they operate on me? No, why would they?* His mind raced. *No, I must have been in some kind of accident.* He tried to focus. What was the last thing he could remember? *Last night, where was I? Wait, who am I?* It was all there, only the night was missing. *There is little enough comfort in remembering one's name,* he thought without humor.

The cadence of the monitors was broken by the intrusion of a rather large, unpleasant looking nurse followed by a doctor. Even in his weakened condition, the old man's empathic abilities remained intact. She radiated something Arthur found disquieting.

"Well," she began, "you're back with us." Her

words and her demeanor put Arthur off, so he simply ignored her. Mustering all of his strength, he looked into the physician's eyes. "Doctor, would you please ask this nurse-person to excuse us for a moment?"

The doctor noted what appeared to be a truncated accent buried in a very commanding, rich baritone voice. The stroke, he judged, had not impaired the old man's speech. The nurse started to object, but he stilled her.

"Give us a few . . ." She hesitated, and then left the room, eyeing the old man all the way to the exit, pulling the door shut behind her.

"Doctor, where am I?"

The doctor found the question typical given the circumstances. "George Washington Medical Center, intensive care unit," he said. The old man started to interrupt, but the doctor quieted him with a raised hand, and then read from a chart. "You were brought in by Metro Ambulance at 11:30 p.m., unconscious, an assortment of bruises and contusions. Your outward physical trauma was minor but you've suffered a significant neurological episode. In layman's terms, a minor stroke." He thought about his statement. "If there is any such thing. You were fortunate an EMT happened on you lying near the cab stand at the Westin."

"Did you say, the Westin?"

"Yes, the Washington Westin on 23rd and Park." The doctor eyed his patient. "You don't remember?"

"No, not precisely, parts of the night are missing, but I don't have amnesia, if that's what you're thinking."

"Oftentimes with trauma, one can develop retrograde . . ." the doctor began, but Arthur was not about to let him finish—"Amnesia, our brain's facility to block out recent traumatic events—just who do you think you're talking to doctor . . . some paperboy, as you sit there dispensing medical pearls of wisdom?" Arthur's eyes took on a momentarily icy look Jack hadn't seen from many people in his lifetime.

The old man was obviously not accustomed to being questioned, nor his mental acuity doubted. The doctor ignored the flare-up and sat, writing silently in the chart. Without looking up, he said, "The Rolex you were wearing is down in the safe. The Emergency Medical Technician saw it. Thankfully he is honest. His honesty allowed me to save your jewelry—and your life. Without such an expensive calling card and no I.D. you would probably have ended up at Mercy Hospital, then, most likely the morgue. Indigent care is not as 'efficient' as we are."

The old man scrutinized the young doctor, gauging his intellect, judging his character. He sounded cynical, but seemed reasonable.

"And, my wallet?"

"Gone."

The old man stared into the doctor's eyes, as if to read his thoughts.

"Do you know who I am?"

"Yes, well I do if you didn't steal that Rolex." The 'joke' was lost on Arthur.

"Who else knows I'm here—who I am?" Concern crept into the old man's voice for the first time.

The doctor did not flinch. He stood his ground. As was his style, the old man liked it.

"Nobody. I mean, who would I call, the President?" the doctor asked. "We rarely speak. Anyway, I'm nothing, if not discreet." The doctor's hard exterior lessened only slightly.

The old man began to accept him. He seemed direct, intelligent and articulate. Perhaps he even possessed a sense of humor.

"What is my prognosis?"

"Well, we're way ahead of ourselves here. So far, your progress, if we can call it that in such a short period, is encouraging. Your vital signs stabilized, but you're still listed as critical and guarded condition."

Arthur looked at his lifeless arm questioningly.

"I can't seem to move my hand . . . a permanent condition?" The old man asked without emotion for it was clearly a clinical question.

The doctor found the old man too self-assured perhaps, though very charismatic.

"Doctor's rule number one: Never guess on long term prognoses to stroke victims. It's much too soon to say . . . your paralysis is obviously the result of the stroke. What you need now is bed rest, and then some tests so we can do a full-blown evaluation. "

Arthur interrupted with a wave of his good hand. "Are you a neurologist?" The question was really a challenge.

"No."

"Surgeon?"

"Not yet, but . . ."

"A little 'seasoned' are we, to still be in training?"

Jack blanched at the 'age' reference.

"It's a long story . . . and I think another time might be better."

"Then I shall certainly require a second opinion."

The doctor stiffened with the challenge, "I expect you'll be taken out of here as soon as it's safe to move you." He clipped the chart to the front of the bed while studying the top page.

He eyed the doctor.

"What is the time?"

"Almost 7:00."

Arthur looked away.

"Did I speak, or say anything during my episode, while I was unconscious?"

"Nope," the doctor replied instantly.

Arthur looked into his eyes . . .

Why is he lying to me?

"What time is it?" The old man's demeanor of total authority and superiority slacked for the moment as he repeated his question.

"It's early, not quite seven."

Arthur had no idea how much time had passed.

The doctor hesitated realizing the breadth of the question.

"It's morning."

"We have no time left, and it may be too late already."

The doctor just looked on and clearly did not understand.

5

Arlington, Virginia.
7:09 a.m.

She lay in bed for what seemed an hour after the alarm went off, her head pounding. Rolling over she checked the time; it was 7:09, so she had actually slept for less than ten extra minutes. She tried in vain to remember the night, but it was hazy. She knew less than four hours had passed since her last drink, and her mouth still tasted thickly of Stoli, and the nasty, all fried, buffet . . . *all of which will end up on my ass*. She hesitated before looking at the other pillow, relieved she wouldn't have to make small talk with some unfamiliar lover. It was a bittersweet relief, as there were fewer and fewer men in her life, bed or otherwise these days.

She walked to the bathroom, stopping to look at herself in the full-length mirror. She compulsively stared at her body; while it was good, she thought, it was changing, and not for the better.

By any standard Kelsey was attractive at this stage of her life. Her overindulgence of alcohol and food from her recent barroom visits had brought puffiness to her hands, as well as adding her most dreaded fear . . . extra weight . . . and it all seemed to be gathering in the wrong places. She decided she would cut back on the booze and food, and wear some extra makeup—to make her presentable. *For God's sake don't weigh . . . it'll only cause me to binge, it's so depressing. Fifteen extra pounds on a woman my height;* she rationalized, without finishing the thought.

As she reached for her toothbrush, she thought back of her painful adolescent years and part of what she endured: wearing a mouthful of metal, in the form of braces, all the while, plump as a Cheshire cat—it seemed an eon ago she was adolescently awkward, as well as fat. In her mind clearly despised, and certainly ridiculed by her classmates. The other students all had 'pet names' which they called her—and the names stuck deeply in her psyche for years. She wondered how long it would be before her body and face that had, come so much later in life, abandoned her. Deeply scarred from memories, Kelsey now, almost resented the 'latter day' attentions of men—she was a classic late bloomer who was an outcast in grade and early high school—the butt of seemingly endless jokes mostly by cruel adolescent 'boys'. This made her life miserable and left her guarded; all baggage that she carried deep in her consciousness, making her self-assured outward countenance, a very fragile facade.

With apparently no hope in sight for physical change, she turned inward; emotionally shut down to protect herself. These events fueled turmoil that very soon, even after shedding an incredible seventy pounds, left her in pain—fighting constant bouts of bulimia; and anorexia—her scars from these days ran deep.

She fought her problem with amphetamines. When she first began taking the drug it was a legally obtained prescription from her doctor. Since that time the potent 'diet' pills had become a part of her daily routine.

She vowed she'd never be heavy again, and sadly,

no matter how 'thin' she actually was, the person *she* saw in the mirror was always just, 'a little too heavy for her taste.' Probably as a result of this deep-seated angst and wariness of boys and men, she never married.

As she finally blossomed into her latter day self—her new found attractiveness as wonderful a gift as it was, the reality was this left her bitter and cynical; *'of course they accept me now; I finally look . . . 'normal' . . .* she had developed this aggressive mind-set and it had become her ruling reality. With great irony she now thought, *at age thirty-six, I'm battling gravity's tug of war, as well as the well-chronicled 'women's' slowing metabolism. It's a fucking conspiracy.*

It was time to call her editor and beg off—something that had become a frequent occurrence; and not her favorite way to start a morning. She reached for the cordless, punching in the familiar number as she continued to stare at the 'heavy' woman in the mirror; her eyes puffy, her fingers swollen. "*Christ, I have to stop sleeping naked or break that goddamned mirror,*" she thought as she grabbed her robe.

Nelson's voice-mail kicked in, "You have reached the editor of the Washington Post, Nelson O'Bryan. Please . . ." She punched *one,* ending his succinct message.

"Nelson, uh . . . Kelsey here, I'm late, but I'm sure you know why . . . I know what you're gonna say, but I spent four hours last night pumping that . . . that pile of shit for more information on the base closings. Christ, even when he says 'no comment' he's lying." She remembered a time, not so long ago when her source most likely wouldn't have said 'no comment.'

"Anyway, I'll be in by nine, nine thirty at the latest . . ." She hesitated, "Thanks."

She walked into her kitchen, which was spotless. A

compulsive neat freak, she never cooked, unless it was an occasional Lean Cuisine nuked in 4 minutes or less—she rarely ever ate at home. She opened the refrigerator and picked up a lonely can of tomato juice. She wrapped her robe and sat down, while propping her feet onto a chair. Grabbing the remote, she turned on the small Sony perched next to her microwave. CNN droned in the background as she continued to think about Nelson. He had watched over her and knew she was slipping into dark habits again. Her work was not crisp, she was a half-step slower than she had been, and the younger, hungrier news bitches were on her heels. She herself had stalked the old timers once, and had reveled at the fear in their eyes. *Life is a cruel circle.*

The television droned the early morning news. The President was leaving tomorrow for what had been described as a military base inspection tour in four states.

"Inspection hell," Kelsey said aloud. "He'll only visit the ones he isn't closing, shake hands and wear a flack jacket—jingoistic bullshit."

She enjoyed talking to the television during the news. She listened a bit more and judged there was nothing extraordinary she needed to know, downed the juice and retreated to the bedroom to start the process of selecting the outfit of the day.

She selected a Ralph Lauren suit, a matching blouse, an Italian scarf, all in her "best" color. The skirt happened to be the shortest she owned; knowing it showed off her legs without drawing too much attention to her growing ass. She dressed quickly and applied makeup as sparingly as possible. She really didn't require much, not yet, even with the unwanted puffiness.

As she pulled her blonde hair back and pinned it up she walked into the bathroom and broke open several bottles of prescriptions . . . everything from legal, to not—

Prozac for her ongoing depressive bouts, Valium to relieve anxiety and bring her down from Amphetamines which she took to curb her appetite. There was also vitamin E to help her skin, and hopefully help her maintain her 'youthful appearance' and counteract the hollow unhealthy look sometimes created by the amphetamines.

The amphetamines had become her 'upper' when she awoke, and then in the middle of the day to give her a midday boost and she even used them before late night interviews to combat the fatigue. She was a 'working addict', but never thought of it really. If this routine could keep her thighs and ass reasonable, so be it. *I can quit any time I want to . . .* pure delusion.

Kelsey thought back to a better time, a few years ago, when she was caught—as alone as one could get—with a sitting President. He had stepped onto her elevator, just minutes before a news conference in the White House briefing room. The President looked directly into her eyes and said, "You know, Kelsey, I think you're the only natural blonde within six hundred miles of this", he paused and said with emphasis, "shark infested hell hole of a town." She was stunned he actually knew and remembered her by name, *and* he knew she was a natural blonde. She had reddened at his attention. The secret service agents smiled graciously, easing her embarrassment, and in her mind, maybe flirting just a bit. Her ego was bent, not broken entirely.

"Thank you, I'll take that as a compliment, Mr. President," she said finally. The doors opened, and he stepped off the elevator, clapped her gently on the shoulder. She had never spoken with him again. She missed the man's quiet integrity and jumbled syntax. To her, he was one of the good guys.

Her daydreaming was interrupted by the harsh signal of the incoming email on her computer. She grabbed her shoe, slipping it on as she hopped over to the burled oak desk. Her face was uncharacteristically lined with deep furrows. She read the message from the unknown source three times.

There was a very sick man at the Westin last night.

6

White House the Oval Office
7:55 a.m.

The report rested on the President's desk. He entered the room through the private entrance, sat heavily in his chair, and scanned it rapidly. It contained nothing unusual, more important, was not helpful. The phone rang with quick bursts and one long one signaling the Director's private ring into the Oval Office.

"Yes, Bob."

"Mr. President, you've seen the report?"

"Yep—not really much of a report—there's not one scrap of new information."

"We ran all the local hotels, hospitals . . . nothing."

"I can only guess you've checked the morgue . . ." The president's voice trailed off.

"Yes, we did that first, actually."

The president's face reddened. "This is going nowhere. Look, debrief Arthur's secret service agents again, Cole's people, and whoever else can shed some light on this thing, and I don't give a goddamn if his people don't talk, press them as hard as you need to . . . kick their asses around a little, you know how. Then, be back in my office by eight thirty, and Bob . . ."

"Yes, Mr. President?"

"Keep this tight."

"Sir . . ."

But the president was already gone.

7

George Washington Medical Center Room 671
8:05 a.m.

The old man could not breathe. The tubes were simply too constricting, and his body was rebelling. The force of will sustaining him through eighty six years gave him the strength to reach down with his left hand and fumble for the nurse's call button. Above his head, a monitor began to sound. His last conscious thought was, *If only I could cough.*

Arthur was spared the code blue panic scene, which is so familiar in intensive care. The stern looking nurse hit the door first, ramming the crash cart through it and up against his bed. She was followed in short order by three white clad bodies. Unknown to Arthur who was now unconscious, one of them was the doctor.

The old man was limp and turning purple. "Another stroke," the nurse was loud.

"Check his oxygen!" The doctor yelled to the team.

"Not breathing, pulse is . . ." The nurse was following her own lead, ignoring the physician in charge.

A second alarm interrupted the team. Too often, stroke victims survived the initial onslaught only to succumb to one of the many side effects. But this looked different somehow.

"Airway constriction, he's choking on his own mucus, pull the tubes . . . running out of time here," the doctor was louder yet.

The nurse ignored the order and grabbed for the suction machine, again dismissing the doctor's instruction. A dark look passed over his face, as he reached and caught her wrist in mid-air, holding it in a vise-like grip. "I don't believe I said 'suction.'" His tone was harsh and he had a fire in his eyes she had not seen before. He stepped forward aggressively; in doing so brushed her aside, so roughly she lost her balance falling backward onto the crash cart, knocking it into the wall noisily. She slid to the floor with a graceless thud. A white clad body reached down for her, only to be rebuked by the doctor. "Don't touch her," he said. "Assist me with our patient or get the hell out of this room." None of the nurses had seen this personal side of the physician.

Just then, the old man startled everyone with an enormous gasp, as his lungs struggled to fill with air. The doctor stepped back and eyed the nurse, still sitting splay-footed on the floor.

"Now, suction your patient." He leaned forward, their faces only inches apart as he spoke in hushed, ominous tones, "If you ever ignore my instructions again, I'll have you before the Hospital Administrator."

Twenty minutes later, the droning of the machines filled the room again; it was as if nothing had happened. Except for the two men, the room was deserted, and dimly lit. The doctor sat by Arthur's side studying the elderly man with remarkably beautiful thick silver hair, frail body, watching the purple veins pulsing regularly beneath his parchment skin.

8

Arlington, Virginia

Kelsey learned early on Washington thrived on two basic elements: power and rumors. Most conversations were about *someone* not *something,* always concerned with Washington's power elite. The city and the power brokers were long past the age of innocence in America. There was a new and even sharper age of cynicism in the mood and tone of everyone, so it seemed. Reporters dug mercilessly for every morsel, and did so around the clock. The youngest congressman, from the smallest district, of the least populated area of the United States arrived in Washington aware of this. The city had become ruthless beyond description.

This turgid atmosphere may have explained Kelsey's uncharacteristic lack of interest. Rabid curiosity had once been her forte—until recently, she would have gone straight to the Westin, interviewed everyone in sight, awakened the night crew with questions, tracked down the best available source, and pinned him or her to the mat.

Today she did not, and time was becoming more precious than she could imagine.

9

George Washington Medical Center Room 671
8:16 a.m.

The old man's eyes fluttered as the young doctor sat and watched. Even though he had been off duty for some time, he felt compelled to remain.

Arthur M. Jacobson's resume was formidable. He had been in government in one capacity or another for as long as Doctor Jack could remember. He had been an Ambassador, Secretary of State possibly, maybe U.N. liaison; several other positions which Jack could not recall, and they were all appointed posts, it seemed. Jack thought it strange Arthur could remain politically viable given the partisan nature of the government. But even in rapidly changing Washington scene, with political parties coming and going, Arthur always seemed to remain above the fray.

God, he might date back to before I was born, Jack found himself thinking, *maybe even before Truman or Roosevelt*.

The old man began to stir. "If this is Hell, I'll have no part of it." His sense of humor, dry as it was, remained intact. "You charlatans could have killed me forty years ago when I was only middle-aged."

"Say the word and we'll have you in the bosom of

private care." Jack chided him ever so gently as he gazed down at the old man.

"Well now, this is a conundrum."

"Hmm?" Jack was surprised. He had not expected Arthur to remain in a public hospital. "Well, I suppose you could do worse. Our staff is better than most, and the food is uhh . . ." he held his hand up and waved it back and forth.

Arthur grunted.

"I suppose we should make some arrangements with your . . . uh . . . people?"

He stared at the ceiling. "No, hold off on . . ."

"Mr. Jacobson . . . Arthur," the doctor said softly, "You were a John Doe to the admitting desk, not registered under your name when you were admitted." As it was well known John Doe's are usually taken to Mercy Hospital, Arthur was confused.

"Actually, I recognized you early on, but as far as I could tell, I was the only one who did—and frankly, was shocked to see you admitted without an I.D. The last time I saw you was on TV; you were with the President, both surrounded by the Secret Service, so I guess I was stunned—so I approved your admission."

"Very good. Very good indeed . . ." Arthur smiled in spite of himself. "How long do we have before anyone discovers our little . . . charade?" The word sounded very phonetically as *sharad*. Arthur still carried part of his mother's accent with him.

"I have no idea."

"Jack, I am very old, very tired, and very sick. Time, once my ally, is now a mortal enemy. Unfortunately, it's not my only enemy. There is a lot I have to tell you, and I suspect quickly if it's to get told at all."

Jack sat back and said nothing. While he found the old man compelling and believable, his training had taught him to be wary.

"There will be another attempt on my life."

It was simple and to the point while compelling—Arthur M. Jacobson's trademark.

"How's a stroke . . . an attempt on your life?" The doctor waited for more.

"Check my blood, Jack . . . check it very closely."

10

White House Lower Level Security Meeting

The Executive staff meeting was on the verge of chaos. The President was anxiety laden and could not yet explain the depth of his concern, the time was not right.

"Mr. President, there's nothing new on Arthur," the Director said. "We can put fifty men on this, but as you well know, that many suits on the street will guarantee a nightly news story, or at least some very curious reporters. Since you've said we need to keep this quiet, we're in a real tight spot, it's gonna be hard to do both." The man giving the report wanted more information. It was in his nature to be cautious as well as curious. He decided to make the President give him some plausible reason for an all-out search for a career politician, who, except for his advanced age, could easily be shacked up with one of Washington's finest escorts.

Time had come for the cover. In a room filled with trained liars, the one who was most adept, and was the most believable was the President.

"He's working on a secure project for me, so not only is he missing . . . there's a protection issue we have to consider here."

Silent groans filled the room. The President was on

the verge of losing his audience. He moved around the table to the Director and stood behind him, placing his hands on the man's broad shoulders.

"Taylor, I don't have a sense you're with me on this."

"Now, Mr. President . . ."

"Naa . . . I can see it in your eyes. Tell me, how long have you known me?" The Director winced; he knew the President was about to travel into some unpleasant territory.

"Uh, well, Mr. President if you count your time as Governor . . ." But the President didn't let him finish.

"The question, Taylor, was rhetorical; nobody gives a shit how long we've known each other. My point is I don't make idle requests of you and your people . . . ever, do I?"

"No sir, but . . ."

"And Taylor, do you think anybody in this room really thinks you are a, ahh . . . dedicated government employee who lives just to benevolently serve his country; or is the kind of person who can actually live on a job description that calls for you to make what, ninety thousand?" On a roll, the President pressed his advantage. "I'm guessing your first two wives get more . . . each, annually."

"Just a minute there's no need to . . ."

"Yes, Taylor, there is a need *to*, after all I'm the man who signs a budget which has, what, four point two million dollars hidden in our discretionary fund, just to pay you." Taylor's face reddened and his jaw pumped but he only stared forward, ignoring the gaze of the president.

The President lowered his tone and volume to a more pacifying level.

"Taylor, today is the day you earn your money. In fact it's the day we all do, or we sure as hell won't be here much longer to do so."

It was a quiet, stunning declaration, made without acrimony. The President was neither loud nor threatening, which made it even more significant.

The Director's red face had paled to ashen white, and he could not speak. The irony of the moment was not lost on the President. Not so long ago, a predecessor of the Director had blackmailed White House occupants and a host of senators and congressmen with great success for more than thirty years. The President relished this moment of absolute control.

"You've got almost no time to find Jacobson."

11

The Post 8:58 a.m.

Kelsey flipped on her screen, sipping her coffee as she waited for her computer to boot up.

"You have 37 e-mail messages."

"Shit, I don't have time." She traced down the list, checking to see which ones were pressing, deleting those she knew to be unimportant. Most were routine, except for one . . . entitled, the Westin.

Our sick friend at the Westin is still alive.

"What the hell?" She picked up the phone and called Nelson.

A Washington old-timer, Nelson was big, balding, and gruff, a rumpled mess of a man who continually pushed Kelsey. His motive was simple; he saw himself in her, twenty years removed, and he clearly saw both the good and the bad.

"Nelson, see I said I'd be in by 9:00."

"Here's a flash, we start work around here at 8:00. So you, little lady can work late tonight," he barked.

"Okay, all right". She hesitated, annoyed.

"Say, you got anything in from late last night, maybe something that could have happened at the Westin?"

It was not like Kelsey to be cagey with him.

"No," he replied. "Not unless you consider half our congressmen getting laid in a five hundred dollar a night hotel room, news. You got names, pictures . . . anyone talking?"

She ignored his sarcasm.

"Seriously, I've had two phantom contacts about something maybe . . . dark, over at the Westin," she began cautiously; "I think I should check it out."

She heard his chair squeak as he leaned back. "We're running a newspaper here. I realize that runs a distant second to your gut instincts, Kelsey, so just for the record, tell me about our base closing story. No, let me guess. I know so far we've got a C-note invested in a bar bill and we'll have to headline with, `No Comment'—I'll put it right next to `Dewey Wins' in my scrapbook." Nelson snorted aloud at his own humor.

Kelsey was not immune to his sarcasm, just prepared. "You'll get the story by two, and actually, it's slightly better than no comment, but certainly no, 'Dewey Wins'."

12

George Washington Medical Center
Room 671 9:05 a.m.

"Close your mouth, Jack, I'm not delusional."

Jack watched his patient closely. He was thinking he should be more careful with this patient.

"And when I 'check your blood,' what exactly will I find?"

Arthur, who was accustomed to having his way with everyone, was not prepared to be challenged. "Indulge me," he said. "Listen to what I have to say. Then, if you're convinced I'm some lunatic old coot suffering from delusions, do whatever you like." He lay back satisfied he had heightened the physician's curiosity.

Jack looked at his watch, "Okay, I'm off duty, so now you're on my time."

Arthur braced himself. This had to be good, and he knew it.

"Jack, whatever your political beliefs, you must suspend them for now. Take what I have to say as the simple truth. Try not to be judgmental."

Jack said nothing.

Arthur Jacobson began a tale spanning some seven

decades and involved the most powerful men and companies the modern world had ever known.

13

Private Residence, Antigua

As the interim director stood in the front of the room, his thoughts were of the legendary Arthur M. Jacobson, who, as chance would have it, had not been invited to this particular meeting of the Committee.

He was thinking, in all likelihood, Arthur was dead by now.

This was only the second committee meeting in more than sixty years Arthur had not attended. The first, five months ago, had set the wheels in motion to create his absence from this and all future meetings. There had been very little resistance to the plan, since most committee members had begun to view him as increasingly difficult.

The new and still unofficial Executive Director called for quiet. He looked around the table and saw familiar faces. Major corporations from all over the globe were represented. In fact, they were the true wealth of the world.

The Executive Director began with the traditional opening, just as Arthur had hundreds of times before him, strictly adhering to Parliamentary procedure.

As the meeting was called to order, his mind drifted back to the last meeting, also held at a private residence in the Caribbean. Arthur's resignation was not sought, nor would it have been accepted. Only death would silence such a man. His earlier genius would be missed; no one in the room possessed his mind or his strategic skills. But he had, in the mind of the Committee, become a dinosaur, an impediment to their bold new path. He had resisted the Committee's recommendation to bring the Military Chief of Staff in for a permanent seat, arguing, 'to broaden the Committee, would compromise security'. "Presidents can act, military types can only react. It's simply not clean!"

There was a case to be made for his observation. The Committee's absolute control over the past eleven Presidents was evidence of the strategic as well as confidential correctness of its original mandate.

"We must rule from the top down," Arthur had argued.

The Committee ultimately saw this ideology as a reflection of an old man's thinking. In reality, Arthur had come full circle in his doctrine, and now wanted to moderate the actions of the Committee he had helped to create. The realities of a global marketplace had sealed his fate. The CEO of a well-known oil company had first spoken the unspeakable: "Arthur . . . has become a *problem*."

The very existence of the Committee ensured quick solutions to such problems. Within twenty minutes, a plan was in place. No one mentioned the result—the price of a human life. It was business. The Committee was negotiating its own metamorphosis. It was very clean.

"Who's our man?"

There were no names mentioned, only references to file numbers. No one in the room really wanted to know the distasteful details, and this made security complete.

A suggestion from the floor for file number three was entertained—a man who had handled the sanitary removal of a judge last year. He had been successful for the Committee on a number of occasions . . . their very best option.

There was a pall over the room, the kind of regret one might only have for the loss of an Arthur Jacobson. Finally, the acting director said, "Any objections?"

No one spoke, or even looked up. The committee-men shifted uneasily in their chairs, each contemplating mortality and the possibility file number three might some-day draw his name.

14

George Washington Medical Center

"I am the Executive Director of the Committee," Arthur began. "The Committee comprises the most powerful and influential people in the world. They represent the really serious money which controls all financial dealings globally. This august body was formed out of necessity shortly after the dreadful financial debacle known as the Great Depression, back in the late 1920's and early thirties. Our government was loath to take care of even the simplest financial crisis during a rather naive financial era. We recognized the time had come for structural change in our government. We realized, of course, common man would not accept the complexities necessary to enact constitutional change, so the group came together through an extraordinary series of strategic preparations."

Dr. Jack Ryan had never been a great student of history, and felt out of his element.

"Arthur, what exactly are you saying?"

"I am trying to be precise and thorough, so try to keep up, Jack. What I am about to share with you is an intensely intricate unraveling, covering several decades. And it shouldn't surprise you none of this has ever been revealed, even though this has been rumored for more than half of the last century. So, in essence, the Committee is a financial entity that has formed the underpinning of our government, world governments really, though clandestinely, since Roosevelt's first term in office. Is this difficult to understand?"

"No, it's not difficult to understand," Jack said, "just hard to believe."

Arthur looked at the ceiling, as if to collect his thoughts and regain his strength. "What would you say, Jack, if I were to tell you the last eleven Presidents worked for me, through me, under the auspices of the Committee?"

Jack did not react to the old man, so Arthur slowed the pace to allow the doctor to absorb the information.

"What if I told you I hold secrets inside my head—answers to questions no one dares to ask? Secrets harbored by our government and world governments throughout the past sixty years. Moreover, I not only know the answers to these questions, there is an excellent chance I'm the person who outlined the plans for these actions—incredible happenings which even your wildest imagination couldn't conjure."

The words sounded delusional, but the old man seemed lucid enough. Still, Jack knew he needed to proceed with great skepticism.

"Maybe you should rest," Jack said. The comment clearly agitated the old man.

"There's no time for rest! Certainly you know my condition. I may have hours, or minutes, there's no way to gauge. You must help me to stop them, Jack. They've gone renegade on me and our government may not survive their latest plan."

Arthur's resolve was considerable, and enough to pull the doctor along—at least enough for him to want more information.

"All right,' he said. "I'm sure your tenure with government placed you in some remarkable situations."

Arthur realized he was being placated, and he knew the doctor would have to be won over quickly or be lost to him. He paused only for a moment, and then moved swiftly on.

"I'm trying to save our government, and allies' governments, as we know them Jack. The Committee has chosen to attempt to assassinate me, and this means they will succeed in whatever course of action they have outlined, unless I can stop them. They never fail, at least they never did while under my leadership. You see, the less moderate faction within the Committee is now apparently in power, and within two weeks, a well calculated shift in military power could lock us into a checkmated military position . . ."

Jack shook his head and leaned closer to the old man. "Slow down," he said gently. "You're still way ahead of anything I'm prepared to understand."

"Yes . . . yes, I'm pressing, I know." Arthur forced himself to take a deep breath. It must be all this dreadful stroke business."

Jack handed him a glass of water, and he eyed the plastic straw warily. "You know, the last time someone handed me something to drink, it didn't agree with me." He then charmed Jack with a smile only Jacobson could conjure.

Arthur tried unsuccessfully to move the straw to his lips. Jack watched him, observing his frailty; amazed a man with such incredible power could be rendered so helpless by the simple rupture of a blood vessel.

Arthur's rich baritone voice belied his condition, as did his sense of humor. "You can watch me die of thirst if you like, Jack, or you can help me."

"Even executive directors are expendable," Jack said, while carefully lowering the straw to Arthur's lips.

"Only those who are very old, and stubborn." Arthur felt an inner rage and a sense of frustration he had not experienced as he spoke. "Oh, they once feared me so, Jack. Actually it was dreadfully embarrassing." He winced, "Obviously, I'm slipping, or they would not have gotten to me so easily."

Arthur paused again, long enough to organize his thoughts in order to share the whole of the essence of the Committee.

"The year was 1933, and the President, 'The Chair,' as I called him, was in the White House. God, how magnificent he was." Arthur shook his head. "The man had remarkable instinctive gifts—charm, intelligence, not at all like the current occupant. Nonetheless, we had gotten Mr. Roosevelt nominated, and then elected, a simple feat given President Hoover's disastrous years. And to make sure we had his complete attention and understanding, we arranged for a tragic and dramatic demonstration of the Committee's—dedication to purpose."

"Demonstration?" Jack shrugged.

Arthur sighed, "You may find this somewhat ghastly but, it *was* fundamental to the beginnings of the Committee and to our subsequent successes. "Check your history books, Jack. The year was 1933. Our newly elected FDR was riding in a motorcade with Anton Cermak, the mayor of Chicago; he then gave a short speech. The assassin could easily have shot Roosevelt any time but chose to wait—then fired a hail of bullets into the crowd—Roosevelt knew it didn't smell right and told the Secret Service as much."

"Frankly, the mayor was a small time player, and certainly expendable. During that fateful moment, he was tragically shot to death, while our new President-elect stood next to him and watched in horror. It was very public . . . very unsettling." Arthur thought for a moment, "More important, it was extraordinarily effective. The 'assailant' wounded six others in the melee. I believe it was obvious to everyone the assassin could have easily killed the President, a fact not lost on Mr. Roosevelt. In some ways, the necessity for this was a shame, really, but we had to make sure our protégée understood the Committee was *his* true master."

Jack was incredulous. "You were behind the . . ."

"Oh don't be so pedestrian, Jack, of course we were. At least we hired the man who did it. The significance of the act was amplified by the somewhat ruthless follow-up. You see, a note was left on the President's pillow. *Your advocates within The Committee will not mourn the loss of Mr. Cermak.*

Roosevelt, who already knew we were his benefactors, understood the depth of our commitment and now, the length of our reach. He fell into place quite nicely, as we had anticipated."

Jack had not reacted in several minutes.

"Are you still with me doctor?"

Arthur waited for an answer, watching Jack wrestle with the possibility and moreover the probabilities. Was it a complete lie? The ravings of an old man? A kernel of truth?

"Jack, what would you say if I were to tell you the man responsible for this 'assassination' was dead within the month?"

"You mean, you hired him, and then killed him?"

Arthur's evil half-smile chilled him to the bone.

"Oh, in a manner of speaking; the man was electrocuted thirty-four days later, after being arraigned, tried and convicted of the crime. It was all quite legal. And for those who care to count, the man Cermak lived for nineteen days following the shooting. So the entire legal episode took about two weeks." He looked directly into Jack's eyes. "Our judicial system can be extraordinarily efficient when it needs to be."

Jack was stunned by the "efficiency" of the Committee—if there was such an entity—and awed by its reach.

"Our properly motivated new President's first act was to close the banks, of course, at our behest. Obviously, the Committee knew the run on cash would cripple the country beyond its ability to heal itself. Not to mention the obvious inconvenience it created for our 'investors'—this was only the beginning. In December of the same year, the ridiculous 18th Amendment was repealed, forever eliminating Prohibition." Arthur sniffed.

"All that simplistic 'noble experiment' nonsense almost ruined this country. Rational people simply don't think that way. Why, the Committee saved the United States!" Arthur said proudly.

Jack took a deep breath and held it.

"After Roosevelt's reelection in 1936, the Committee decided to make its boldest move to date. It became my job to convince the 'Chair' that, though obvious from all financial indicators, the crisis was not over. Coming out of the mess we were in would take some exquisitely timed planning . . . extraordinary, indeed."

15

Washington, D.C. Oval Office 1937

"**M**r. President, this is our first meeting since your re-election. The Committee sends its congratulations for such a resounding victory. We all consider this to be a mandate for your programs." Arthur paused, and looked at Roosevelt. "You have the power, Mr. President."

A much younger Arthur sat across the desk from the Chief Executive, who squinted through his bifocals and nervously tapped his cigarette holder against the side of the ashtray while eyeing his visitor.

"Oh, come now, Arthur, get to the point. You didn't come here just to stroke my massive ego." The President's words were well thought out. He chose not to create an ugly confrontation with Arthur, though God knows he dreaded these meetings.

"Well, then, let me get directly to the point. The Committee has decided, while your economic programs seem to be taking hold, unfortunately, we don't have the luxury to grind this financial recovery out for ten more years."

"Just exactly what solution does the Committee suggest, Mr. Jacobson?" The President considered Arthur painfully young to be ordering him around, especially since he was a second term President.

Arthur forged ahead.

"We must allow the maniac in Berlin to be successful, in a calculated way, and under our watchful eye, of course. So, we recommend we accede to Germany's projected alliance with the Japanese. We foresee a moment in time, Mr. President, and reasonably soon, when a plan will become clear to our people detailing a full scale attack on all of the Allies."

The President sat motionless for what seemed an eternity, barely holding his inner rage in check. He was not a man given to violence, but he had a well-documented venomous temper and a penchant for world-class sarcasm.

"Very well, I'll draw up the papers for the sale of the White House. It needs some redecorating, a splash of paint here and there, but even so it should bring top dollar from Mr. Hitler. Or do you recommend I just hand him the keys? Let's send him a telegram. 'Save your bombs, just bring a check.' You people are madmen. And by the way, Mister Jacobson, for your information, I don't foresee an alliance with the Japanese. With all this Aryan race nonsense, our Japanese friends are clearly second class citizens . . . at least according to Mr. Hitler." The President exhaled.

"Oh, they *will* align with Germany if we do our jobs correctly, Mr. President. We need to cut them off economically, and isolate them, cut off their oil flow. They will come around to Mr. Hitler, after all, they are the ultimate pragmatic thinkers, you know."

"Yes, and my people, and it's not a well-guarded secret, tell me our Jap friends want us to give up our positions in, what, Wake, and Pearl Harbor, and recognize the New Era, or Modern Era, or some such thing! Arthur, goddamn it, sputtering wildly now, "why war, when we're just recovering from a decade long Depression?"

The man across the desk remained calm and was amused by the President's naiveté. "Mr. President, do you know how many people it takes to build just one naval destroyer, how many jobs . . ."

"What is this, a fucking riddle?" The President was red-faced.

"No, no, no . . ." Arthur said evenly. "This is a matter of carefully planned financial execution. Our 'investors' have calculated our financial recovery based on your most optimistic projections, versus what can be gained through an economy running full steam ahead, building armaments, planes and bombs."

"War . . ." now ghastly white again.

Arthur did not respond.

"You're talking about trading American lives for financial recovery."

How basic this man can be, Arthur thought.

"Mr. President, our investors don't care about a simple recovery. They are capitalists looking for good, sound, long-term investments. The American war machine should do nicely."

The President stared helplessly into space, unable to face Arthur.

Arthur looked at his hands, as if to examine his manicure. "Trust me on this, just as I shared with you the great Huey Long wouldn't be a problem for anyone . . . in the 1940 elections. He looked up at Roosevelt, whose face was ashen.

The President retreated. "Arthur, please . . . I have nowhere to go on this. The isolationists will have me impeached. Honestly, I think these people would have to bomb sovereign United States territory for us to move against the Germans or the Japanese."

Arthur stifled a smile. "Oh, Mr. President it could

come to that. Don't worry; we'll position you carefully, so you appear to have made every effort to avoid a preemptive declaration of war. As a matter of fact, at our last meeting, we concluded our military needs a good bit of time to prepare for meaningful action. So, in the interim, we can gear up in preparation, and supply our allies with armaments, all under the guise of remaining neutral."

The young director placed both palms on the president's desk in an apparent effort to contain his excitement. "How does the phrase 'arsenal for democracy' strike you?"

The President bit down hard on his cigarette holder.

16

George Washington Medical Center

Jack took great delight in the old man's reference to him as 'young man.' When he questioned Arthur on his choice of a nickname, his logic was beyond question.

"At my age, Jack, anyone who's not a young man, is either a young woman or dead." While somewhat humorous it was gallows humor.

Jack reflected on the events of the past few hours, which were strange and frightening for him. He knew instinctively he and Arthur might be moments from discovery, and the events detailed to him over the past hour were enough to create havoc. Only two years ago, he was languishing in private practice—coasting intellectually—becoming complacent.

It had only been a special promise, a desire to use his 'surgeon's hands', which had brought him back to academia and a residency. .

The promise had been the fruit after many years of a marriage, ending tragically. Sarah had been the girl of his dreams. He met her in his last year of college, while chaperoning a freshman 'beer blast.'

As they worked their way through the first awkward moments, they felt a mutual attraction—discussed politics, war, abortion, family size. And to their surprise and delight, they found nothing to disagree upon. Jack proposed three months later—they were blissfully happy. Jack entered medical school and Sarah taught. It was an idyllic and bohemian existence for two people in love.

Sarah ended their happiness with a simple announcement on New Year's Eve, "The test results are back."

Those were the last words he could clearly remember. Eight months later he was standing at her bedside signing the release, allowing the hospital to turn off her respirator, Sarah's only link to life.

The next several months he grieved for Sarah, cursing her goodness as well as her physical beauty. He felt guilty, even shallow. But the passion he felt—the love and anger—was undeniable. At the cemetery, he vowed to keep her memory alive by living a 'normal life.' But it was a hollow promise. He immersed himself in work and never looked up. Her absence had crushed his spirit.

Jack then worked his family practice, thinking always of his first mentor. "Jack, you have a surgeon's hands and mind," the man had told him. "Quit wasting your time diagnosing ring worms in that posh family practice."

But his words were not the deciding factor, Sarah's were. "Go back, Jack, become a surgeon."

The night Arthur was admitted to the emergency room, Jack was working as a surgical resident. It was the end of his training, the beginning of the fulfillment of his promise to Sarah.

17

Washington, D.C. The Post

Kelsey picked up her phone and dialed the Westin, searching her memory for the name of the Antonio Banderas look-alike parking attendant she had enjoyed flirting with on numerous occasions. He had become a good informant—reliable and discreet—and, from Kelsey's perspective, the price was definitely right, he worked on testosterone, not heavy tips.

"God, he's cute—what *is* his name?" she thought, as the phone clicked. "Roberto . . . yes, that's it."

Four voices later, he answered the phone, somewhat breathlessly, as if on the run.

"Roberto here."

Kelsey loved the way he rolled his r.

"Roberto, Kelsey at the Post."

"Kelsey, every time you say that, I think of a horse race, especially with those long slender legs of yours."

She was always in control, and got what she wanted—information. Roberto was after more than flirting and the exchange of confidences, but then, so were most of the men she knew.

"Say, Roberto," she began, "did you see anything unusual last night, anybody sick or hurt?"

"Oh, yeah, we had some excitement here; a fire in the kitchen, one of our chefs got burned."

This didn't smell right to her. "Anything else?" She was pouring it on a little heavier now.

He had guessed she really didn't care about a grease fire; he was just making her earn this one. "You know, Kelsey, we still haven't had that drink."

"Roberto, you read my mind, I was just going to mention it."

He paused just long enough to let her know he was working her now. "I think, Kelsey, what you're looking for is the old gentleman who fell, or had some kind of attack out by the cab stand late last night. He was unconscious. The Bell Captain said he was pretty sure he wasn't a guest, and I don't think they found a wallet. And, oh yeah, I heard the ambulance guy say the old man had a Presidente on his arm, and was wearing a four thousand dollar suit. Smells like money, money. "

"A what on his arm?"

"A Rolex, Kelsey. You know, about twenty-five thousand worth. Anyway, it all happened about the same time as the fire, so we were really jumpin'."

Kelsey was back on top, confident, examining her nails. "So, where'd they take him? What happened to him?"

"Don't know—'Cap' said he never came out of it and he looked real bad . . . so maybe the morgue."

"Who took him?"

Roberto was not about to pass up his opportunity. "You know . . . I think maybe we're up to two drinks and dinner . . . but on me . . . of course."

Kelsey was much too quick for the likes of young Roberto. She had played this game many times before, and played it better than him. "Sure, drinks and dinner"

Roberto rushed ahead, just to keep the moment alive. "Metro Ambulance Service . . . I think. Anyway, it's the one with that funny lookin' green cross on the side. There was two guys—one black—real big and tall, like maybe 6'5". And the other guy was . . . a kid, you know, like maybe twenty. He just watched, mostly."

Kelsey wrote it all down. This was one twosome that ought to be easy to find.

"Roberto, how about you, me . . . dinner Friday night at The Tarmac, that new restaurant at the airport?"

Roberto hesitated, his Latin macho facade idling for the briefest of moments.

"Really?"

Kelsey smiled at his reaction. "Sure, I never kid about dates with handsome men."

They both hung up the phone satisfied. Neither had heard the faintest of clicks on the line.

18

Arthur M. Jacobson was a "whiz kid" long before the world celebrated child geniuses, sending them to college before puberty, working on their doctorate before the legal driving age. His intellect would have given him the latitude to pick from any of a number of high profile careers. He was to political science, as Mozart was to music, truly one of the world's most gifted.

Throughout his tenure in Washington, those least threatened by his enormous intellect admired his endless capacity for both acquired knowledge and stored information. Others were curious about his social life and sexual and preference—all speculation, with no answers. Arthur was an enigma. Through necessity, he was not widely recognized, and he had no public profile, which only fueled the firestorm of curiosity. Cocktail parties were breeding grounds for speculation, and when the Washington social scene was revitalized in the early 1960s, with an influx of Ivy League intellectuals, the pseudo-intellectuals all claimed Arthur as their colleague. Perhaps the shortest, most accurate assessment of Arthur came from "The Kid," the fourth President to serve under Arthur.

As two of his very gifted aides ruminated over Arthur's intellect based on his writing and academic abilities, "The Kid" ended their game with one short sentence.

"Arthur's I.Q.? Probably 180—200; anyway, who gives a fuck? He's the brightest star to grace Washington . . . ever." With that he spun on his heel, leaving female mouths agape. Such frankness and language was not suitable at cocktail parties, even in Washington during the early 60's.

George Washington Medical Center

Arthur could be condescending, and was, when he dropped his guard."How could you pull all that off, Cermak and Roosevelt?" Jack asked him.

"People are sheep, easily led by liars and thieves simply because they *want* to believe in something. It was truly a different world in those days. You must think of the America that existed in the late thirties. We had roughly half the population that we now have. The rural parts of America were woefully backward. It may come as a surprise to you to find out that only a third of the people on farms had electricity. Electricity, Jack, not computers or televisions for heaven's sake!" The old man had become agitated at the thought of such ignorance. He caught himself and backed off slightly, softening his tone.

Jack was still reeling from the thought of the last eleven Presidents taking orders from this man. Arthur watched him wrestle with the information he was being given and thought about what his own father had taught him. "Don't interrupt a man deep in thought unless you can improve on the silence." But as time was not a luxury they enjoyed, Arthur was compelled to break that silence.

"For me to proceed, I must have some assurance that you believe me and that you are prepared to help. Otherwise, I really must stop now and pursue another course of action. Prudence dictates as much."

Jack considered his options. Incredible events were unfolding, and yet, they were somehow believable. And the old man was passionate and eloquent if nothing else. He also rationalized that Arthur had little to gain by spinning an intricate web of deceit. Still, he needed better insight into the man.

"Arthur, I don't know anything about you . . . your background. Why do you have a British accent?"

Arthur smiled wistfully. Jack had taken him back to a better time. "Because I am British, that is, my mother was. She was a proper English lady, brought to this country by my father, who lived in Boston. He was a man with a great deal of money."

Arthur stared up at the ceiling, his eyes aglow as he remembered. "Oh, I was quite the little lord as a lad, precocious, a terrible show-off, as you might imagine. And Boston was a wonderful place. My father was always entertaining associates who were deeply involved in politics. Our home was filled with his contemporaries."

"I remember one particular election eve; the precinct captain brought the vote count to the house. I tallied the candidate's percentages as they were called aloud. And the men were astounded. By the age of seven, I could multiply and divide to three decimal places in my head. I really thought everyone could do it . . the calculations. When I found that they couldn't, it was probably the first time I realized that I was different."

Arthur studied the doctor, then changed directions quickly, one of the many weapons in his arsenal of seduction. "Enough of the reminiscing, Jack, do you believe me or not?"

Jack took stock of the tubes and monitors keeping

Arthur Jacobson alive. He knew his patient required constant medical care at a level only available in an intensive care unit, or that, which could be administered by a full time in-house physician. He had little time to think, but his instincts were clear, his convictions growing stronger.

"Can I afford *not* to believe you, Arthur? I can't condone the course of actions you and The Committee may have taken . . . but I'm willing to help you."

"Then we have a beginning,' Arthur said wearily. He lay back on his pillow, as if to gather new strength.

"Now, Jack, I would like to explain to you why the Committee found it necessary to eliminate the Chair."

19

Washington The Post

Kelsey hung up the phone. She was bristling with excitement. She had not felt this level of passion for her work, for a long time. Who in the world could this old man be? His only identification was a Rolex watch. Not just a Rolex, a *Presidente*. She reached for the phone book. Two minutes later, she was still listening to the telephone ring – eight, ten times—an eternity to be waiting for an ambulance service to answer. She was double-checking the number, when on the fourteenth ring, a woman's voice answered.

"Metro Ambulance."

"This is Kelsey Richmond at the *Post*. I would like to speak to one of your drivers, but I'm afraid I don't know his name." She could hear a commotion in the background and sensed the story growing in importance.

"I'm sorry, ma'am, is this a medical emergency?"

"No. . . ."

"You'll have to call back. We have an emergency." The phone went dead.

Kelsey was ecstatic. She rang Nelson immediately. Before he could answer, she hit him with a blast.

"Nelson, I'm onto something big. I haven't a clue, yet. My notes for the base closing are on my computer, finish it for me, or roll it over till tomorrow . . ."

The editor pondered the day. Kelsey had not fin-ished the base-closing story. She had come in late, and had spent too much on liquor to get a simple story. She had called him, sounding almost incoherent and screamed on the phone about some vague story.

He smiled; he had not seen her this involved in over a year.

20

Washington Near Metro Ambulance Service

Thankfully for Eric, Roberto had supplied the information he needed. Kelsey, Eric's unwitting accomplice, had found the possible path to the old man in a remarkably easy way, as he knew she would.

Step one was to find out who had made the run, a name, any piece of information could or would do wonders . . . an angry call—a complaint from an apparent red neck.

He dialed . . . moments later a chipper young female voice—

"Metro Ambulance."

Eric braced himself. "Look here, Goddamnit, I'm calling to complain about some stupid fucking nigger, who cut me off in traffic over on K Street this morning!"

"Excuse me?" The girl was bewildered by this attack.

"I said, this jerk cut me off in traffic . . . and, who is that idiot?"

Sealing the fate of the steady, intelligent John, she gave up the fatal piece of information. "Sir, you must be mistaken, Big John is the best driver on our force, he's been here . . ." But by then Eric had hung up in what appeared to be a fit of rage.

Step two was obvious, a simple yet effective disguise . . . a red, then blue, reversible jogging suit, under which he wore a strapped on 'pot belly'. He would go out, without his typical hairpiece, showing a shaved head. Eric looked ten years older than normal, and thirty to forty pounds heavier.

He approached the neighborhood of Metro Ambulance cautiously; without a precise plan in place for interdiction, but he knew that if he persisted, only good things would happen.

The fates smiled on the assassin that cloudy day—because as he jogged and walked through the area, he spotted Big John carrying a bag, coming out of a Dunkin Donuts two doors down from Metro Ambulance.

The best approach is always the frontal approach. 'Hey . . . hey there," Eric waved and shouted to the big friendly black man. "Hey, John."

The big man stopped and smiled at Eric. "Do I know you?"

Eric stuck out his hand. There's something irresistible about a smiling man with his hand out. John stuck out his big paw—and Eric grabbed it, a tiny needle pumping a deadly elixir into his hand.

"Damn, static electricity, it's a killer, huh?"

Eric feigned an out of breath attitude, and to sell the jogger façade, bent over, placing his hands on his knees.

"Well, I was just out tryin' to lose some of this," patting his belly and laughing. John was sold. *God this is easy.* "And I wanted to thank you, John, they tell me you picked up my Grandpa at the hotel last night . . . you know, over at a hotel cab stand. They say you saved his life."

"So, the old gentleman made it?" John's natural warmth came through as he smiled and shook his head at Eric. "Don't mean to scare you, but I didn't think he would make it . . . I'm so happy to hear that he's ok."

"Yeah, my mom called and told me . . . but didn't tell me where he is, John."

John stopped short with a puzzled look on his face. "Yeah, but how'd you know my name?"

Eric the assassin hadn't expected John the ambulance driver to be so clever. He hesitated only a second, put both hands on John's chest, pushing him back into the alleyway between buildings.

"What?"

"Look, I just need information. Where'd you take the old man?"

John started to give the confidentiality speech, but Eric had other plans. "Look, that little 'shock' you felt wasn't static electricity, but a needle . . . I've injected you with a remarkably deadly drug . . . if you don't tell me what I need to know, so I can give you this antidote, you'll be dead in less than five minutes."

"What did you do to me . . . ?" John moaned, his breath already starting to gasp.

Eric held up a small vial with a clear liquid inside. "We trade, John, information for your life . . . you decide."

"I don't know man, we made six hot runs last night . . ."

Eric shook the vial in front of the big man, taunting him.

"Mercy . . . no wait, it was George Washington, yeah, that's it, now give me . . ."

"You wouldn't lie to me now, would you, John?"

"Please, man . . . ."

Eric looked at him, knowing that he would not lie, not under these circumstances. He tossed the vial to John who twisted the top open, and hungrily gulped the three ounces of tap water.

It would be some time before they found the big man, slumped against the wall of the building, his bag of donuts in his lap.

Moments later, Eric was gazing out the front window of the bagel shop located three doors down and across the street from the Metro Ambulance Service. His physical appearance was remarkably different now. The large potbelly was gone; the dark jogging suit was reversed, now showing a bright red. His baldhead was now covered with an amazingly realistic hairpiece. Essentially, he looked fifteen years younger and thirty-five pounds lighter. No one who saw him talking to John could possibly recognize him as the same person.

He munched a bagel and nursed a cup of coffee, absorbing any details that might prove useful. His instincts were razor sharp, and they told him he should watch and wait.

The commotion across the street began with the discovery of John's body to a passerby. Predictably, John's coworkers sprang into action. But it was futile. John was quite dead. It appeared that an overweight forty-eight year old man with chronic hypertension had died of an apparent heart attack. There would be no autopsy.

Inside the bagel shop, a young waitress eyed Eric. She couldn't guess his age—maybe thirty—but she thought he was somewhat attractive. She attempted to start a conversation.

"What's up over there?"

Eric did not turn. He hoped she would simply leave him alone. She walked his way, and casually began wiping the window table with a soiled cloth. "Did anything happen over there?" she repeated.

Eric watched her reflection in the shop window without turning his head. Large breasts were his weakness, but not today. Nevertheless, she had cornered him, and he had to respond. *"Parlez vous francais?"* he asked in excellent French.

The girl vaguely understood that the language was French, but had no idea of what the man had said. She hesitated, as if her question could become obvious just by looking at the action across the street. Eric was amused by her forwardness, as she was plainly flirting. *Why*, he wondered, *would a cute kid like this hit on some stranger in a bagel shop?* He held up his coffee cup, eyebrows raised in a questioning look.

"Oh, sure."

She turned to go behind the counter. Eric thought she looked even better from behind. It was indeed a shame that he was so distracted.

By the time she returned, coffee pot in hand, the door was swinging shut. Eric was gone.

Outside the bagel shop, Eric blended into the mass of bodies on the sidewalk. A minute later, he was standing next door to Metro Ambulance. A small crowd of people was witnessing the crew that hefted John's large body onto a stretcher for his one last trip in the ambulance. This time, the destination was the morgue.

After the convoluted conversation with Metro Ambulance, Kelsey, realizing the story had built to a new level, and being only seven blocks north, almost ran to the site, but decided to drive—she was there in ten minutes, and arrived at the height of the action.

Eric spotted the blonde woman in a peach colored suit, talking to a Metro employee and taking notes. He moved cautiously, drawing closer to hear what was being said. The man was obviously John's partner. Eric recognized him from Roberto's description. He filed the man's face in his memory for future reference.

Meanwhile, the reporter, realizing no one had seen anything, had become disinterested in the Metro employees and had begun to size up the crowd. She had a strange feeling, a 'reporter's chill' as she called it, as if someone were watching her. She scanned the faces in the crowd, as she reviewed the details of the story she was hoping to get. A Metro driver picked up some mysterious old guy, and then hours later, was dead. A tragic coincidence?

Eric monitored Kelsey's movements with practiced ease. He watched her shift her attention from the Metro employees to the crowd. She looked directly at him. As she did, he was careful to not engage her with eye contact. Still, she couldn't shake the feeling of being watched, but Eric was quite capable of disappearing, and at this moment he felt invisible. He had known many women in his life, and making assumptions of someone he knew to be a powerful woman like Kelsey was easy for him. He admired her stealth, and if she got in his way, he would enjoy their struggle. She seemed . . . worthy.

21

Washington Director's Office

As a man of virtually unlimited power, the Director had become accustomed to giving orders—never taking them—and based on his station in life he despised even the vague possibility of being threatened; certainly in front of his underlings. He fumed after his meeting with the President, and vowed the insult would not be easily forgotten. The President, he concluded, lacked finesse. The Director rued the day the new breed in Washington had taken over. They were not merely young, they were "wrong thinking." He smiled grimly as he realized that even Arthur M. Jacobson would agree with that. Perhaps it was even the reason that Arthur was missing.

With each successive political regime, Arthur had enjoyed security supplied by the Secret Service, with the President's approval and no one had ever questioned the unusual practice. Each President was careful not to assign active Secret Service men. The agents were special agents hired from a pool of former Secret Service and C.I.A. operatives. Since the White House enjoyed a wide berth in its budgeting, the process was quite simple. Many assumed that the special security was a tribute to Arthur for his distinguished career in government service. Others assumed that it was due to his advanced age. In any event, Arthur was so respected and feared; no one dared question the arrangement.

Of course, none of this explained the heat generated by Arthur's disappearance. *If he were working on something sensitive, why didn't the agency know it*, the Director wondered? He had come close to asking the President, but thought better of it. He had made that error once before, several Presidents ago, when "The Actor" was in office. That President had turned on him with a vengeance. In a voice that shook uncharacteristically, he ended any further discussion.

"Arthur M. Jacobson is my most trusted personal advisor, also, my confidante. As such, his work is invaluable to me. He has been in the catbird seat of government for more than fifty years, serving Presidents in an absolutely bipartisan way. The chances are very good that he'll be here long after we're both gone."

While the speech had sounded curiously rehearsed, it was of no consequence. The Director never again questioned Arthur's existence or his security.

He would not question it now, even though the priorities had clearly changed. The current occupant of the Oval Office wanted Arthur found and neutralized, and he was exacting a heavy price. Twenty-four hours, or his neck was probably on the chopping block.

Who is the most qualified to find Arthur—my people have been worthless.

On an outside hunch he thought of the best mind he had met—and while not in the daily service, could probably locate the old man.

The Director picked up the phone, glanced at his computer for today's security code, and punched in a fourteen digit number. The number accessed a secure line that appeared to originate in Rensselaer, Indiana. Several clicks later, the phone rang and he received a recorded message. "You have reached the offices of Plantation Food Limited. If you know the extension of . . ." The Director punched in a second fourteen-digit number. Several clicks later, it accessed another secure line out of Bella Coola, British Columbia—a computer driven line that converted his voice to binary code, permitting a second written message to be sent by modem, while simultaneously creating hundreds of thousands of 'blind alleys' along the way, for anyone nosey enough to want to snoop into his business.

The Director thought of the operative he had chosen. Though known primarily for wet work, he was the most successful of all the operatives the agency had used.

Twenty-eight blocks away from the point of origin, a phone rang once. The Director was connected. The coded message was the same as the last time: *I have an excellent offering on the Stock Market. We must act quickly to purchase at a price I consider reasonable. Number of options unlimited.*

The modem in Eric's apartment switched off.

22

George Washington Medical Center
Arthur Continues

"The 'Chair', Roosevelt's code name for obvious reasons, was wonderful throughout his first three terms, Jack. He played his part magnificently. Little did we know that he would begin to believe his own press clippings and that he would forget the depth of his commitment to the Committee. We should have known he was such an ego maniac, an incredible intellect bowed but not broken by polio."

"You said you found it necessary . . ." Jack prompted.

"Yes, yes, it became apparent as the war went on, that he had become truly unmanageable. At the Yalta Conference in February of '45, he befriended that Russian peasant, Stalin, the single largest source of most of our post war problems in Europe, especially in Germany. That one 'harmless concession,' as Roosevelt dubbed it, took more than forty years to correct.

"It was immediately after Yalta that the committee elected to make its boldest move to date. Having served his dual purpose—pulling us through the worst of the Depression and holding the country's hand during the war—we felt the need for a man who was easier to control. The vote of the Committee was unanimous.

"We simply arranged for his well-known health problems to escalate. Of course, as was always the case, we had to set the stage for the new man. So, one week before Roosevelt's 'stroke' in Warm Springs, Georgia, the Vice President, received proper notice from the Committee that he would become the nation's chief executive. When the' Chair' died, and right on schedule, the Vice President— even with his, shall we say . . . less limited vision—got the picture. He was, I remember thinking at the time, woefully out of his league compared to Roosevelt. And quite frankly, Jack, he was not in the least prepared for the job."

23

White House Oval Office 1945

Arthur sat in the Oval office, across the room from the President. The 'Hat' was cornered, and clearly agitated.

"What in God's name is this Committee and who the hell are you?" Arthur handed him an envelope, which contained the, agreed upon "In the event of my death letter," written in the recognizable hand of the former occupant of the Oval Office. Truman's natural pallor grew more pronounced as he read the document.

"You people seem fairly astute at predicting . . . strokes." Truman sat poker straight in the massive chair, which had only days before belonged to Franklin Delano Roosevelt.

The 'Hat' lacked sophistication, but he was 'street smart'. And Arthur was at his eloquent best. He detailed the workings of the Committee, its role in government for the past decade, and the successes that both they and the country had enjoyed. Of utmost importance, he detailed the role that the new President was expected to play. "We are planning a course of action that will move us from a wartime economy into a prosperous peacetime economy, Mr. President. With that in mind, the Committee has taken the position that, now that we have Europe somewhat in check, we must end the conflict in Japan as quickly as possible. The best course of action would be to use the Bomb against them."

The 'Hat' did not respond. Arthur simplified his message.

"Mr. President, I am suggesting that we go ahead with plans to drop the Bomb. We think it will end the conflict in the Pacific immediately."

"How the hell would dropping one bomb end the entire conflict?"

Arthur hesitated. He was unprepared for Truman's total lack of knowledge in the area of the military.

"Mr. President, are you aware of a government program known as the Manhattan Project?" The President remained blank, pursed his lips and shook his head.

"The Atomic Bomb, Sir?"

"No. Apparently, there is a lot that my predecessor didn't see fit to tell me." Truman spoke sadly, but without resentment. He truly never expected to be president. Arthur sighed, realizing this could be more difficult than he had anticipated.

The 'Hat' stood slowly as if the weight of the world had been laid on his shoulders. He surveyed the well-groomed lawn outside the Oval Office window.

"You know, not long ago, I owned a hat shop, and was a not so successful businessman at that. And now I'm the president of the most powerful country in the world. You have just informed me that I am to take orders from you and some goddamn committee. It doesn't smell right, does it?"

Truman turned to face his visitor. He was visibly shaken. Arthur studied the president, but remained quiet.

"I'll tell you something, Mr. Jacobson, I love my country. Those aren't just words. I mean it. So hear me when I tell you this, before I do anything that I consider to be wrong . . . you folks can arrange one of those goddamn 'strokes' for me, too!"

Arthur admired Truman's valor. He had balls. Whatever his shortcomings, he was a patriot, and Arthur knew that it would ultimately make his job easier. Arthur simply moved into a mind-set that he calculated which Mr. Truman could most appreciate.

"I'm sure you'd like to bring an end to this war?"

"Indeed, I would, Mr. Jacobson . . ."

"Our military experts have calculated that our new atomic bomb will save millions of dollars and hundreds of thousands of American lives."

Still unconvinced, Truman stood behind the desk square-jawed, wanting more information. Arthur started slowly, working his way through all the rudimentary elements of atomic fusion, Oppenheimer, Einstein, and the whole of the Manhattan Project. He was patient with the new and patriotic president from Missouri, and it paid great dividends. It was the basis for grudging respect from the "Hat". Even though he did not fully understand the breadth and depth of this committee nonsense, he accepted Arthur and the premise enough to coexist with him through the remainder of Roosevelt's last elected term, and through his, upset of Jack Dewey in 1948—a feat impossible to imagine, without the Committee's backing. Arthur was proud of his handling of Truman. It was a hallmark moment in his career.

Within a few months, the nuclear age was born. The two bombs dropped on Hiroshima and Nagasaki, ended the war in Japan and began the conversion to a peacetime economy—an economy ripe for the Committee's picking.

Just as Arthur had predicted.

24

George Washington Medical Center Present Day

Arthur found it difficult to hide the delight he felt in playing such a prominent role in the nation's history.

"I was the one who orchestrated the firing of McArthur. It was absolutely imperative that we get rid of him; he was an impossible man to deal with. Good Lord, he had a bigger ego than the 'Chair.' If he had made a serious run for the Oval Office . . ."

Arthur paused abruptly, as if a draft had entered the room, chilling him to the bone. "Jack," he began, turning his head to make eye contact, "my instincts tell me that we must leave this place at once."

25

Washington, D.C. Near Metro Ambulance

John's partner Phillip was torn, saddened by the loss of his friend, yet intrigued by the reporter's interest in him. Even though he was not blessed with a great mind, in his simplistic way, he wondered what a reporter with the Post wanted with a story about a dead ambulance driver.

Kelsey decided to be as honest as possible with him. "Look, I really came here to ask about a run that you guys made last night to the Westin."

Phillip was a serious smoker, and the events of the day had increased his need for nicotine. He asked Kelsey, for the second time, if she would like a cigarette. She declined graciously, as he lit up again.

"Why do you need to know?" he asked. "Who was he, anyway?"

"That's what *I'd* like to know." She knew it would be a tactical mistake to elaborate.

"Why do you care *who* he is?" Phillip wanted a simple answer to a simple question.

Again with the "why," she thought. But she had worked on much tougher eggs than Phillip. The timing for answers was critical, and some questions were often best ignored, so she pressed on. "I have some details on him, much older man, frail, thin, white hair, very expensive watch, no identification. So, where'd you take him, Mercy General?"

Phillip shook his head. "Not with that arm wear he had on. We took him to George Washington Medical Center. The old guy may have lucked out on that one."

"How'd he luck out? I don't get it."

"Because the doc in the ER seemed to know him—like the old man was his patient or something. That might've saved his life, like if he was his patient, or something, he already knew his medical history."

Kelsey took note of yet another coincidence. "Did this doctor happen to mention the old man's name?" she asked.

"Not to me, I do the grunt work. But he might have talked to John. Everybody talked to Big John; they liked him." Phillip looked distant, remembering his dead partner.

"Who was the doctor, did you know him?"

Phillip looked thoughtful. "I didn't pay much attention. He was a lot older than most of the doc's working the ER."

Phillip was rewinding the tapes in his mind, still puffing on the cigarette. Kelsey smiled at him, and he noticed. "What?" he said grinning awkwardly.

"It's just that most people don't work this hard to remember, and I really appreciate the help."

"Yeah, maybe I do remember a name . . . not for sure. A Dr. Jack . . . something."

"You say he was pretty old?"

"Well, just older than most of the other guys in emergency, maybe 40."

Kelsey winced. She could reach out and grab 40. "One more thing, before I go," she said. "Had John been sick lately, or did he have a history of . . . ?"

"What, you mean like heart trouble that could kill him at any minute?"

Phillip was bitter. He would miss his partner. Kelsey did not respond immediately. She was giving him a bit of space.

"No, not John," Phillip said finally. "He was big, heavy, hell he was just overweight, but he was an unbelievable athlete, really just unbelievable. You see that basketball goal over there? He'd take me over there and wear my ass out . . . five, six games at a time, you know, one on one, just me and him. Hell, he could still dunk the ball . . ." Phillip's voice trailed off. He puffed on the remainder of the cigarette, and then stopped to examine the butt. "Shit, he used to tell me these things would kill me." He flipped the butt angrily into the street.

Kelsey let him vent, knowing it would cement their relationship. Philip needed someone to talk to as much as she did. Finally, she held out her hand, thanked him, and started to walk away.

"One other thing," Phillip said, stopping her. "I don't know if this means anything, but the old guy we took to Mercy was in and out of consciousness, and talking, you know, like someone talking in their sleep. He was incoherent—it didn't make much sense. We get this a lot with head injuries, so it may not mean anything."

"What'd he say?" Kelsey could barely contain her composure; she knew that this was it.

"Well, it was like 'presidential committees' or something like that. He just kept repeating it."

Kelsey caught her breath. The next few steps would lead her to a hospital . . . and with any luck, to the White House. The story was now official.

"Phillip, do you know what a 'scoop' is?" she said

smoothly, while dropping her reporter facade.

"You mean, like at a newspaper, when you get the story first? Sure." He shrugged.

"Yes, and if you tell anybody else, anything, I may not get the story . . . and I'm not exactly on a roll lately."

Kelsey's confession was more candid than she expected, and she blushed. Phillip noticed, and warmed to her honesty. He understood.

26

George Washington Medical Center

The nurse steamed silently, her thoughts venomous. *Just who does that arrogant little cocksucker think he is?* She sipped her coffee and stared at the closed circuit monitor of the old *man's room. Aren't they cozy . . . Ryan hasn't left his side in hours.* Dr. Ryan, who had embarrassed her in front of the code team, she would get even.

She looked at her watch. The old man's medication was overdue by exactly one minute and forty-three seconds; a record for her after twenty years on the floor. *Let's see how long before those son-of-a-bitch super doctor notices.* Beads of perspiration formed at her temples; her heart thumped loudly in her chest. Jack cared about the old man, that much was obvious. *What if they were good friends . . . ?*

The nurse stared into space, and saw nothing but blackness.

27

Washington D.C.

Whenever Eric worked the District, he alternated between two residences. He would leave from one and return to the other. That way, anyone who might see him leave, would be unable to witness his return.

He had chosen today's arrival point carefully, an apartment in an area busy enough to support anonymity, but one that did not present a traffic problem. There were only two other tenants in the building, and Eric had sublet the original apartment to himself a year earlier under an alias.

The neighbors were elderly, perfect for Eric's purposes. Insofar as Eric could tell they had never figured out whether he was a visitor or a resident.

Eric entered the room with his usual cat-like movements. He put his keys on the hook next to the door and looked at the room. He had created a beautiful oasis in the middle of a fairly modest section of D.C. Even though his needs were typically simple given his financial status, he was careful, as always, as to how he redistributed the enormous sums of money he collected for his work. He had chosen a large apartment that was built in the 1920's, and offered architecture that he could savor.

Since he never entertained guests, the inner sanctum of this refuge was his to enjoy as he liked, and it offered an escape from his real life. He had appointed the interior with comfortable, functional, and certainly tasteful furniture, but nothing of great value.

He grabbed a towel and mopped his brow. Even though the weather was cool, he was sweating.

He paused, surveying the room and its comfortable look, and smiled as he approached his only indulgence—his audio system. He had purchased some of this equipment shortly after his first job. He had then become, as many hobbyists are, smitten by the technologies, the look and feel of the equipment. The last time he had calculated, he had spent more than two hundred thousand dollars . . . for him, not much.

He flipped the switch and watched the bluish-yellow vacuum tubes of the amplifier begin to glow. As the voltage increased, they became brighter, a fascination for Eric.

Often, late at night, he would sit and listen for three or four hours, mesmerized by that bluish glow of the tubes, and, of course, by the music. This solitude was his escape—a respite from the dark inner thoughts that followed him everywhere.

This time, he selected Sarah Vaughn, recorded live, in 1961 at the Tivoli Gardens. The disc was one of several thousand classics he owned. It took several minutes for the equipment to warm up, but he did not mind. In fact, he relished the interval as part of his slowing down process.

Eric walked to the bathroom; shed his reversible jogging suit and the expensive hairpiece. Later that night, he would deposit them in the fireplace, and in the morning, they would leave as ashes in a plastic bag.

Soon the apartment filled with music, and he began his sit-ups. He would work on his body while he contemplated his options.

He thought of Kelsey and Phillip, talking outside Metro Ambulance Service. He would begin to follow her closely. Humans were tragically predictable, he mused, so the chances were very good that she would lead him directly to Arthur.

He flipped on his computer screen, and was mildly surprised to see an e-mail message from the Director. He read it, noting the time would be a problem. *We must act quickly* meant the job was extremely time sensitive. At this juncture, he would have to pass or stall.

He entered a series of numbers, accessing a computer in Billings, Montana. *Please enter my order for $5 million of recommended stock. This transfer of the balance will take longer than usual. As much as two weeks. Will the price still be acceptable?"*

At this price, he reasoned, he would attempt to make room for an unexpected, and at this time, inconvenient job. He was compelled to finish the assignment he had started some ten hours ago. His reputation required no less; unfinished work could prove disastrous. Loose ends were not part of Eric's life.

Next, he began a telephone search at George Washington for a patient named Arthur M. Jacobson, but it soon became apparent that either an alias had been used, or the old man had not ended up at George Washington, after all. Why would, John, a man facing certain death, have lied to him? No, the ambulance driver had spoken the truth. The old man was a John Doe, or he had acquired some friends along the way. It was only another piece to the puzzle, which each job presented to Eric. He knew that now he would for sure have to track the old man through Kelsey, dogging her every step of the way.

    The delay had cost him dearly.

28

Washington, D.C. George Washington Medical Center

Kelsey wandered into the emergency room, knowing that she would need all her feminine wiles, and a great deal of luck to discover the identity of the man transported from the Westin. She decided a frontal attack was in order, and approached the charge nurse with determination, and a kernel of truth.

"I'm Kelsey Richmond, with the Post, and I'm doing a story on emergency rooms in the D.C. area." A white lie, small, she waited for the nurse to respond.

"We have a public relations staff that handles all press." The nurse was neither friendly nor helpful.

At that moment, a man with a very bloody compress against his forehead and a dazed look appeared at her side. Kelsey looked at the man, then the nurse. She eyed the man with the same disinterest as she had Kelsey, and then looked back at her as if the man had disappeared. "Look, we have some sick people here, Ms. Richmond, so . . ."

Kelsey used the man to leverage a hurried response from the nurse.

"Sorry, I really only need the roster of E. R. residents who work the night shift. It's kind of a human interest thing, and good press for the hospital." The nurse's shoulders drooped, ever so slightly. "Rosters for shifts are posted next to the door that says, 'No Admittance.' I guess nobody will notice if you take a quick peek."

The nurse frowned tiredly, and pointed Kelsey toward the door, relenting.

Five minutes later, Kelsey had hospital administration on the phone, even as she worked her way through a list of four names. They were more than happy to supply a Post reporter with the first name of a doctor for a human-interest story.

"Dr. Jack Ryan, is a resident physician, and quite experienced. He rejoined our staff and is studying to be a surgeon. He might be good for your story. Let's see, he's working third shift—let me give you his pager number."

On her cell phone, six floors below Arthur Jacobson's room, Kelsey paged Dr. Ryan. The little black box that never left his side vibrated silently against his hip. He studied the number, it's prefix was an easily recognizable as a mobile phone. He glanced at the old man, whose breathing was regular, punched in the telephone number. It didn't even ring as she answered immediately.

"Kelsey Richmond here."

"This is Doctor Jack Ryan returning your page."

Kelsey's heart raced. She felt the story, knew she was close, and this was her chance. She went for the jugular, hoping to catch him off guard.

"Dr. Ryan, I understand that you treated an elderly gentleman in the emergency room last night . . . sometime around midnight."

Jack shifted uneasily in his chair. *How in God's name did this woman, whoever she was, find them so fast?*

"I'm sorry; I didn't catch your name."

Kelsey gripped the phone. *This is good*, she thought. He's stalling because he's knee deep into something. She tried desperately to keep her voice casual, but thought she could hear herself tremble.

"Kelsey Richmond, with the Washington Post, Dr. Ryan. I'm an investigative reporter."

Jack was non-committal and cold. "Patient treatment is confidential, Ms. Richmond. Certainly you can appreciate confidentiality." Jack separated the syllables on confidentiality, in order to rub Kelsey's nose in it.

Kelsey stiffened. *He's smug, even for a doctor.* She knew that she would have to work this man in person. Otherwise, she would not have a chance.

"I know, but this is very important . . . urgent, Dr. Ryan. If I could just speak to you in person."

Jack was about to end the conversation, when he felt the old man's watchful eye at his back. He turned around and found Arthur staring at him, nodding his head. Jack's pulse quickened.

"Excuse me, Ms. Richmond."

There was a faint click on the line as Jack hit the hold button. He turned and found Arthur smiling.

"So. . . they've sniffed us out, have they?" the old man said.

Jack was stunned by his intuition. "How'd you know?"

Arthur, even in his weakened condition was thinking much too quickly for Jack. He was taking control, as he always had.

As Jack waited for an answer, Arthur's smile faded. "Who is she?" he asked impatiently.

"A Post reporter named Kelsey Richmond."

Arthur's wheels turned quickly, he smiled smugly. "Undoubtedly a good one, too. Jack, you must talk to this woman . . ."

"Not unless you give me a reason, Arthur. A compelling reason."

"We may be able to use her. Meet with her, divulge nothing, just find out what she wants, and more importantly, what she knows. She can't possibly know who I am. That is our plan, Jack, we must be in control."

The old man was right, and he could be very persuasive. Jack looked at the phone and regained his composure.

"Ms. Richmond, can you meet me at George Washington Medical Center?"

"Yes, I can be there in ten minutes." Kelsey did not want to explain that she was already inside the hospital, six floors away. Jack was edgy enough.

"I'll be in the cafeteria," he said. "How will I know you?"

"I've got blonde hair and I'm wearing a peach—colored suit . . . five seven, one twenty-four . . . ok, maybe one forty." She laughed lightly, already flirting with him.

"I'll be the doctor with a white coat, Ryan on the name tag."

"I'll find you. . . . And thanks, doctor."

Arthur was already on step three of his plan, when Jack hung up the phone.

"Jack, we have a very important mission for our reporter friend. She could provide a solution to parts of our predicament. That is, if you keep your wits about you. If you'll take a word of advice from an old man, who still remembers meddlesome lady reporters who think they have a Pulitzer waiting for them. Don't let your little head do all your thinking. Ms. Richmond from the Post already thinks she's in control."

29

George Washington Medical Center

Arthur shifted gears the moment Jack turned off his phone.

"I distinctly remember telling you that we need to make a move, and quickly." Arthur was feeling stronger. Jack's pulse was still racing from his telephone encounter with the Richmond woman.

"We have options, but we could easily end up looking like the Macy's Thanksgiving Day Parade if we're not careful. We need to think about this, where to go, treatment protocols, emergency strategies; in case there's another attempt on my life . . . you do realize by now that my illness was drug-induced?"

"Could be, Arthur, but your condition . . ."

Arthur tried not to be abrupt, but he was pressed for time. "I'm willing to risk a real stroke to make good our getaway. What we need is a safe-house."

Jack skipped past the obvious, to the only solution that made sense. "When Sarah died, I ended up with the beach front home her parents once owned."

"Splendid, but who knows of it? Better yet, is the property in your name?"

"I don't know. I can't remember the legal parts this

long . . ."

"Think, Jack, you must keep up with the enemy. If our friend, Ms. Richmond, found us, they are not far behind. This is problem-solving at its exquisite best!"

The old man was right on target, and Jack found himself digging deep into the well of painful memories. "It's still in my wife's maiden name," he said at last. "I never had the title transferred, and the tax bills have always come in her name."

"Good, then we have an option."

30

Washington, D. C. The Oval Office Present Day

The President leaned back in his chair. He was remembering the first time he met Arthur. God, what an intimidating old bastard he was! To take the oath of office, then to find out that he was beholden to some group of people he had never met. The letter from his predecessor had been succinct, and sincere.

The harsh reality of your situation is that you are now in the world's most powerful office, but dealing with the world's most influential people, who simultaneously wield the most power of any group ever assembled. Take some comfort in the knowledge, that, as you do their bidding, as your ten predecessors have, you will ensure your personal safety, as well as wealth beyond your wildest expectations. Frankly, they won't ask you to do anything that you probably wouldn't do anyway. Keep in mind that the Constitution was written by a group of gifted men, none of which were more gifted than Arthur M. Jacobson. Follow his direction, and keep our democracy safe.

It had been the greatest shock of his life. He found himself in complete denial, rejecting the existence of the Committee until he was forced to acknowledge it.

Arthur's first visit was unexpected.

31

White House the Oval Office January 23rd 2001

Arthur Jacobson was the essence of charm. He declined tea, and took a seat across the room, so that the President was forced to peer down at his frail form.

"Welcome to the Oval Office, Mr. President."

What an arrogant bastard, to welcome me to my own office. The President immediately was on edge and felt overmatched.

"There are several changes that we have planned, based on the change of administrations and parties. Here are the appointments we have arranged for you . . ."

"Just hold on there, Mr. Jacobson."

Arthur ignored the sophomoric protest from one of the nation's youngest chief executives.

"You'll see that these appointments are all financially sound, and therefore, essential and logical for the illusion of transition."

By the time Arthur was finished, beads of perspiration had formed on the President's forehead.

Present Day

The President looked at his watch. It was close to midnight, twelve hours since Arthur's disappearance. *Maybe we have another Jimmy Hoffa, complete disappearance— forever unexplained.* He then realized that it hardly mattered in the long run. The Committee would be alive and well, and in charge, regardless of the relative health of a very old man. What if the old bastard talked or went public? The President's next thought was a little less pessimistic, but offered retribution. What if Arthur was alive and well, aware of an attempt on his life, and gone to ground, planning some reprisal?

Alternate realities began to work their way into his thoughts. What if Arthur somehow wrestled control of the Committee back to himself? He himself could be in real danger. And what of the new Committee, why hadn't they contacted him? What precautions had they put in place in the unlikely event that their attempt failed?

The President's face had turned a pasty white. He was covered with perspiration and breathing rapidly. The phone rang, startling him. He knocked it to the floor in his haste, and it made a loud resonant clang as the handset hit the floor. The door to the Oval Office flew open and two secret service agents leapt through the doorway one on either side, an obviously well-rehearsed move. They crouched, their eyes searching the room, their hands just inside their lapels.

"God-dammnit, close the door . . . get out, go!" the President yelled. People in the adjoining office strained to see the commotion inside.

The President exhaled slowly and tried to calm himself. Clearly, it was time to issue another summons to the Director, he thought, and maybe a Valium . . . or two.

32

George Washington Medical Center
Near the Emergency Room, Women's Restroom

Kelsey looked in the mirror for a long time. With very little makeup to repair, it was mostly an exercise in vanity. Her early morning puffiness had disappeared, leaving a beautiful unlined face. She knew how to use her attractiveness to keep most men captivated long enough to get what she needed without being obvious, but she sensed that Dr. Ryan would be tougher, and realized that she would have to go farther than just superficial flirtatious talk to position herself.

Her two "white lies" of the day, nagged at her. She tried to be scrupulously honest; a throwback to her Southern Baptist upbringing, but it was a difficult task, given the nature of her work.

"What should I say to him?" she said aloud.

"Tell him to kiss your ass Honey, and tell him I said so," came the unsolicited reply from a woman in the first stall. "Men are pigs."

Kelsey was at first startled, not really expecting an answer since she thought she was alone, but she smiled, "This one's a doctor."

"Even worse, he's an egomaniacal pig."

Kelsey laughed with the stranger. Women, she mused, have the capacity to make casual friends in the strangest places, and on the spur of the moment. She made the sound of a loud wet kiss, and they both laughed heartily again. But, in truth, it was gallows humor; she was simultaneously frightened and exhilarated at the looming prospect of her meeting with the doctor, and what he might tell her.

Her fingers trembled slightly as she put on her lipstick. She evaluated the situation as rationally as possible, placing known facts and speculation in separate files. She had been running near the edge of exhaustion all morning, with too little sleep, too much adrenaline, and remnants of a vodka hangover as well as the side effects of 'her medicine'. She knew she had to remain rational to be effective. Whoever the old man and doctor were, they were both involved in something extraordinary. That, she could feel. She remembered the brief telephone conversation, replaying the moment—why had he put her on hold?

She looked at her watch, as an idea came to her. Maybe Roberto had something more by now. She pulled the cell phone from her purse.

"Roberto, Kelsey again. . . ."

"Calling to break our date, beautiful, and so soon?"

"Of course not, I have one more question about last night."

Roberto could hear the echo of the tiled bathroom in the background.

"Where the heck are you?" he asked.

"George Washington Medical Center"

"George Washington, what are you doin' there?"

"I'm following the old man from last night, listen . . . this is important, I need to know. Did you see the old man; I mean . . . could you identify him if you had to?"

Roberto thought about it. He had seen the man, but only from a distance. Still, the old guy was memorable. "Yeah, Kelsey, I'm pretty sure I could."

"Great, look why don't you meet me for coffee— what time do you get off?"

"Well, we're short of people, that's why I'm still here . . . wait, hold on, Kelsey."

In the background, she could hear him talking to a customer.

Roberto took the keys of a rental car from a man with mirrored sunglasses and a deep scar across his left cheek. The man spoke to him in a heavy east European accent, and was about six feet tall.

33

George Washington Medical Center

The nurse sat in the bathroom stall for several minutes after Kelsey left. Their interchange about men had exhilarated her. *The dumb bitch was talking to me—like we were old friends, and all the time I was watching her.*

Nothing that happened in the hospital escaped her watchful eye. As soon as Kelsey had asked about the old man, the emergency room nurse called upstairs to the sixth floor and gave the duty nurse the full run down. It was part of the nurses' network, "them against us" mentality, which operated with a basic tenant that doctors are overpaid fat cats and *we're the healers that get little or no credit*—or money for that matter. *They make all the money, while nurses do all the work.* This nurse exacted her revenge by exercising control over them as often as possible.

She opened the door slightly, and peered out into the hallway. The reporter had disappeared. It was her chance to talk to the old man alone.

* * *

Arthur was fatigued, catching naps and talking to Jack as much as his strength would allow. These sessions were more draining than he would admit, but he had to keep up a strong front, to ensure that this new alliance would get him out of the hospital to safe harbor. Now, as Jack checked in on other patients he rested.

His unfailingly accurate internal clock told him that his medication was late. Even in his diminished state, he could recite all his treatment times, number of pills, colors.

He made a mental note of an eighteen-minute delay, when the nurse entered the room carrying his medication tray. She looked at him

"It's time for your medication."

"No, my good nurse, the medication was due exactly eighteen minutes ago."

His rich baritone voice caught her off guard . . . he looked so frail. Eighteen minutes hardly made a difference on a busy hospital floor. Her body stiffened, she despised the upbraiding.

Arthur had been gauging human reactions since he was four years old, and he knew that he had hit the nurse where it hurt the most. And though her obviously disgusted reaction startled him somewhat, the words gave him pleasure. He sensed she was an inveterate meddler and a misanthrope—*a healer, indeed*, he thought. *This woman could easily kill and had probably done as much.*

What happened next left him thunderstruck. The nurse looked back at the door, and slowly and purposefully walked over to his bedside. She tilted her head slightly, reached up and grasped the IV bag in her hand. She looked at him, through him, her eyes glassy. Arthur tried to gauge her mental state. He had atypically yet woefully miscalculated her reaction. Clearly, she was enraged. When she spoke, it chilled the old man's normally cold blood.

"Listen to me, you dried up old fuck . . ." Spittle flew onto his nightgown. "One squeeze . . . just one simple squeeze and you'll be dead in seconds. Who are you . . . really . . . old man? And don't lie to me."

* * *

The nurse was the one unforeseeable element in the equation of escape that neither Jack nor Arthur could have anticipated. She had been married to three husbands over a period of twenty years, all of whom were emotionally disabled to varying degrees. Two were alcoholics with a propensity and liking for violent behavior. The third was now in prison for killing a bartender and two patrons with the jagged neck of an Old Milwaukee bottle.

In her personal life, she attracted miscreants and losers like a magnet, but at her job she was obsessively neat and efficient. Her uniforms were precisely starched, her unattractive gray and mouse brown hair pulled back severely. To the casual onlooker, she was the picture of the committed, middle-aged career woman, who had no home life or outside distraction. She trained and intimidated young nurses until they became 'her girls' emphasis on 'her' as she ruled their actions and thoughts through intimidation. Her work allowed her a respite from all, the personal pain of her home life through the years.

The nurse had first realized her capacity for murder with her second husband. He died badly at her hand over a period of several days, in what became a prolonged execution. Because of his severe alcoholic state, and his usual physical rundown condition, no one really questioned his death.

The nurse prepared for his demise by purchasing several bottles of his whiskey of choice, Jack Daniels; she then systematically began to ply him with a great deal more than even he could handle. After two days of a non-stop drinking binge, his stomach had begun to rebel and he began hemorrhaging. She continued to force the bourbon down his throat. Of course his blood alcohol level was so high he was hardly aware of her actions, let alone her over-all plan. Toward the end, she actually envisioned herself as something of an angel of mercy, delivering him from his misery. The fact that the man had a sizable life insur-ance policy softened her grief. The added "insurance" of no more broken ribs or black eyes at his hand, was the catalyst for her actions.

She enjoyed remembering his death, the sound of liquor bubbling from his lips, and the low gurgling sound.

34

George Washington Cafeteria

It had been eight months since Dr. Jack Ryan had been engaged in a truly personal conversation with a woman. He had buried himself that deeply in his work. The extra time he had, he volunteered in the ER; a reflection of his obsessive work routine and his lack of a personal life.

Now, as he waited for Kelsey Richmond, wondering what he would have to say while one on one with a woman, regardless of the circumstances, he realized how deeply he had been drawn into a dangerous, and potentially deadly political game. He felt terribly isolated. Inexplicably, he'd begun thinking about Sarah.

His eyes finally came to rest on an attractive blonde at the coffee urn. She looked like Sarah—tall, well proportioned—it was several moments before the peach suit registered along with the realization that the wearer had to be the reporter.

Jack approached Kelsey tentatively and extended his hand.

"I'm Dr. Jack Ryan."

Kelsey stared at him for an instant, smiling as she took his hand in a firm grip.

"Thank you for meeting me on such short notice,"

she said. "I think we should find somewhere more private to talk."

35

Washington, D.C. Westin Parking Garage

Eric heard the name George Washington Hospital and smugly reminded himself of how clever he was for being in the right place at the right time. It was fortunate for Roberto, as well. Had an interrogation been necessary, a tragic accident surely would have accompanied their meeting.

Eric retrieved his car and left the garage on a tear, his tires squealing on the slippery pavement as he pulled into traffic. First, he would confirm Arthur's presence at George Washington, and then he would eliminate the reporter and the old man. She would be first, he thought. That way there would be no one to question Arthur's death.

Eric calculated that he was three or four hours away from completing his job and a five million dollar payout. Though, by now, the money was secondary in his mind.

He smiled as he peeled the "scar" from his cheek. *Sometimes it's just too easy,"* he thought.

36

George Washington Medical Center

The old man had negotiated everything conceivable in his sixty odd years with the Committee. Trillions of dollars had changed hands, world wars had begun, regional conflicts ignited, presidents and countless others had died—all for the good of the Committee. However, the one thing he had never negotiated, he realized, was his own life.

He watched as the nurse held the IV bag and stared vacantly into space. He realized she was certainly, quite insane.

Though the room was a mere sixty-eight degrees, the bed sheets under him were wet from his perspiration. He was frantically searching his vast intellect for some advantage, however slight it may be. In her state of mind, anything could happen, so he realized that, somehow he must bring her back to some semblance of reality. *What was the focus of her anger*, he considered? *The young doctor, all doctors, all men?*

Arthur played his only card.

"You know, nurse, he almost let me die," he barely whispered. She ignored him, but he kept talking, and was careful to soothe her, trying desperately to sound calmer than he was.

"I understand that you tried to help me and that he turned on you, too." Arthur allowed himself some excess. "Who do these men think they are?" He lay back and looked at the ceiling. "I desperately need your help. Will you . . . will you, nurse, please help me?"

She was looking through Arthur with vacant dead eyes. She said, "Don't fuck with me, old man," she gritted her teeth as she spoke, leaning forward, grasping the IV bag even more tightly.

"Do you think a friend would let me die?"

"But you both blamed me for that . . ."

"No, nurse, not I, how could I know such things, it was *him*. I really need your help, someone I can trust to tell me the truth . . . if I ask another doctor, they'll just agree with each other, you know how they *all* are."

She finally looked at him . . . saw him. She lessened her grip on the bag, just slightly. "Why should I help you?" she said, with just a crack of uncertainly in her voice.

The meticulously starched uniform and tightly woven hair had not been lost on Arthur. "Because my fine nurse, you are a healer, not a doctor, everyone realizes that, and understands the difference in the motives of these two very different professions. One, that is the doctor, loves only money; the other, the nurse, loves people." The words coming from his deep and resonant voice sounded very much like prose.

The nurse loosened her grip and let the bag swing away from her hands. Arthur had said the magic words. His remarkable gift of knowing people, and being perceptive enough to know what to say at precisely the right time had paid off once again. This time though, importantly, the payoff was his life. He pressed on, though carefully.

"Can you do it now before he comes back, we may not have much time? You've noticed how he never leaves me alone?"

The nurse looked confused and bewildered now, and not at all like the mad woman who had entered the room. She looked at the bag without remembering why she was holding it, and she repeated Arthur's words, as if she was mesmerized. "We don't have much time . . ."

"I'm counting on you to save my life . . . nurse." The last word, *nurse* was again recited to her almost like poetry.

A bead of perspiration dropped from Arthur's left cheek, onto his blue and white hospital gown. The nurse released her grip, and he finally exhaled.

37

George Washington Medical Center Cafeteria

Kelsey followed the doctor to a table in the corner. Jack pulled the chair out for her. She said, "My goodness, a man with manners. Some woman must have trained you properly."

Jack's face reddened. Kelsey noticed his reaction and tried to recover.

"I like chivalrous men; they're certainly rare enough." Kelsey really meant that one. She smiled sincerely while Jack fought to resist her obvious charm.

"So how can I help you, Ms. Richmond?"

"Kelsey, please."

"How can I help you . . . Kelsey? By the way, that is an unusual name, where did it come from?" Jack wanted to let her talk, so he could watch and learn about her. He knew that people loved to talk about themselves. He sat back and waited.

"Yes, it's fairly common these days, but not from 'my era'. Mine is simple enough though, it was my maternal grandfather's last name. His people came from Scotland, and he inherited quite a moniker, James Trelewyn Kelsey . . ." she stopped short, "This is more than you wanted to know, isn't it?"

"No, I do or wouldn't have asked. I like to know these things, my minor during my early beer drinking days, was English Lit, so I like words and derivatives."

"English Lit was one of my majors", Kelsey said, not really wanting to go there as Lit was one of about six Majors, and fortunately for her, her last.

She quickly recovered and said, "I don't want to be curt Dr., but I really am on a mission here, and you're in the middle of what looks like a mess, or so it seems—so let me begin by telling you about what's taken place from my perspective since about 7:30 this morning."

Jack only nodded—then did not take his eyes off her as she detailed the morning, the two E-Mails, followed by her circuitous route in finding the "mystery man" that Jack was treating. Considering that the best investigators and half the governments best "spooks" in Washington were probably looking for the old man, he was impressed and rightfully so.

Kelsey hesitated when she got to the "John the Ambulance driver" part of her story, and stopped in mid-sentence.

Jack noticed, "What's wrong?"

"Look, I'm a firm believer that there is no such thing as coincidence, so this may mean nothing. Do you know an ambulance driver who works for an ambulance service—a tall black guy?"

"Sure, John—hmmm something, I remember he was driving back when I made my *first* trip through residency. He still works for . . . Metro." Since he knew where she was headed, he added, "And yes, John was here last night."

"Was he a friend of yours?" Kelsey asked.

Jack instantly realized that the past tense referral was going to make the story grim, and cringed, "Why, what happened?"

"Heart attack. At least that's what they said."

The blood rushed to Jack's head. "Who's they?" he asked.

"Metro Ambulance. They found him this morning. It looked as if he had just come back with some food, and just sat down next to a building and . . . died. The odd thing is that Phillip, his partner, said John seemed to be— in good health. I realize that apparently healthy people die every day, but this adds up to a coincidence that I'm having trouble with."

Jack recalled the big friendly man, and how he had spent time behind the hospital playing basketball with the guys. John had once told him that he had played college ball somewhere, *maybe Kentucky*, he remembered sadly. Kelsey interrupted his recollections.

"So what's the coincidence?"

"Well, I get emails about a 'mystery man' then the guy who brings him here ends up dead . . ."

Jack sat.

"Jack?"

"Sorry, I was just thinking about John."

"Look, like I said, I'm not much for coincidences. This whole series of events, just doesn't add up to me."

Jack mentally added Arthur's "stroke" to the list. Was it a coincidence? He also remembered the old man's warning: divulge nothing.

"That brings me to the heart of the matter, Dr. Ryan. Just who are you treating upstairs? Why is he here, and is it somehow connected to John's death?" The words she used were harsh, but as always, Kelsey softened them with her casual presentation.

Jack was not ready for an interrogation. "Wait a minute here, who said I was treating anyone like this?" he asked.

Kelsey had learned, almost fifteen years ago, that the best interrogation was the silent question. She watched him, waiting for the moment of truth.

Jack was no amateur, but he was also no Kelsey Richmond. Her stare made him uncomfortable, and he shifted uneasily in his chair.

She knew she had him. "Who's the old man who came in last night around midnight—the old man who had a seizure or whatever, at the Westin?"

Jack leaned back; he had been only inches from her face. He took time to regroup, realizing that she still had nothing concrete. "Well, Ms. Richmond, I think we're back where we started. Patient information is . . ."

"I know, confidential." Kelsey leaned into him. "But I won't accept that, doctor, too much has happened, mysterious e-mails, people dying. I'm a reporter, and I'm naturally curious, and God knows I like intrigue. Hell, I thrive on it. But this time I didn't ask for it, it came looking for me, and somebody wanted me involved. Who, I don't know. But now that I've been put in the middle of it, you can bet your ass I'm gonna find out everything there is to know. And you can help, or you can get in the way. The choice is yours."

She folded her arms across her ample breasts. There were tiny beads of perspiration at her temple. Her green eyes looked directly into his, and Jack knew she wouldn't budge until she had what she wanted.

38

New York, New York Penthouse Upper East Side

The unofficial Executive Director of the Committee sat at his desk, waiting. Had everything gone well, he would have been notified in the early morning hours of the tragic passing of Arthur M. Jacobson, but he had not. That meant there would be no coded message to the President, explaining the transfer of power within the Committee.

As he sat in the darkness, he waited listening to the antique clock on the den wall. It seemed that it had never ticked more loudly, or slowly.

An empty bottle sat before him, a vintage brandy—in the ashtray, a half-smoked Cuban cigar. This night was to have been a celebration.

Reality began to sink in shortly after four o'clock in the morning, when he sobered up and began to pace the floor. The great Arthur M. Jacobson was not dead he realized, nor would he be dead in *his* lifetime. He feared Jacobson more than any man. Now, given the circumstances, he understood his position—saw himself as the "sacrificial lamb."

He thought back on his life; he was one of the wealthiest men on the planet, but the money held no allure for him. What he really wanted was power, and with it, respect. If only God had graced him with good looks or an articulate tongue, he would have gone into politics. At age sixty-four, and divorced for some twenty years, life was uncluttered, even women were arranged for.

When the Committee approached him to succeed Arthur, he coveted the opportunity. His first meeting had been a complete success. He had carefully positioned his closest allies on a single point—the dangerous decision to get rid of Arthur. He had put everything on the line; now he realized that "everything" included his own life. Consequently, some two months later, he sat by the phone in a death watch.

He looked blankly at the .357 Magnum, wondering if he would see the muzzle blast in the dark.

The maid heard the gunshot.

She walked the long hallway in silence, unhurriedly stopping outside his room, to straighten the original Picasso, thinking to herself that it looked ridiculous.

She opened the door and saw the man. He had slid onto the floor, and was wedged between his prized Jefferson desk and the red leather chair. The blast had removed pieces of the man's skull—a grizzly scene, but the woman did not react with any shock or emotion. She had been carefully chosen for this position.

As she walked over to the desk and looked at his plump gray body, the smoke still hung heavily in the room. She shook her head as she reached for her blue directory which contained the fourteen digit number that accessed a secure line in Lake Geneva, Wisconsin. The phone rang once—a lifeless voice answered with a simple, "Yes."

The maid steadied her voice. "This is Amanda in housekeeping; I need cleanup assistance in the office."

There was no hesitation. "Our people are on the

way."

The phone went dead with no dial tone.

39

Washington, D.C. Pennsylvania Avenue

Eric looked at his watch—he had just enough time to change his appearance before going to George Washington Hospital. He contemplated his mission—Kelsey Richmond—and the most efficient way to accomplish it. This must go off without a hitch, and with no trace or suspicion of foul play. The worst scenario he could imagine was that of another investigative reporter looking into the death of a colleague.

It was still early in the day—too early to take chances—and too urgent for an elaborate plot. A simple hit and run, well executed, was probably the best course, he had decided.

He mulled over the problem, how to get her out of the hospital, and into the open. But how could he possibly accomplish that? There was only one way he could imagine—her editor.

Eric reached for his cellular phone and punched in the telephone number of the Post. Three voices later he had the editor on the line.

"Mister Jefferson," Eric began. "This is Andrew Arnot. I am a principal contributor to the Fund for Performing Arts here in Washington."

"Good for you," Nelson said rudely. He hated interruptions, and he particularly despised being solicited while at work.

"I would like to meet a reporter on your staff, a Ms. Kelsey Richmond, to discuss her being an honoree at our upcoming celebration."

"Why call me? Mr . . ."

"Arnot."

"Yes, well, she's out on assignment right now. Why don't you call back, say tomorrow?" Nelson lifted the receiver from his ear to hang up on the man, but Eric spoke quickly.

"Well, I just have a moment and . . . could you be so kind as to give me the number of her cell phone?"

Nelson was suspicious. "Sorry," he said. "The mobiles are private, but I can have her call you when she has a chance."

"I'll call back," Eric said thoughtfully. "By the way, please share with Ms. Richmond how much I value her work, and that this is a very special honor."

"I'm sure it is, and I'll let her know."

Seconds after Eric hung up, Nelson dialed Kelsey's cell phone.

40

George Washington Medical Center

Arthur trembled; his world had turned upside down.

Over the past few hours, he changed from being the most powerful man in the world, to bargaining for his life with a schizophrenic nurse. Even by his most optimistic estimates, he did not have long to live. An assassin, random bad luck, and a crazed nurse had conspired to create three "near death" events in the last ten hours.

Where in Christ's name was Jack?

Helplessly, he looked at the clock and realized only eighteen minutes had passed since the young doctor had left his room, though it had seemed an eternity. He knew that to have any chance of survival, he needed to get the good doctor back now.

The door opened, and Arthur strained to see his visitor. He was not expecting to see Kelsey Richmond peering into the room cautiously, as if entering some forbidden place, with Jack right behind her.

"Ahh, Ms. Richmond, please come in, and Jack, I'm relieved to have you with me again."

Kelsey was taken aback that the old man knew who she was.

"Please come in, Ms. Richmond, over here. . . .my,

you are a vision." Arthur looked at Jack. "No doubt, my friend and colleague has told you everything." Jack started to protest. "No, no, it's perfectly alright, I knew that Ms. Richmond would have the ingenuity to, shall we say, get past you, Jack. Even I, am surprised at her alacrity"

Arthur gazed at Kelsey, judging her to be formidable.

"Jack, please give Ms. Richmond and me the courtesy of a proper introduction." Jack complied with the request, though feeling somewhat staged.

Kelsey was surprised. *"The Arthur Jacobson?"* she said.

"If your question is, am I the same Arthur M. Jacobson who has clattered about Washington for the past sixty odd years, then the answer is . . . yes."

Arthur smiled at her, and patted the bed with his good hand. "Come, sit by me, and I'll bring you up to speed. You see, Ms. Richmond, you've walked into the thick of things, and by my estimate, we have ten minutes, or we may already be out of time, either way, time is of the essence. Jack, do be so good as to close the door, thereby shielding us, however momentarily, from would-be assassins and killer nurses.

Jack blinked at the last remark.

"Yes, your friend with the equilibrium problem paid me a visit. It seemed she wanted to know who I was. She was quite forceful in her questioning."

Jack moved toward the door, a reflex action. But the old man stilled him with a single motion of his good hand. "No time for that, Jack. We have to leave this place now, if we're to survive the day. Let's start with our priorities; do you think anyone saw you come back into my room?"

Jack thought for a moment. "Maybe, no, probably not, we came up on the back elevator. The nurses' station is hidden from that angle."

"Good. Then please arrange for our immediate and clandestine exodus, while I regale this young lady with stories of presidents, kings, diplomats, and of course, money, the root of all that power and evil."

He winked at Kelsey, and succeeded in charming her. He was prepared to do anything to encourage her, since she was so essential to his newly conceived plan.

"Your first priority, Jack, should be to shield us from the maniacal nurse as quickly as possible."

Jack silently agreed. He removed his tiny cellphone from his coat pocket and contemplated the options. He needed transport capable of handling the old man and a diversionary tactic. The diversion was simple, transportation was not.

He walked to the window, the farthest point from the bed. "I can avoid the nurse," he said. "But transportation is trickier. We need an ambulance."

"I think I can take care of transportation," Kelsey interrupted.

Kelsey used her phone to call Metro Ambulance and to ask for young Philip. With the impression Kelsey Richmond made on the young ambulance driver, arranging for a vehicle to transport a special patient was easy.

While Kelsey spoke into the phone, she watched Jack out of the corner of her eye. His admiration was obvious, and she found herself looking at him with new interest.

The attraction was not lost on Arthur, and he recalculated, thinking that this could be important to the success of his plan. He ran a quick tally in his head of their current status, and everything appeared to be in better order than he could have hoped for just minutes earlier. The elements would soon be in place for his escape, after which Jack would provide the necessary medical care and a domicile that was safe and secluded. And Arthur knew that a reporter, certainly this reporter, could convey his story, convincingly—the documentation necessary to leverage him back into power, as the rightful Director of the Committee.

41

Washington, D.C. The Oval Office

The President had never before felt this uneasy. The phone rang, a coded sequence, and oddly, continued to ring. He dreaded this call, though he knew it to be inevitable. He reached for the receiver, and could hear the caller's voice even before he put it to his ear.

"Trotter?"

It was the President's code name, short for globe-trotter, and a reference to his constant travels. The call was clearly from the Committee.

"We need to talk in person. There have been . . . complications."

The President cringed at the word. "What kind of . . . complications?"

The President was breaking security by engaging in a detailed response. "Check your calendar," the voice interrupted, and the line went dead.

The President's chest heaved. Heart pounding, he checked the calendar. The eighteenth. He searched his memory to decode the contact location designated as one-eight.

Eight plus one fixed the location as number nine, a dreadfully simple, yet very effective code, placed the meeting point within the Presidential limousine. "Trotter" needed to be mobile and secure while speaking to The Committee. He would be contacted with instructions while en route.

James L. Drake, the Chief of Security, was not surprised at the informality of the president's call. Many times during the past three years, the president had called on the spur of the moment to "venture" out, as he called it.

"We'll be ready to hit the street in five, Mr. President."

The President hesitated; he needed to travel privately. "We're on our own on this one Jim, I don't want *any* company. Chick can sit up front with you. Drake knew that this meant that he did not want agents, or even a follow car, and he was a man of few words who took direction well. It was strictly against protocol to travel without Secret Service escorts, but he reminded himself, it would not be the first time for his quixotic boss. "This is not protocol, sir," he said weakly.

"Maybe not, but they can't be tougher to deal with than me. Just do it, Jim."

The President's voice had an unusually tight edge, and Drake was not accustomed to arguing with the man who controlled his future. "Yes, sir," he said with conviction.

The President checked his security code. He would take his scrambled mobile phone, so that when the Committee called, it would forward into the secure limo line. No witnesses, a scrambled phone, a soundproof shield between him and the driver, number nine was indeed a good location.

The phone rang as the president stood to leave his office—two long and one short ring, the Director.

"Yes."

"Mr. President, we now have a complete list of all ambulance activity city wide for the specified time."

"And?" The President was not about to let up.

"Well, of all the runs, there are only four possibilities that night, and we're in the process of working them. Two went to Mercy, one to the Morgue, a third to George Washington. I have personally dispatched men to all locations. We'll have an answer within the hour."

"Taylor, I don't require any details on how you do this—just do it!"

The Director gritted his teeth. God, how he hated the arrogant son-of-a-bitch.

"I'm mobile for the next hour or so, but I'm forwarding if you need me," the President said. "Make that, if you need me for anything important," he jabbed.

42

Washington, D.C. Director's Office

The two men assigned to track Arthur were given information on a "need to know" basis, and were, as far as they knew simply investigating a "John Doe." The credentials issued to them were the same as issued to local police; the Bureau did not want official involvement and a possible security leak.

Both agents, seasoned veterans of the Bureau, resented what they considered "grunt" work. The tall one was the first to express his disfavor. "Eight years with the Bureau and my new I.D. says I'm a street cop." He pulled the nondescript Black Chevy SUV into heavy traffic. They were a half hour away from the hospital.

The older man was more forgiving, mellowed by years of working the streets. "It's not the Lindbergh kidnapping, but if the Chief assigned us, it must have some heat on it."

The tall one thought about it. "We in a hurry?" he asked.

"Naa, like I said, it's not the Lindbergh Case; we ain't lookin' for Bruno Hauptmann, or his stash."

43

Washington, D.C. Metro Ambulance

Phillip was not particularly curious about the upcoming trip, or about the passengers. Kelsey had asked him if he could get an ambulance for a forty mile trip, and he had agreed, borrowing an older vehicle that was used for training.

Reporters, he thought, they're always into something. He was secretly glad she had called. He figured that the 45 minute trip would kill three or four hours of his day, and he could use the distraction. He was thinking too much about his friend, John, who had always treated him fairly. John was, in fact, the only one of the drivers willing to work with the new kid. Phillip had not forgotten big John's quiet acceptance.

They had made several "hot runs" the night before, but the most memorable was the old man. A sharp dresser, Phillip remembered, with an awesome watch.

Absently, he began to piece the events together. The reporter must have found the old man she had asked him about, he concluded, and wanted to stash him someplace.

It was an intriguing thought—an old guy and a reporter—but soon his mind began to wander. He would have to explain the extra miles on the ambulance. The dispatcher never missed things like that. Kelsey had offered to pay, and Phillip accepted. He told her ambulance drivers didn't make much money, and she told him she quite understood.

44

Washington, D.C.

The President looked at his watch. It was 10:20, so he had just enough time to circle the inner city, take the coded call, and be back for lunch. Drake had assigned his favorite driver, a man who rarely spoke . . . the perfect man for a private occasion. "Use your imagination, and keep us out of traffic," the President said, as he settled back and waited for the call. "And Jim, put up my screen."

"Yes sir," James complied raising the soundproof divider.

As the driver took him past the Senate Office Building, the phone hummed in the President's pocket. He punched in.

"Mobile?" the caller asked.

"Yes, and scrambled," the President said.

"What is your name and location?"

"Globetrotter, secure in number nine."

There was a delay, as a rather large computer began to confirm the information.

"Trotter, we have two problems. The first is that the target is still on the move. We did not confirm success in our attempt."

The words were factual, not apologetic, and the

President was annoyed by the arrogance. "I knew that hours ago. Why wasn't I called?"

"Problem two," the voice of the Committee said. "Our acting Director was found dead this morning."

The President leaned forward and gripped the tray in front of him. Don't feed me bits, you arrogant son-of-a-bitch, he thought. I'm the president.

"It seems he had an . . . accident with his own gun."

The President winced. "We seem to have a preponderance of accidents." The President's head throbbed. He was terrified. He knew these people were capable of anything, but the timing seemed wrong. It gave him pause to wonder if Arthur was pulling strings from the "grave", and if so, how?

"What is the likelihood that the acting Director was . . ."

"Self-inflicted," the voice replied. "No question about it."

"Who's in control?"

"You are," the voice replied, "until we elect a replacement."

As it should be, the President thought smugly.

"And when will that be?"

"As soon as arrangements can be made, no more than two days."

"What about the target?"

"We have no word from our man. Our contract is explicit. If we don't have confirmation within twenty-four hours, the contract is void." The voice hesitated. "However, the problem may be worse than anticipated."

"How could it be worse?" the President barked.

"The possibility exists that the target interceded with 'Hunter', code name for File #3, the assassin, and that he exceeded our offering for the assassination." The word describing Arthur's contract was spoken, an unfortunate breech in security, but the President did not even notice.

"You're not serious?" The President was alarmed. His greatest fear was Arthur alive and hell-bent on revenge.

"Never more serious. It is understood that "File#3 the assassin" aka "Hunter" *must* perform . . ."

"Or he could become the next target?"

"Yes."

"Well, as acting Director, I suggest that we proceed immediately with that option."

"Our bargain must be maintained. It's only been eleven hours."

"Very well. Give him 'til six, Washington time, to update. If he fails, elect a second Hunter. That being the name or code of the intended assassin . . ."

"There is no precedent," the caller argued. "And there is an obvious reason to hold."

"I can't imagine what that could be," the President felt the power of his newly gained position in the Committee, and was posturing.

"Simple. He's the best."

The President felt a surge of power. "You mean he *was* the best. Report to me, and make it on the hour."

45

Washington, D.C. George Washington Medical Center

Kelsey's phone rang. It was Nelson.

"Some guy called looking for you . . . wanted your mobile number. He says his name is Andrew Arnot. Something about an honor bestowed by one of those artsy groups. Kelsey, he doesn't fit, and I'm worried."

"You're right, it doesn't."

Nelson snorted, "I know I'm right. So, what the hell is going on?"

This was so wild and convoluted; she couldn't begin to explain, so she didn't even try.

"If he calls back get a number," she said. "I'm with you, so far—he's not what he said he was."

"He's not going to call back. He only wanted your number. And, goddamnit, I'm your boss and I want to know what you've gotten yourself into."

"Nelson, it's big, really big, I just can't . . ."

He would get nowhere. "I've been where you're going, kid . . . just be careful." He softened as he always did with Kelsey.

"Sure." Kelsey hung up, sadder for shutting Nelson out. She turned, and Jack was standing in her shadow.

"My editor," she said softly.

"I wasn't listening . . . it's just a small room."

Kelsey wanted to clear the air. "Look, I don't know what we're getting into here, but I think this really has some heat on it, the kind of story that comes once in a lifetime."

"You don't owe me any explanation."

"Let me finish, Jack. Whatever this thing is, we're a team if you want to be. We all do what it takes to get Arthur to the beach house. That way I get what I want." Kelsey thought for a moment, looking closely at Jack. "Like I said, I get what I want, but I can't figure, what is it that you get?'

Arthur watched Kelsey laying down the ground rules, and asking a very tough question. He interrupted, not wanting the doctor, perhaps the most important team member to reevaluate his own motives.

"Jack, do you know what to do?"

The question went unanswered, as he nodded. "I'll take care of the nurse, while Kelsey wheels you down to the side exit."

Jack alerted the nurses' station that he was shutting off the monitor, in order to take his patient down to X-ray. It was a believable story. Arthur had bruises everywhere, and he made a pitiful sight after they had carefully placed him in the wheel chair.

Jack exhaled deeply, calming himself. "I'll see you in exactly ten minutes," he warned. "Under the canopy. Very few visitors come or go from that side. We'll be more visible to the staff, but we'll miss the uh, potentially un-wanted traffic." He winked at Kelsey.

"Call me." She smiled.

He looked at the old man one more time. "Are you going to be alright?"

Arthur looked squarely at him. "That, is precisely the question I was going to ask you."

Jack smiled and squeezed the old man's hand. The moment was not lost on Kelsey. They had forged a friendship in a few short hours, and each seemed inexplicably committed to the other.

Arthur ended the moment. "Let the escape begin," he said. Coming as it did from him, it was very much royal decree.

Jack left the room and headed toward the nurse's station, walking slowly. He stopped and opened his cell phone when it beeped.

"Jack, are we clear?" It was Kelsey's voice.

"Yes, doctor, I'm fine," Jack feinted. "What can I do for you?"

"Jesus you're a horrible actor, lighten up." Kelsey was amused but concerned. Jack sounded tight.

Kelsey began pushing the wheelchair to the door. "OK," she said. "We're on our way."

She opened the door, searched the hallway for any sign of trouble, and navigated the wheel chair around a corner and toward the elevator. Her heart pounded with every step. She punched the down button eight or nine times, in a futile attempt to speed the elevator. The loud clang of the elevator bell sent a shock wave through her. Arthur watched her closely, her eyes darting in all directions. He could feel her tension. He placed his hand on hers, and squeezed it, and the gesture helped to keep her from coming unglued.

At last, the elevator door opened. It was filled with residents, who eyed the unlikely pair with open fascination.

Kelsey's spontaneous cover was perfect to diffuse any nosey onlookers. "Don't you worry, sugar pants," she told Arthur. "I'm not going to let this spoil our honeymoon. We'll be home in time for . . ."

The door closed with her in mid-sentence as she had hoped, leaving its recent occupants to exchange looks followed by a burst of spontaneous laughter.

Inside the elevator, Arthur huffed, with mock indignation. "Sugar pants . . . indeed!"

46

Washington, D.C.

Eric fumed after his call to Nelson, realizing the utter futility of his effort. The editor, it seemed, was much too cautious to fall for such a clumsy story. He evaluated his recent actions, knowing he would have to approach the next part of his mission with greater caution and stealth

He looked at the overnight bag containing everything he needed: two guns, a blue oxford cloth button down shirt with triple starch, an old school tie, (red blue and gold), khaki Docker pants, and a long stem red silk rose; an odd but necessary combination. For now, he wore golfing attire suitable for a doctor making last minute, pre-golf rounds. He counted on hospital traffic to make him invisible. He pulled into the parking lot of George Washington, just behind an ambulance with a green cross on the side.

* * *

Jack stood at the nurses' station, pretending to talk to a colleague on his cellular phone, while scanning the station for "the nurse." He wondered where she was as he signed the necessary paperwork for Arthur's fictitious trip to x-ray. Avoiding that maniacal nurse was his primary goal at the moment.

Meanwhile, the unlikely couple arrived on the first floor. Kelsey waited inside the elevator, quickly examining the lobby for anything that looked remotely suspicious, as Arthur sat in silence.

The long hallway adjacent to the elevators was only seventy-five feet, but to Kelsey it was treacherous as a minefield, and longer than a football field. She waited so long that the elevator doors started to close; then at the last moment, she reached out and stopped them, having located a possible momentary safe haven in the gift shop across the hall.

At the front of George Washington Medical Center, the revolving door swung open, and in walked a man casually dressed as a golfer. He carried a doctor's bag and sported dark sunglasses, which he did not remove. He appeared appropriately bored and preoccupied. He cut a diagonal path, taking him to the information center.

Kelsey had chosen that very moment to dart across the hall to the gift shop, and to position herself behind a rack of tee shirts. Eric looked in that direction, feeling a tug that only his sharp powers of intuition could feel. He only caught a glimpse of her back and blonde hair, but it did not register. He was after all preoccupied with the business of locating his prey. Any other time, he would have followed his instinct and pursued his gut reaction. Kelsey safely ducked into the shop.

At the information desk, Eric interrupted two ladies in pink-and-white striped pinafores "I'm Dr. Levin. Someone just paged me to consult on a stroke patient, but my pager cut off, and I didn't get the patient's name. I do know he was admitted late last night through emergency, and is quite elderly."

"Do you have the name of the attending physician?" one of the women asked. It was a routine question. Eric pulled his glasses down and stared at the young nurse, something he did not want to do, but it helped him make his point. He continued with biting sarcasm.

"No. Let me repeat what I have already told you, my pager cut off, and I only know that I was asked to consult on this, so if you could just accommodate me, I want to keep this as short as possible," Eric said. "This wasn't part of my schedule today." He looked at his watch pointedly. The nurse was as intimidated as Eric had hoped.

"I'm sure he's on the sixth floor in critical care, doctor." She punched the computer for recent admissions. "This is probably your patient . . . a John Doe—the entry must not be complete.

Eric hesitated. "That must be him." But he was still troubled. "Any other admissions that fit that description?" he asked.

The woman scanned the page, and shook her head. "No, doctor. As far as neuro admissions last night through emergency, that's it."

Eric decided that either way he was now within striking distance. "What's the room number?" he asked.

"Six seventy one, doctor."

Eric did not bother to thank the nurse, but simply turned and headed for the elevator.

Inside the gift shop, the conversation between the doctor and the aide was audible to both Kelsey and the old man. She was putting the pieces together, and Arthur recognized the man's voice, even without the lisp and the practiced southern draw that Eric had used at the Senator's home. "My God," he told Kelsey, "its him. Alert Jack, quickly."

Kelsey punched the phone, and Jack answered. "Jack, unless you want company, you'd better get the hell out of there. Be sure to take the elevators opposite the central bank."

"But we said . . ."

"Just do it, Jack, and hurry, he's on his way up."

As Jack walked past the nurse's lounge, the door opened, offering a surprise glimpse of the stern nurse, sitting, and staring into space. Jack turned his face away and picked up his step. But he would not have the extra time that he wanted. He was standing just a few feet from the elevator bank when Kelsey called.

The doors opened.

47

George Washington Medical Center Nurses Lounge

The nurse was still in a state of confusion. Mental lapses and near catatonia typically followed fits of uncontrolled rage. She tried to put the pieces of the morning together, but was at a loss to explain exactly what had precipitated the confrontation with the old man. She looked at the bulletin on the wall without thinking, still holding the medicine tray with the name Blanchard on the pill dispenser. A younger nurse walked into the lounge and saw her, but dared not question her.

Finally, it began coming back . . . *The son-of-a-bitch, Jack. He's the one to blame . . .*

Jack stood, almost paralyzed, but the man he saw looked ordinary enough, and certainly did not look like an assassin. He stood face to face with a man who appeared to be a slender young physician sporting a dreadful hairpiece. "Excuse me," he said, side-stepping the man.

Eric's antenna sounded another alarm, so he slowed and eyed Jack from behind his sunglasses. He did not know why, but he felt compelled to engage the man. "Critical care?" he asked.

Jack thought a moment, and tried to calm himself and look casual. "Who are you looking for?" Sweat began to form on Jack's brow, as his pulse quickened from the adrenaline rush—his head began to pound.

"I'm consulting, just need to check a patient file." Eric was, for some unknown reason, suspicious of this complete stranger. It was as if he could feel Jack's angst.

Jack realized that the man had not answered his question. Simultaneously, his phone began to hum.

"Just a sec . . . Yes?"

"Jack, where the hell are you?" Kelsey pleaded.

"On my way. . . ."

"And Jack . . . our man is wearing a bad hairpiece. Arthur's sure he saw him at the central bank of elevators."

Jack avoided Eric's gaze. "Yes," he told Kelsey, "I know."

Outside George Washington Hospital, two agents in a black Chevy SUV, pulled onto the emergency ramp and parked illegally.

48

At the opposite side of the building, Phillip waited patiently. He had rolled the window of the ambulance down and was smoking, a strict violation of company policy. What the hell, he thought, who was going to know? He glanced at his watch, remembering Kelsey had told him to be there at 10:30 sharp. If she was late it, was not by much.

He flicked the butt out the window, and got out to open the side doors. He began lowering the wheel chair lift, and halfway through the cycle, it stopped.

'Shit,'' he swore aloud. "This damn truck is still fucked up." He began the annoying process of turning the key off and on again several times, until it caught.

He thought about the incoming passengers. The old man was undoubtedly in a chair, more likely, horizontal, he thought. Either way, Phillip wanted to be ready.

He gave thought to the supplies he had on board, remembering that Big John had taught him well, "Always carry what you use, not what they say you'll need." As usual, his friend's advice was right on target.

Phillip lit another Camel, leaned against the side of the truck and watched the door and thought about how much he would enjoy watching Kelsey's long legs walking toward him.

49

George Washington Medical Center Patient Information

The two agents used the same door Eric had used five minutes earlier. Their instructions were to attract as little attention as possible, but find the old man. The tall agent, the more aggressive of the two, quickly found a young nurse.

"Good morning, Ma'am, I'm Detective Lanier, and this is my partner Detective Walcott." He displayed his phony ID. "We need information on a possible John Doe that would have arrived last night by ambulance."

"We don't usually admit John Doe's without a sponsoring physician," she said evenly. "They're routed to Mercy."

The tall agent changed his approach and his demeanor. "Look, Miss, I need to see all emergency admissions of a Caucasian male, elderly, let's say, between 10:00 p.m. and 6:00 a.m. . . . now!"

The nurse hesitated, but knew any resistance would be futile and time consuming.

The older agent leaned over to the tall one, and whispered. "My, you are a smooth silver- tongued son-of-a-bitch, you really are."

The tall one grunted and did not take his eyes off the

woman, as she retrieved the admissions sheet. She handed it over and he quickly scanned it. It was unfortunate for them that they did not have as tight of a search to work with as Eric.

"We've got twenty-odd names here. Just give me . . . white, male, old, last night after 11:00p.m. before 4:00am."

In less than a minute, the woman returned with a computer printout identifying two admissions, both John Doe's but only one sponsored by a local physician.

As they walked to the main elevator bank, the older agent decided to go with his gut feeling.

"Let's try this John Doe who's on the sixth floor."

50

Langley, Virginia, CIA Headquarters Comm. Center

The young cryptographer fidgeted nervously in his seat. The Director had agreed to see him personally, but had kept him waiting for more than twenty minutes. It was not a good sign; the Director was compulsive about everything, especially time.

He looked around the office. It contained professional memorabilia of all kinds, but nothing of the man's personal life. There were no family photos, vacation shots with a wife and kids.

No one but the eager assistant would have noted the oddity, for the same reason that he had ferreted out the scrambled communication between the Committee and "Trotter." Quite simply, he never missed a detail, no matter how small.

The Director entered, having just been briefed on the state of the world, while the assistant was still mulling this over. Throughout his career, the Director had frantically searched for anything that might push him closer to the top of the Washington inner circle. He was annoyed at the possibility that, if this classified message were correct, some flunky had actually ended up, almost by accident, with an incredibly important coded transmission. Life was strange, he thought bitterly.

After the first report of the random call, he had put all resources into a frantic search for "relative substance," as it was called. He was careful to discourage any scrutiny as far as the contents of the message were concerned.

"Well," he began, "what is it that brings you in to see me?"

The Director knew, of course, but he loved to hear his people explaining things in great detail. The conversation also gave him the opportunity to evaluate his visitor. This man's speech had a halting cadence, and he was unsure of his words.

"Today, not long ago, I . . . received a 'random scramble'."

"A what?"

"Uh, we call it a random scramble, sir. It's a mobile, with scrambled communication from somewhere inside the District. They're unusual, so we dissect and decode them. Typically, they're military and can't be decoded except by the Pentagon. This one was different, though; it came across a mobile phone line and was coded through a *complex X* based sampling."

He waited and watched the Director, and was using just enough gibberish to gauge the man's understanding of his work.

"Go ahead."

The reality was that the cryptographer had tapped into a secure mobile line quite by accident.

"Anyway, I have the transcript and I think you should read it."

The Director stared at him. "Have you read it?"

"Sir, I recognized it as a high-level security transmission between two people, from somewhere in the Capital, near the White House and Senate Office Building. But the meaning of the dialogue escapes me. The young cryptographer was being careful; he had not really answered the question directly.

The Director looked at the cryptographer for a full minute without speaking, which seemed an eternity for two people closeted in a quiet office. But he did not flinch.

Finally, the Director smiled. "How long have you been with the Company?"

"Four years next month." He shuffled slightly in his chair. He had begun to feel gut level fear, inexplicable but real, and he wished he had not come to the Director.

"What do you think this message is all about?" the Director asked him. "What's your interpretation?"

The cryptographer was out of his element. He looked down at his feet before speaking.

"Sir, may I be completely candid?" He winced at his own question, and proceeded without an answer. "It has to do with a failed assassination attempt . . . wet work. I wouldn't have a clue as to who the people are. It also contains references to some committee." He trailed off.

The Director had to make a decision. "Who has seen this?" he asked.

"Just me, sir. Then I requested a meeting with you." The assistant rubbed both his knees, trying to dry his sweaty palms.

"Did you make notes of the transcript?"

"No, I was very careful. The translation of the scramble is only in my computer, filed under 'Transit'."

"Hmm, why transit?"

"Short for transition, until I could determine exactly what it was."

"Logical."

It was time for the deception.

"Son, we know the origin of this piece of work," the

Director said. "Its organized crime, my best guess is, we're about to see a 'hit' that has been rumored for several days."

The cryptographer could not accept this, even though he knew he should have let it go. "Sir, if it's someone outside top security clearance, we still have a problem."

The Director looked dead pan. "How so?" he asked.

"The scramble required the highest order of clearance. I recognized it from other top secret transmissions."

The next step was painful, even to the Director. The assistant had stumbled into something enormous, and was much too young and naive to be trusted. It could blow the roof off Washington.

"You're convinced?"

"Absolutely," the assistant said.

"Then we'll need to debrief you thoroughly." He winked at him and nodded, "I can see your career moving quickly, son."

The analyst allowed himself the slightest smile. Five minutes later, "Transit" no longer existed in his computer, and twenty minutes later, he was taken to a debriefing room, never to be seen again.

51

Arthur M. Jacobson was cautiously optimistic. Since everything seemed to be in place, his only concern at the moment was the medical disaster he felt looming.

In spite of his tough outward attitude and appearance, he could feel that his lungs were filling with fluid, and his breathing was becoming shallow, becoming increasingly difficult. As he sat in the hospital gift shop, he tried valiantly to keep his condition hidden, but Kelsey recognized his distress.

"What's wrong, Arthur?"

"I don't know," he wheezed, "Maybe pneumonia . . . heart failure. I expect neither one would be good."

She looked at him carefully. "Will you be alright until we get outside?"

He sidestepped the question with a terrifically direct answer, "I think, perhaps some oxygen is in order."

Kelsey looked down the corridor, her face a study in determination. They were less than fifty feet from the door.

Jack was alone in the elevator. He had met Eric and eluded him.

Meanwhile, Eric walked the hallway in search of Arthur. He was here to kill the old man. The contract called for as much. If he failed, he knew that, as is the case with any work of this kind, he would become the target. He had no doubts about the motives of his clients; they were notoriously ruthless. But in the end, he thought no more than he.

* * *

Nelson sat in his office at the Post, knowing Kelsey was involved in something very big, and if it was, it could also be very dangerous. His heart and mind raced—an agony of excitement and anxiety. Every instinct told him she was in grave danger.

52

George Washington Medical Center

Eric walked the hallway without taking his eyes off a large nurse. She appeared to be unsure of herself, out of step with the efficiency of a bustling hospital floor. Eric was always aware of anything that appeared unusual.

He hurried to check in at the nurses' station, again banking on the simplicity of his disguise, and the likelihood that nobody would remember him later. He maintained his late-for-golf attitude.

"Nurse, I need to see the file on John Doe, also known as a, it looks like Mr. Blanchard."

The nurse barely looked up. Even Eric was amazed at what a stethoscope could do, in lieu of credentials. She simply handed him the clipboard.

"What is his current status?"

"Stable, Doctor, but, I think he may have already been taken down to radiology." With that, she looked in the direction of Arthur's room, just as the door closed behind the large, maniacal nurse.

"Can you give me more details on his condition," Eric asked, searching for any information to confirm his target.

"Well, he's stabilized . . . but there's left side paralysis."

Eric scribbled an illegible note on Arthur's chart and left the station for the old man's room. As he approached the door, his mind was racing. He would inject a second and certainly lethal dose of the drug he'd used before. This time it would flow directly into the IV drip. And after he was long gone from the hospital, the old man would simply die as many stroke victims did. This, he thought, was a clean plan.

Inside Room 671, the stern nurse looked at the empty bed, unsure of where her patient had been taken. The door opened, and Eric stepped inside. "Where's our patient?" he asked.

The nurse's thoughts were a curious mix of contempt and anger. She did not bother to look up.

Eric watched her as she hit the intercom button on the wall behind the bed. The reply came back almost immediately. "He's probably down in X-ray, a wrist fracture, they think. Dr. Ryan signed him out."

Eric did not have the luxury of waiting for the full medical answer. But he did need confirmation that the stroke victim was really Arthur Jacobson. So far, the pieces fit.

As he reached back and locked the door to the room, the nurse did not seem to notice. He withdrew the syringe from his bag. He was now committed.

"The old man," he began, "what did he look like?"

The nurse was confused. Why would a doctor refer to a patient as "the old man?" And why should he care what the patient looked like?

"What?"

Eric moved with amazing speed, and was at her side, his arm around her neck before she could utter a sound. The essence of logic and authority, he again asked about the patient.

"The elderly gentleman that was in this room, what did he look like, exact details, height, face?"

He grabbed the nurse's hair roughly, pulling it back, exposing her neck. His strength was incredible, enough so that she could not move.

She studied his face carefully. "Who are you?" she was barely able to whisper.

Eric did not answer. He exposed a syringe, and held it against her neck, but did not speak. He was in his element—calm, breathing slowly.

The nurse was more fascinated than afraid. "Fuck you." she whispered.

Eric hesitated. "I can make this easy or painful," he said. "All I want is information."

"Who is he?" she asked desperately.

"Arthur M. Jacobson, I hope." Hearing the name gave her a perverse sense of satisfaction.

"Are you going to kill him?"

"If it's him," he said simply. "Now, what did he look like?"

The nurse bared her teeth and spit in his face. She felt the needle tear through her skin, and tried to jerk free from her killer's vise-like grip. A moment later, she was unable to move, but her eyes never left his face. Her breathing soon became labored, as her diaphragm jerked involuntarily. Eric held her tightly and watched, as she became the weight of a corpse.

Down the hall at the nurse's station, two men with police credentials approached the duty nurse. Again the tall one led off, flashing his phony I.D.

"We're here to see John Doe #1. We also need to see his attending physician, who might that be?"

The nurse casually wondered about all the activity

surrounding the patient, but did not comment. "Dr. Jack is his attending physician," she said. "He has ordered a full battery of tests, starting with some X-rays, but the patient may still be in his room. I think his neurologist just went in, that room seems busier than most . . . check, if you like, it's that way," she said pointing left.

The tall man moved quickly toward the door of Room 671; the older man hesitated, flirting with the nurse, just long enough to fail to back up his partner.

Inside the room, Eric cradled the dead nurse in his powerful arms dragging her toward the bathroom, her rubber soled shoes squeaking against the waxed tile floor. He carefully balanced her on the toilet, her head tilted upward. As an afterthought, he put a tissue in her hand. Then, jerked at the sound of an ill-timed knock at the door.

The tall detective did not expect to find a locked door, not in a hospital environment, where privacy did not exist.

Inside the bathroom, Eric froze. He knew he had to answer the door, or alert the entire floor. "Yes," he said, sounding old and tired.

"Doctor?"

His plans had changed again. This witness would be one too many. Reaching into his case, he pulled out a 9mm with a silencer—realizing that he had by necessity been reduced to the tactics of "amateurs and thugs."

"Coming."

He walked toward the door, the gun concealed behind his leg. He opened it cautiously, thinking he would lure an unsuspecting orderly in, hit quickly, and then escape. The last thing he expected was an FBI agent posing as a street cop.

The tall agent failed to penetrate the disguise. "Doctor Jack," he said. "I'm Detective Lanier . . ."

Eric allowed the door to swing shut silently.

"No, I'm the neurologist, Doctor Levin. I was called in to consult on this patient." Trying his best to sound perplexed, he continued. "Instead, I find this nurse."

Eric glanced toward the bathroom. The agent turned his back to him, and stepped toward the open door. Eric moved stealthily, positioning himself behind the man, raising his gun in one fluid motion, he discharged a round into the back of the agent's head. The man fell like a marionette cut from its strings.

Eric's heart rate never fluctuated. He calmly stepped in front of his victim, noting the man's vacant eyes. His only option now was immediate escape. He opened the door, checked the corridor, and headed for the elevators.

At the opposite end of the hallway, the older detective caught a glimpse of someone rounding the corner. In the distance, he could hear the elevator doors closing.

53

George Washington Medical Center

Jack punched Kelsey's number. She answered immediately

"Where are you?"

"Ten feet from the door. How about you?"

"A minute behind you," he said breathlessly. "Jack, Arthur's having breathing problems, says he needs oxygen."

"Chest pains?"

"No. . . . well, he didn't say that, just tight and full."

"Tell the ambulance driver to start oxygen immediately. Check his pulse, blood pressure, it could be anything."

"Hurry, Jack."

Phillip had been watching the sky turn a depressing gray. He leaned forward when he saw the hospital doors open and the reporter wrestling awkwardly with a wheelchair. He left the van and bolted to her side startling her. "Shit," she said, grabbing her chest in a panic.

"Sorry, I saw you dragging the chair and . . ."

"That's okay. Look, he needs immediate attention. The doc's right behind us. He said to start oxygen and check his pressure."

Phillip was an average thinker with a gift for healing. He took charge of the chair, and started moving at a normal pace.

Kelsey grabbed his arm. "Look this is not what you think. We have serious problems. We're being chased by a man who tried to kill this old guy. He may be right behind us. I should have told you all of it, but I was afraid to."

Phillip looked at her without missing a beat. "So what are we waiting for?" he said, a broad grin stretching across his face.

The driver shoved the chair toward the ambulance, and Kelsey did her best to keep up. Then Jack hit the hospital door running, and their getaway was almost complete.

Upstairs, the older agent walked the last few feet to Arthur's room, hesitated, and then knocked. His gut told him something was wrong—he opened the door that had been left slightly ajar, immediately.

The scene was grizzly. His dead partner was sprawled, like a broken doll, limbs askew, face forward, in the bathroom doorway. He had taken the 9 mm shell at close range in the back of the head. It had ricocheted, exiting through his left temporal lobe, spraying brain tissue, bone fragments and blood onto the wall next to the bathroom door.

The agent knew the murderer was gone, but he upholstered his weapon anyway. He stepped around his partner and looked at the nurse. She seemed to be asleep, sitting on the john. Her face had a confused expression. He put his fingers to her throat, knowing that it was pointless. Her body was still warm to the touch, but he could feel no pulse. He noted slight discoloration on her neck.

He left the bathroom, averting his eyes from his dead partner. These were no ordinary murders. These were obvious hits, and very professional.

The agent's hands shook as he removed his cellular phone from his pocket and dialed a number that bypassed the switchboard.

"Director's Office."

The agent was breathing in shallow gasps. "I have a code red for the Director."

Code red was top priority, rarely used, and never to be questioned. The woman did not respond, she simply followed procedure, putting him through to the Director's private line.

The Director's phone sounded an ominous triple blast. "Yes," came the immediate reply.

"This is Detective Walcott," the agent said, using his street cop name for security purposes—the Director, always aware of minor details, knew who he was speaking to.

The Director stood behind the desk. The code red signaled critical news. "Get to it," he said abruptly.

It was then that the agent abandoned all bureau protocol. This was to have been a simple John Doe investigation. Danger had not been a part of the equation, and he was livid.

"Listen to me, you rotten motherfucker, what have you gotten us into?"

The Director, far removed from the daily dirty work, was unprepared for an agent talking to him in this way.

"Are you crazy?" the Director screeched. "Who in the hell do you think you're talking to?"

"Do you know what I'm looking at, you asshole," the agent's voice shook. "My partner's brains are splattered all over the wall. Just what in the fuck did you get us into? We had no warning . . . you've violated procedure . . ." His jaw was clenched tightly enough to cut through steel. The man had never felt such rage.

The Director, gaining his composure replied, "Is the area secure?"

There was no response. Had the older agent been thinking more clearly, he would have realized that the assassin was most certainly still in the building.

The Director took control. "Give me your location . . . and secure the area immediately!"

Eric moved quickly to the third floor, and into a secluded restroom. Gone immediately were the bad hairpiece, bright golf shirt and stethoscope. In the stall, he opened the briefcase, removed the heavily starched, blue pinstriped oxford cloth shirt and expensive tie. He removed an overnight bag from the suitcase, exposing the briefcase he had carried into the hospital. He donned a pair of thick lens, horn rimmed glasses. He was now a baldheaded young husband with thick glasses, visiting a wife who was in need of overnight garments. He carried a rose to complete the picture. He studied himself in the mirror, pleased with the illusion.

Moments later, he sauntered through the doors leading to his car and made his escape complete. He knew the damage to the mission was significant. Another hour had passed, and there were two more dead bodies. Worse, he was now left without a clue to lead him to the old man.

54

George Washington Medical Center

Inside the ambulance, the activity was at a fever pitch. The doctor had begun the oxygen immediately. Phillip was a very good assistant, but they needed a driver to get the vehicle headed toward the beach house, so Kelsey assumed the role of head nurse.

The magic of any team is its ability to be flexible, with all parts interacting and performing as needed. Such was the case. Kelsey was completely at ease assisting Jack, as if it were the most natural thing in the world for her to do.

Arthur, now resting more comfortably, was almost back to speed. He wondered aloud, about whether anyone had seen their hasty departure. Kelsey pointed to the obvious and laughed. "Probably everyone. We made for one hell of a sight with my mini skirt, high heels pushing a wheel chair at illegal speeds."

Jack offered sound advice, "You're probably right, so, let's keep an eye on the rearview mirror. We'll know soon enough."

Jack gave Phillip the most circuitous route, yet safest, to the beach house—the one he had taken with Sarah so many times with the top down on their convertible. This route would avoid all major traffic arteries, though it added almost half an hour to what should be a one-hour trip.

Phillip watched the group with interest, but did not question them. He knew the time was not right. As he drove in silence, he also scanned the rear view mirror, but saw nothing unusual.

Soon the ambulance began to drone a steady highway sound, and the frantic conversation slowed to a halt. Everyone was alone with their thoughts, yet comfortable with one another.

They were less than half an hour from the safe house when Arthur broke the silence.

"Jack, there are things I need to tell you and Kelsey. And at the risk of being obvious, I may not have much time. We can put the time to good use by bringing Kelsey up to speed." He looked at the reporter. "How should we proceed? Do you take notes, or record on tape?"

Kelsey pulled out her pad and pencil, and a pocket Dictaphone. "I leave no margin for error, Arthur. I do both."

55

Washington, D. C. The Post
11:47

Nelson rarely took a lunch hour. His routine was predictable. He would usually get a snack from the concession machine, sit at his desk and relax while reading a magazine. Today, however, his mind was on Kelsey. He wondered where she was, the nature of the story she was pursuing, and the level of danger. He couldn't shake the uneasy feeling he had felt because of the call from the man named Arnot. Something was wrong, and he knew it.

He leaned back in his chair and looked at the gathering clouds outside his window. Unlike most editors who want to be in on everything, Jack liked his privacy. He liked to think his way through complex issues in private.

When he'd convinced himself that Kelsey was in real danger, he decided to call in some "markers." In his position, he could snoop around the Capitol without arousing much suspicion, calling on "old timers" and getting the latest gossip. His well-developed sense for an unfolding drama usually led him straight to the top.

Today, he started by calling the president's deputy press secretary, who happened to have a 'thing' for him. She knew Nelson to be honest, and that he had never betrayed a confidence, something that could not be said for anyone else in his position.

Janet was fortyish, and had once flirted with the possibility of being his steady date.

The phone rang only once. "This is Jan."

"I understand you like the ponies," Nelson liked to kid her about her record at the track. She was the world's worst handicapper, but loved racing.

"Well, I'm no Catherine the Great," she quipped, laughing aloud.

Nelson loved her sense of humor. "You are one crazy woman, and that's what I love about you," he said, as he executed the routine again today.

"It doesn't hurt. In the White House it may even be a job requirement."

"So, what's up in this cesspool of a town?" He tried to begin casually. "The hair on the back of my neck has been standing up for days. Something's shaking."

There was hesitation on the other end of the line. "Let's talk, but not here," she said finally. "Where can we meet? Do they leave you alone over lunch in your office?"

"Usually," he replied, "but, Jan, come up through the garage, just to be sure?"

56

Outside Washington, D.C.

Arthur brought Kelsey up to speed with astonishing clarity and focus. Jack was impressed with the old man's recollections, and with his consistency. Kelsey, if astonished by the revelations, was not showing it.

Jack was surprised at the questions she asked. She was obviously well schooled in history, and comfortably conversant with most areas of presidential politics, a fact that had not escaped Arthur's keen eye. He was pleased that they were making progress ahead of his self- imposed schedule.

Arthur looked at her. "Kelsey, exactly what do you think we're going to do with this remarkable tale of a secret government within our government?"

Kelsey's personal agenda ended with thoughts of a Pulitzer. Arthur's did not. She knew this and thought about her response carefully.

"Arthur, this thing is so big, so incredible, that even if . . . rather, when I write it, I have no idea what I can do with it. It has the potential to tear the government apart, so I guess I'm afraid of it. But at the same time, I'm intoxicated with the possibilities. It tops Woodward and Bernstein and Watergate, even the Kennedy assassination. What would you expect a reporter to do with that kind of information?"

Arthur ignored the question, a technique not lost on Kelsey.

"I can help you with Watergate, since we know most of the official details. As for the Kennedy, uhh, removal, *all* the lurid details are in here." He tapped his head with his good hand.

For the first time, Kelsey was truly shocked. While it was obvious that Arthur had played presidents like pawns for some sixty years, it had never occurred to her that the old man could give her some ultimate truths about that infamous day in Dallas.

Arthur watched her wheels spinning out of control. He knew the magnitude of his confession would present her with the most difficult question of her life.

"If you discovered today the elusive truths we all seek, would it be enough to merely know the truth, or would you be compelled to tell it?"

He knew the answer, but he needed to watch her reaction to such a question. She thought seriously about it for the first time. Her life was driven by a desire to investigate, and then to report. It was the fabric of her being. She waited and did not answer immediately, knowing he had more to share with her.

"What if everything I tell you is only a tool to save our government, and can never be reported—could you deal with that?" He watched her closely, waiting for the answer that would set his level of trust.

Kelsey answered honestly, as she always tried to do. "I don't know, Arthur, I simply don't know."

She was not aware that she had passed one of his many tests. A simple yes would have been too easy.

"Kelsey, the Kennedy assassination is but one piece of the puzzle that comprises the Committee."

She thought about his statement. "The assassination is the greatest mystery of our time, Arthur. It's painful to even think about having that information and not breaking the story." She chewed her lips.

Arthur looked at the roof of the ambulance. "Painful. Yes it is painful, not in the sense that you see it. But it is painful for me personally, even after all these years." He turned inward, alone with his memories.

57

Washington, D. C. F.B.I. Director's Office

The Director's mind ran amok. He knew that the president had to be notified immediately, but he did not know where to begin the story.

What in the name of Sweet Jesus could have happened at the hospital, he wondered. One of his most experienced field agents was practically in shock, from what was obviously a professional hit.

Containment was easy; the Director took care of that with two quick calls—the first to remove the dead agent's body, the second, to a cleaning crew from the Bureau.

The nurse, he decided, would be left as she was found, dead from "natural causes." The sealing of the room was tricky, but not impossible to manage. Only hospital scuttlebutt would remain of the ordeal.

The real issue for the Director was the whereabouts of Arthur Jacobson. Given the commotion created by the murders and the old man's escape, there were bound to be leads. But all the bureau knew at the moment was that an old man had disappeared, and one of the hospital residents was missing.

The Director thought about the patient, Blanchard, who was most assuredly Jacobson. Two people had died in the room he occupied. Arthur was most likely being attended by the missing resident. . . what was the name? Ryan. But why would the doctor disappear with the old man. Maybe he was being held hostage.

The Director leaned back in his chair, imagining the scene at the hospital, the death of his agent. Hell, how could he have briefed his men, when he himself did not know what was going on. It was the president's responsibility, he concluded, as he continued to wonder what Jacobson was involved in.

Clearly, somebody owed him an explanation. "One of my men is dead, and I want to know why," he said aloud, as if hearing the words would strengthen his resolve. Then he picked up the phone and dialed the Oval Office. His call was forwarded to the presidential limo, where the president answered the car line, not the mobile phone.

"Yes?"

"This is the Director."

The President leaned forward.

"What do we have?" he asked, clutching the receiver tightly.

The Director had waited years to have a go at the man he routinely called that upstart son-of-a-bitch.

"What we have, Mister President is one dead agent, apparently a professional hit."

He waited for a reaction, but none was forthcoming, so he proceeded.

"Let me give you the full picture. The man's brains were splattered all over the wall. Coincidentally, it happened in what was most likely the hospital room that was being occupied by Arthur Jacobson, who was apparently admitted under an alias. Did you follow all that . . .? Mister President?"

"Wait . . ." the president began.

But the Director was on a roll.

"No. . . . you wait. Tell me and tell me now, before I commit one more man to this fiasco . . . this fucked up mess, exactly what it is we're dealing with."

A subordinate had not chastised the President since he had taken the presidential oath. He was being tested.

"Are we secure on this . . . uh problem," he replied.

"Sir, if your question is, do any civilians know about the dead agent, the answer is no, not even his widow. From what I hear, the poor bastard will have to have a closed casket. We'll need one hell of a cover story on this goddamn mess."

The president was momentarily lost. The implications were frightening, the possibility that Jacobson could be pulling the strings, and pulling them with protection now. Who else would have pulled the trigger on the FBI agents?

"Taylor, let's work together on this. I told you the old man was priority one."

The Director was not that easily placated.

"With all due respect, sir, that's bullshit. Priority one is a bullshit story, and I know it. Priority one is . . . a trade deal, a threat of some economic sanction, and people don't get killed for that shit and we both know it. Please level with me, so I'll know what I'm dealing with."

No president had ever breached the security of the Committee. "Taylor, this is a 'need to know'," the president said. "That is all I can tell you. If you can't proceed, I'll understand. If you want out, just say the word. I have an assistant director who wants your job."

The Director was ready to explode, but years of service and hundreds of 'need to know' scenarios had taught him to be patient. The president sounded sincere.

"You can't afford to lose me now, and we both know

it," the Director said. "So, here's where we go on this one. Number one, I'm changing all alert status for our field people, so they're at least at the proper readiness level."

"Agreed. I'm assuming there's a number two?" The President was calm and quieter than he expected.

"We will personally see to it that Agent Jeffries' widow is comfortable . . . for life."

"It's the least we can do, so it's a given. I'm sure you have contingencies . . . I'll sign off on them."

The Director was surprised at his reaction. Maybe the bastard had a soul after all, he was thinking.

"Taylor, we desperately need Arthur, and we need him now. Plus, we can't afford to draw any attention to this; its dark shit . . . trust me on it."

The Director realized the magnitude of the problem. Jacobson was into something so sensitive that not even the Director of the FBI could know. Dead bodies and a surprisingly submissive President made damn good evidence, and thoughts of what it could be chilled him to the bone.

58

Washington, D.C. The Post

Nelson's stomach growled from two days of too much coffee and not enough food. As usual, he sought the comfort of the snack machine adjacent to his office.

The night before, his menu had consisted of a bottle of Silver Oaks, his favorite Cabernet, and some Wheatstone crackers. The only problem was that he had not eaten any food to offset its effects. This was a typical evening, for him, living alone. Nelson was an antisocial purveyor of news and gossip, but disliked the Washington scene he covered. He preferred his small apartment, always in disarray, a good ball game, and a bottle of great red wine. His health, in the form of elevated blood pressure, suffered from a habitual lack of nourishment and exercise, but there was little motivation to change.

Oddly, Nelson had a roguish charm and a rough-edged charisma that women found interesting. Certainly, Jan, the President's deputy press secretary found him appealing, and they had much in common. Jan liked her privacy, and preferred a good book, along with an icy pitcher of vodka martinis to virtually any social gathering in the city, unless she was required to do so. The editor and the secretary were suited to each other, but so wrapped up in their mutual loneliness that they failed to notice the opportunity. At least, if they did, they did not act on it. So, Jan, possibly seeking to expand to the next level, took Nelson's call as something of a lunch date. A pathetic lunch date, but conversation with a man, nonetheless. While she had sensed the heavy atmosphere in the White House all morning, her real interest was focused on what Nelson had to say.

* * *

Eric was also thinking about the Post editor. He estimated that Nelson had to be somewhere on the up side of fifty, probably overweight, and maybe a heavy smoker. In other words, easy prey, if it came to that physically, and it might. With the old man, the doctor, and the reporter gone to ground, the editor was his only link. His course of action was now clear. He would approach the editor as Mr. Arnot.

He was still wearing the blue oxford cloth shirt and khaki pants that were completely unsuitable for an "artsy" character like Arnot. Changing would cost him precious time, but it was unavoidable. He pulled into the parking lot of the most exclusive men's clothier in Washington. He knew that with his size and weight, he could buy right off the rack. Planning was a wonderful thing, he thought.

59

Near Baypointe

Jack took the old man's blood pressure, which was surprisingly good. His recuperative powers seemed to be truly amazing. The administered oxygen had abated Arthur's breathing problems, and the symptoms had not returned. Jack was not an advocate of the theory "If it doesn't happen again, it never happened in the first place." But that logic was under new consideration.

Kelsey was sitting across from Arthur, with her notebook in hand, completely immersed in the old man's story.

Jack felt a slight twinge of regret. He was drawn to Kelsey, and like much else in his life, the timing was bad. Still, he found himself following her every move and expression.

Deep into the old man's history, Kelsey was getting important details. Arthur was remarkable and thorough. His photographic mind allowed for exact dates, even exact times, which astonished her. She had just asked about the years of 'The Eagle', Eisenhower, who had followed Truman, code name 'Hat' into office, when, she noticed Jack studying her intently. Embarrassed, Jack looked away immediately,

"Was the 'Eagle' your first choice?" Kelsey asked.

The old man did not hesitate. "Yes, he was a war hero and a patriot, so we knew he would fall into line."

"What about the change of parties, did that create a problem?"

"Oh, we never concerned ourselves with party politics. Politics, and the two or three party system, are simply part and parcel of the public illusion, supporting our democratically chosen form of government, which happens to be a republic. The committee deals only in financial realities."

Kelsey hesitated; she was simply a student learning what was for her, a new reality.

Arthur continued, "Let me be more basic. And please don't be offended, I'm not used to being . . . socially graceful at my age. Time only allows me to be purposeful." He smiled, and as if his explanation cleared the air completely, and blunted any condescension, he continued.

"In my opinion our basic system is so flawed, it requires that we offer the masses a choice, however dismal those choices may be. This allows the voters to convince themselves that any common fool, however disgraceful, is worthy to be president. The criterion for this choice can simply be that one candidate outshines the other. The sad reality is that even in our position of enormous power; our choices are appalling most of the time."

Kelsey smiled. "So, as a result, less than half the population votes."

Arthur looked at the reporter, deciding whether or not to ask the question.

"Do you vote, Ms. Richmond?"

She hesitated just long enough to answer without speaking.

"Not always. But I wouldn't have selected either

party's candidate as my first choice in the past election." She tapped her teeth with the ink pen and pondered, "And, that is usually where I end up . . . a limited choice."

"But because you have a 'choice,' you become wrapped up in the process and end up convincing yourself that one candidate is *wonderful*. God! Have you not witnessed those rubes, those sheep at party headquarters on election eve, acting as though some dolt is Woodrow Wilson? It's appalling."

Arthur hesitated and calmed slightly. "Think of it this way; advertising companies never—and I repeat never present just one idea to a client, no matter how good it may be. They always present . . . *choices*. This allows the client to decide on a campaign pulled from a set of choices, many of which may actually be deplorable."

Kelsey slowly shook her head, "You're right."

Arthur sniffed indignantly, "Of course I'm right."

Kelsey was fascinated at the possibility of exploring the Committee's 'real' choices for the Oval Office.

"Arthur," she began, "your 'ideal' candidates— were they the ones who usually made it?"

"That's a wonderful question. Unfortunately, there were very few of our choices who were electable, because of issues that the public would have considered character flaws. You know sexual deviancy, questionable financial dealings, unhappy former wives and mistresses. But on the whole, I would say that our first and most glamorous candidate, Roosevelt, code name, 'Chair' was a true genius, and unquestionably a first choice. His charm and strength were simply unmatched by anyone before or since. He also grew in the position to become better than even I had predicted. His death was a shame." He again stopped short, allowing her to interrupt.

"Are you saying . . . ?"

Arthur glared openly.

Kelsey probed. "Have you ever felt guilt over the . . . uh . . ."

"Ask the question, Kelsey. Have I ever felt guilty that we, the Committee, had presidents removed for what we considered to be the good of our country?"

Kelsey looked at him keenly. "Yes, Arthur. Have you?"

He looked at the roof of the van again. "The question is much too complex to answer based on so-called feelings of guilt. First and foremost, ours was always a democratic process, the Committee's, that is. While I was and am very persuasive in committing votes to my personal view, I would say that the majority always ruled. I take full responsibility for my actions, and while I may have disagreed on certain decisions, I stand by the principles of the Committee, even in its present state of rebellion."

Arthur let this sink in. "Let me ask you, Kelsey, do you think that General Eisenhower thought about the individual element of death when he planned the Normandy invasion? Did he calculate individually, the hundreds, nay, thousands of casualties, as he ordered men to certain death? As the history of the world is written, can we afford to, or will we afford to value the life of a promising young inventor, or father, less than some cigar-chewing politician? Casualties in the somewhat enigmatic name of political progress emanate from all levels of mankind."

Kelsey understood Arthur's logic, yet resisted the enormous cruelty of his seemingly pragmatic words.

"I'm not sure I understand."

"What I am saying, Kelsey is that each casualty is a man, whether he is the president or a foot-soldier dying in the trenches. In our search for progress, people die. This is tragic, but true and unavoidable. Perhaps you feel that General Eisenhower was a hero for 'winning' at Normandy, even though he personally ordered thousands to their deaths. Am I, then, a killer for condemning one man to death, simply because he is a president?"

Kelsey's conundrum: Was this man a sociopath or simply what he claimed, a world leader for uncounted decades? She realized that in the clear light of day many of the decisions made through the years by presidents and leaders might sound hard, maybe even maniacal, but this was clearly beyond her grasp. She had no answer; however, she was sure of one thing. She was not prepared for this kind of reasoning, from Arthur, or anyone else for that matter.

60

Baypointe

They traveled in silence for a time, Kelsey and Jack lost in contemplation, while Arthur napped. Finally, Phillip broke the silence.

"Doc, is this the turnoff? It looks kinda deserted to me."

Jack craned forward, eyeing the beach road.

"Well, that was the original idea, Phillip, isolated, but reasonably close to the hospital."

Jack looked at the once familiar foliage, and as he did, a flood of memories made him realize how much he missed that time in his life.

Kelsey watched him, sensing his thoughts, and wondering what his life had once been like, when he came here with . . . her. She snapped away from the feeling, thinking that it was ridiculous to be concerned about how Jack felt about some woman she had never met. Especially, since she had known Jack for all of about two and a half hours. But she realized that she really did want to know. She also understood that she was drawn to him, and in a way that she had not felt for as long as she could remember.

Jack's mind was elsewhere now, concentrating on the lay of the land. "Pull into the drive, over there, on the left," he told Phillip. "It makes a circle and there's a garage on the side. Hold on, I'll open the door."

He hopped out of the van and ran to the firebox. Inside a false stone was a garage door opener. Not exactly Fort Knox level security, but sufficient for such a secluded spot.

Inside the ambulance, Phillip leaned forward to catch a glimpse of the sky, which was now almost gunmetal grey. He carefully navigated into the garage, as Jack closed the door immediately. The troupe then began the process of moving their patient into the house.

Kelsey elected to remain behind to explore the property. The house was both beautiful and tasteful, but the weeds and overgrowth indicated that the doctor did not come here regularly. She looked down, and noted the beautiful stone walk, and admired its elegance. Everything, she thought, was very well planned.

At the front door, she read the etching on a small brass plaque which read, *Jack & Sarah*. A simple plaque, yet to Kelsey, it established the territory. She felt like an intruder when Jack opened the door.

"Come in," he said brightly, as if their circumstances had nothing to do with her visit.

Many women had graced the Baypointe house, but none, seemed to affect him the way Kelsey did. He felt a strong twinge of guilt, and tried to brush it aside. This feeling was more than a mere attraction to a beautiful woman, he reasoned. He silently wondered if she shared anything like this feeling.

Architecturally, the house was a lovely, Neo Classic beach home. The front foyer displayed an enormous vaulted room that ended in the rear with a glass wall, a floor to ceiling stone fireplace, separating two French doors that led to a pool overlooking the ocean. The hallway to the right of the foyer accessed the large master bedroom, offering a view of the ocean. The kitchen was to the left of the foyer, spilling out into the great room, with counter-top seating at the bar.

Jack made room assignments and set forth a plan. Fifteen minutes later, Arthur was settled in the master bedroom.

As the action wound down, Arthur quietly rallied his troops for the most important strategy session of his life. Jack had recommended at least an hour of quiet and rest for the old man, but he would have none of that. He asked Kelsey to sit at his bedside, telling her, "We can lose no time." It was not a request, but a command.

Kelsey needed more tapes and supplies, so Phillip was dispatched in the "beach car," as Jack called his Jeep. While the house offered plenty of canned goods, Jack's prolonged absences had depleted daily staples. Phillip was admonished to speak to no one, attract no attention, and to buy what they needed with cash.

As Kelsey and Jack gathered at his bedside, Arthur took their security needs to the next level. "Jack, you must call the hospital and give some completely plausible reason for your departure. Make it believable."

Jack nodded.

"Kelsey, what is your situation, will you be missed?"

As a loner, her only tie was to Nelson. "My editor is the only person who would possibly question my absence. But, something strange . . ."

Arthur's impatience surfaced. "Come out with it, whatever is on your mind."

"Well, it may be nothing, but my editor said that someone—an 'unlikely someone'—was looking for me earlier today. I didn't mention it because I didn't think it was important."

Arthur interrupted, "You didn't mention it because you're an inexperienced young woman who could easily end up dead!" He sighed dramatically. "These people who are after us are the world's best. They *will* find us. It is only a matter of time. Have you not already realized this?" He shook his head.

Kelsey just stared at Arthur, who seemed different than the charming old man she had met hours before. She wondered which was the real Arthur—the charismatic old gentleman or the cold-hearted strategist.

"Jack, do you keep the phone connected here?"

"Yes."

"Have you pulled each phone from the wall, so that no one can call in or out?"

Jack shrugged. "Of course not."

"No. . . . .no, you haven't." Arthur was harsh. "You people have lived in a fantasy world until now. Our nemesis, that is, the man who is pursuing us is quite extraordinary. If I know my colleagues on the Committee, it is safe to assume that they have chosen File 3 to eliminate me. And, of course, that now applies to all four of us. File 3 is 'Abraham,' the code name for a young operative who has been employed on numerous occasions. Only I have seen the man, his dossier and details of his life. Actually, I created him. He was a talented young man from a wealthy family, bored with life, and seeking thrills that do not exist within the confines of acceptable social behavior. He was educated at one of my alma maters, pre-med at Harvard, and he left for the military after achieving a perfect 4.0. He soon became a Navy Seal. He learned to kill and decided he liked it. He was dismissed for using 'excessive force' during several military exercises, all covert.

"I maneuvered him into a career as a mercenary. He is cold-blooded and brilliant. He will prove a difficult match, especially for us."

"For anyone," Jack concluded.

The old man weighed the doctor's comment. "It's worse than you think, Jack. The code name Abraham was chosen because he lacked any trace of conscience, even when it came to his own family." The room was silent.

"God asked Abraham to sacrifice his only son," Kelsey said flatly.

Arthur nodded. "In this instance, not a son, but a father; financier whose business dealings became problematic for the Committee."

"He killed his own father, for money?" Jack was shocked by the thought.

"Why are you so surprised? He knows that I was his original benefactor, and he did not hesitate to come after me."

"Are you sure it was him?" Kelsey asked.

"The details of the cocktail party are not as clear as they should be,' Arthur snapped. "But I saw his eyes, and even though he was disguised, I knew it was him. And now, what I am about to share with you will help you to understand the desperation of our situation, as well as our limitations in terms of time." The old man pursed his lips, as if to brace even himself for the news he was about to share.

"The decision you made, when you elected to help me, changed your lives forever. You know too much, especially if I'm unable to regain power. We are all fugitives from our own government. Remember, those in power make the rules, declare the enemies, and then prosecute them.

"Ms. Richmond, you'll want to start taking copious notes and recording now."

The request sounded very much like a royal decree.

She sat at his bedside, her tape recorder on, her pad and pencil ready. Arthur's eyes no longer focused on the objects in the room, she noted, as he began to recall the information placing each event in its proper chronology.

"The Committee wants me dead, which seems obvious. Their reasons are quite logical from their perspective. You see, they see 'opportunity' in the chaos of the New World Order, mostly through the turmoil that exists in the former Soviet Union, Middle East, Korea—China's emergence. Even though we have made superficial progress, which has been mostly for show, to placate the American people—they are convinced. And because of this, they have become certain that we can now rule the world by dictating our realities to all cultures and peoples. They are recommending that we annex—yes, annex sovereign world territories as the first step toward our so-called 'Global Program.' Even with limited successes in the Middle East against Iraq and Afghanistan they are convinced we are now ready to become an empire, as opposed to just the world's moral watchdog. Sovereignty, as we have known it, will cease to exist under this plan. These are preparatory procedures necessary for a declaration of the New World Nation."

"Why else do you think our president threw the election of 1992? He had no stomach for what was to come. While privately, I admired him and felt that he was in many ways, a true American hero, he was one of the few to ever hold the office and leave on his own terms. It was a masterful plan on his part, and disconcerting to the Committee."

Remembering the man as she encountered him in their brief meeting, Kelsey could only nod in agreement.

"The 'Redneck,' who followed him, was shameless. He didn't flinch. I believe the man would . . ." He stopped short of describing his innermost thoughts.

"The Committee sees the great abundance on the planet: the oil rich Middle East, the forests of South America, the fresh water supplies of Canada. They see all of this as future assets of the United States. Their appetite is insatiable, whatever resource is worthy of having, they are willing to steal. By the way, Kelsey, just as a matter of record, do you know why Canada is so valuable in their minds? Better yet the question should be, 'Do you know how much of the world's fresh water supply is available through our friendly northern neighbors'?"

Arthur's tone had become cruelly sarcastic. He caught Kelsey with her guard down.

"No," she replied. "A lot . . . I guess."

"A lot . . . a lot," Arthur mocked her cruelly. "You sound like a school girl." He paused, calming slightly, taking the edge away from his tone.

"Roughly seventy-five per cent. Of course with this information, you can begin to see the picture. The world is ours for the taking, at least, according to the Committee, and frankly, who could deny us if we really pursued this course?"

Arthur shuddered a quick but perceptible shudder.

Kelsey spoke first, as the old man suspected she would.

"Then, our only hope is to end the Committee or to have you regain your old position." It was both a question and a statement. "I'm assuming that you resisted this whole line of thinking, which is why you became . . . expendable?" Arthur smiled and quickly became charming once more.

"Kelsey, my love, you are indeed brilliant. The Committee was never conceived to rule the world, in the sense of empire. It is madness, but they were close to reaching a consensus at our last meeting." He thought a moment. "That was the last Committee meeting *I attended.* The attempt on my life confirms that the plan was indeed ratified."

Kelsey noted the rapid movement of Arthur's eyes, but said nothing. She was stunned by Arthur's manic view of her as a naive schoolgirl one moment and brilliant in the next.

"Only I can stop this, and that's assuming I can regain control."

Jack offered a rational option. "Arthur, who are your allies? Who within the Committee, can we appeal to in this?"

"There are a few . . . malleable under the right conditions, but we must have a very strong inducement. In a word, blackmail. Such an ugly word, don't you think?"

Neither of them answered, since this entire situation was ugly to them.

"The fates must have brought us together for this very purpose," Arthur continued more cheerfully. "As soon as we were cornered by Ms. Richmond, I decided that she could write the history of the Committee in such convincing detail as to be completely believable. Then, when properly committed to paper and tape, we could leverage it, gaining concessions from the Committee, and even perhaps, full control."

Arthur grimaced and lay back on his pillows. Jack, the doctor, took over.

"What is it?" he asked.

Arthur tried to deflect him, "My God, have you not noticed that I'm nearing a hundred years old?" He forced a convincing smile, but Jack was not buying into it.

"Now it's time for some rest for you," he said.

Arthur obliged, allowing Jack to check his vital

signs. Kelsey walked to the foot of the bed, and looked at the old man. She had judged him harshly for the actions born of an ideology, which she could only evaluate in hindsight. He had ordered people murdered, toppled governments, maybe even acted as a de facto world ruler, though behind the scenes, and had done so for decades. With that power came the inherent baggage. Her simplistic viewpoint had put him in a category of his own. How much worse, she wondered, would the world have been without him? Or, from her perspective as a dispassionate collector of information, could it not have been better? There was no way for her to draw any conclusions.

He looked up and smiled at her. Then, almost immediately, drifted off into the deepest sleep since his stroke. Apparently, the words he had shared had temporarily emptied his mind, lessening his burden for a time.

61

Langley, Va. CIA

The CIA Director pondered his dilemma. With the cryptographer now out of the picture, the "random scramble" was his personal property, and he would use it to his best advantage. He dialed the number, not bothering to use the private line. He wanted to gauge the President's reaction to a surprise attack. The Director did not have an appreciation of his leader's intellect. And, did not think him to be particularly savvy on most of the critical issues, he thought contemptuously.

The phone rang in the Oval Office and was rerouted to the limo.

"Yes."

He had not expected such a quick response using the regular line.

"Mr. President, this is Cole." The Director attempted to begin with pleasantries.

"I'm about to go into a meeting, Cole. What do you have?"

"Mr. President, given the tumultuousness of our time . . ."

"Cole, for Christ's sake just say what you mean!"

"Sir, we have a random scramble."

"I'm enthralled, Cole, what the fuck is that?"

"An encrypted scrambled mobile transmission."

The President put his hand to his face, tired of this endless stream of techno babble. "A phone call?" The President made no secret of his impatience with the ways of the intelligence community.

"Yes, sir."

"Then just spit it out. Is it just me or do you fucking people in intelligence have some secret goddamn language?"

The Director, in spite of the President's irritability, was exactly where he wanted to be.

"We have uncovered an attempted assassination. And, any time there is an act of violence referred to as an assassination attempt, within the D.C. area we go on full alert."

The man in the limo listened more closely now. "Yes, I know," he said sarcastically, "and I fully endorse that procedure."

"In the call, they reference a 'Hunter' and target."

With this the President froze his mind racing. Those damn Washington "spies and spooks" must have somehow intercepted his scrambled conversation with the Committee. It seemed to him, as it often did, that though he was privy to everything, sometimes he knew nothing. He wondered if the Director was playing with him, by giving him partial information, or actually confused.

"What's your take on this?" the President asked, gauging the man's knowledge of the conversation.

The Director owned the text, not the voices, and he explained as much to the President.

"It's as I said, a failed attempt, yet we have no information on anything out of the ordinary as far as your security is concerned. These things require top priority and close scrutiny."

The President wanted time to sort out the events, so he stalled, cleverly.

"Look, I'm really in blitzed for time, but I have just prioritized your call. Go ahead and contact my Secret Service people and tell them to go on full alert; then, meet me in the Office in one half hour, and we'll look at this together."

The President didn't want to alert the Director, but he did want to short- circuit any investigation. "By the way, who else has seen this information?" he asked.

The Director was chilled by the similarity to the conversation that he had with the young cryptographer and not about to make the same mistake, he lied.

"Well, it's all there, in the official log of the entry, sir."

The President was prepared to be blunt.

"Who else has seen this?" he asked abruptly.

"Only I have seen the text, but it exists in the computer for anyone with clearance to look at it."

"Secure it. . . .now!"

"Yes, sir. And I'll see you in the Oval office at, what did you say, 12:30?

The President hung up without signing off or confirming the question.

62

Washington, D. C. Near the Post
12:44p.m.

Eric sported a pencil thin moustache and shoes that were expertly crafted to give him an additional two inches of height. He had also purchased pants, pleated in the front, and loosely cut at the hips giving them a bloused look. The illusion was that of a gaunt looking man well over six feet tall. The appearance was close to the truth, in fact, for during the past twelve hours he had dropped five pounds from stress and lack of nutrition. He was running that bitter edge that one reaches, when desire overtakes logic and rational thinking. He could not recall being at such a point of distress in his entire life. He thought critically about his own performance over the last few hours, and concluded that even though rushed, he had done most things correctly. Of course, in his occupation, just getting most things right was potentially a death certificate.

The killing of the detective couldn't be helped, he reasoned, it had been his only option. His choices had been very limited.

He figured the editor could locate this reporter, and in turn she could lead him directly to Arthur Jacobson. So, his next line of attack would be to show his face at the

Post, as Arnot, and present the bait in the form of a check. He would offer a considerable sum of money from a blind account to press home the sincerity of his action. Nobody shows up with fifty thousand dollars without making an impression. Surely, he reasoned, common sense would prevail, and the editor would relent.

* * *

Kelsey sat on the white sofa admiring the spectacular view that Jack's home offered of the ocean. She thought of Nelson, alone at the Post with his corn chips and Diet Coke, or whatever; and while she understood Arthur's security admonition against calls from the beach house, she felt that a call from her cell phone could be safe enough.

She punched the number, but got Nelson's voice mail. She decided to leave a carefully crafted message.

"Nelson, I just got a free minute and wanted to update you and let you know that I'm okay and I'm on to something big. The timing is all wrong to try to tell you more now. Look, we've always been completely honest with each other; this thing is so convoluted and runs so deep I can't explain," she trailed off. "Plus there are some bad—really evil—people involved and you could be in danger, just by being my boss so . . . be careful. Oh, that guy that called you earlier . . . he's probably connected to this . . . hell, anybody could be connected, so . . . watch your back." She thought a moment, then simply hung up

* * *

Jan entered the Post the back way, as Nelson had sug-

191

gested. She reflected on the paradox that this clandestine approach represented, in a country that has freedom of the press as one of the basic tenants of its government. *Oh well, I've done sneakier things in my life in the name of a free press . . . and certainly, sneakier things for a date . . . or to try and get laid.* She giggled at her silliness.

Over the years Jan had developed people skills to the point that she was able to read colleagues like a book. Her empathic abilities while legendary, seemed almost a job requirement for someone in her position. Yet Nelson, a man she was very familiar with, remained an enigma to her—partly because he was in fact, precisely what he presented himself to be. Since Washington was replete with agenda-laden people, she had not, even after all these years, adjusted to his candor and honesty.

God, this place is like a morgue, she thought, as she made her way down the corridor toward the editor's office. Rounding the corner, she hesitated long enough to open her purse and pull out her compact and lipstick. *Why not, he's worthy of the full treatment.*

At the exact same moment, from the opposite direction at the front of the building, in broad daylight, ironically, the assassin was approaching Nelson's office, too. He hesitated to take stock of his surroundings, reading the names of the office occupants listed on the building directory in the outer lobby. He stopped when he saw the name Nelson O'Bryan, Editor. The building had no security to speak of, only a young woman in the receptionist's chair, casually reading the latest *Cosmopolitan* sex survey. She did not notice the openly gay looking Eric, a man with an expensive coat draped over his shoulders, sporting a pencil moustache, a wide brimmed hat, and sunglasses. He looked as if he had escaped from a 1940s Hollywood movie set. As he strutted by her desk, she did not even bother to look up.

* * *

Jan leaned inside the editor's office and looked at Nelson affectionately. Rumpled white shirt, open at the collar, tie askew, pants two weeks overdue for pressing, he stood behind his desk holding a Diet Coke and pretzels.

"How are things in the bowels of literature?" she asked, with a fiendish smirk.

Nelson fancied himself clever. "Shitty." He smiled a crooked smile.

Jan was smitten. Who could imagine that this man was Harvard educated, and could have written his own ticket in corporate America, almost anywhere? "Well, Nelson, why the hell am I here and why did you call?"

Their personalities ran parallel. He knew she would work him, so he started with his typical opening salvo: direct unfettered honesty, in order to establish credibility, but with just enough misdirection to trap his audience.

"What the hell is going on with the base closings?" he asked gruffly.

Jan set her purse on his desk and plopped down in the chair opposite. "Gee, you're quite the host. Since you didn't ask, a Diet Coke will do nicely."

"And by the way, I happen to know that you don't give a tinkers fuck about any base closings."

She put her hand under her chin to show resolve. It gave her a feminine look that appealed to him. That, coupled with the fact that he liked people who knew what they wanted, especially women, made him smile.

"Tinkers damn, Jan. If you're going to use profanity, at least get it right."

"Nelson, get in touch. It may have been damn two

hundred years ago, but this is the twenty-first century."

She sat back, waiting, and not about to budge.

Nelson studied her for a moment. "Well," he said, "I guess I thought we might trade."

"Trade? What are *we* going to trade Nelson? What could you possibly have that *I* need?" she said, flirting openly.

The middle-aged editor just grunted and changed the subject back to refreshments, choosing not to lose control of the conversation. She was good though, he thought, with admiration, very good. This should be fun.

"Diet Coke I've got. Beyond that, we'll play it by ear. Make yourself comfortable, I'll go get one." He stopped at the door, and looked at her with raised eyebrows. "We could go out?" It was not really a question, just a half-hearted gesture.

"Nelson, other than the obvious fact that we shouldn't be seen together if you're trying to pump me for what most people would consider confidential information, what makes you think I'd be seen in public with you?"

Nelson grinned. "You'd pay good money for a date with a man like me." He opened the door and eased out slowly, not taking his eyes from her.

From down the hallway, just far enough away to be out of sight, Eric watched Nelson leave his office. He had not really expected a break so soon, and was glad for the opportunity to study his prey. He had sized him up correctly as a powerful man, very different from Big John. This man would require some of Eric's best work, and it had to be done without his normal preparation time. This had the potential for sloppy and dangerous outcomes, he reminded himself.

The whole Arnot persona, he decided, was now inadequate to his need. He rethought the whole plan, knowing that he would need to move this man from this public location. Either that, or wait to catch him alone in his office, but he had no time for that, he would have to act now.

He reached beneath the coat, upholstering his 9 mm. He disliked the feel of the weapon with a silencer; it was much too long and bulky. He cleared himself to the rear, held the gun close to his side, hidden underneath the coat that was draped loosely over his shoulders.

As Nelson entered the deserted concession area, Eric glided into the room right after him, noiselessly positioning himself directly behind the editor. Nelson was deep in thought about Jan, and did not bother to look up.

"Mr. O'Bryan?"

Nelson turned and saw the tall man dressed in an oddly feminine fashion, holding a rather large gun, which was pointed directly at his head. But to Eric's surprise, the man did not react, nor did he seem frightened. In fact, he continued to feed coins into the Coke machine. When he finished, he calmly looked at the assassin with questioning eyes. Eric spoke with absolute clarity and authority.

"You will want to come with me," he said, nodding, and pointing the gun toward the exit.

As Nelson looked at the gun, he found himself thinking of Kelsey. He wondered if this animal had already visited her, and if so what had happened.

63

Baypointe 12:48

As Phillip returned with the provisions, Kelsey took the opportunity to warn him again about the dangers of anyone finding them. Phillip nodded and proceeded to unload medical supplies from the ambulance. He was very businesslike outwardly, but had a hard time hiding his excitement. These people and the situation they were in made for the most intriguing adventure he had ever been involved in.

Kelsey returned to the kitchen, where she was alone with her thoughts, torn by her personal desire to be the best reporter she could be, and troubled by the realization that Arthur's story could bring the country to its knees if brought to light—worse yet, if it died it would only became a vehicle for Arthur to wrest power from the new leaders of the Committee. Some of her angst was guilt for feeling this way. The dead story was best for the country, but added up to zero gain for her.

Jack came in to the kitchen for coffee. It was the first time they had been alone since they met in the cafeteria.

"How long before I can get back with Arthur?" Kelsey asked.

"I'm not sure. He's resting well and that's what he needs, but, probably when he wakes up. His body will tell him when he's ready to go."

"Jack, what is his prognosis, I mean long term, with the paralysis and all?"

"Normally, I'd say not great . . . he's very old. But . . . his vitals are remarkable; that works in his favor. The only thing I can be sure of is that he needs therapy and pretty quick—and rehab. This stroke won't kill him, that's for sure."

Kelsey needed to know Jack's take on their new friend. She'd wanted this information earlier, but this was really their first chance to discuss it privately.

She was direct. "Do you believe him; I mean the whole thing?"

Jack did not answer right away, but paused as he relived the past several hours. "There is a lot we still don't know, Kelsey—for now, clinically, I don't think he's delusional." He waited for her to respond, but she was silent, so he proceeded.

"So, all the things that he's told us, at least represent his version of the truth—reality." Jack could feel her excitement of his evaluation—it solidified her book potential. He knew she was completely taken with her newfound opportunity. He decided not to put a quick damper on her, at least not now.

Kelsey did nothing to hide the fact that she was in awe of the old man. "He's unbelievable, and so . . . powerful . . . charismatic." Jack agreed.

"Well, that explains that's why *I'm* here. That's how this whole thing got started. I got him admitted to the hospital, started all normal procedures, and he began talking, mostly gibberish. We get that with head injuries, and you just sorta block it. But then, he looked at me . . . I can't describe it . . . it was almost as if he was completely lucid just for an instant—and said 'You must help me.'"

She understood. Arthur's power was intoxicating.

"So, on a hunch I approved John Doe admittance, a cardinal no-no, telling admissions he might be a patient of mine in private practice. Then, I stayed close to him until I could find out more. You know most of the rest."

There was nothing else for Jack to say. They sat quietly. Kelsey looked out the back window toward the ocean, knowing that it was her turn to tell Jack a little more than he already knew, and under less guarded circumstances than in the hospital cafeteria. She could be more open now, and talked non-stop for half an hour. The time went quickly and easily. They were comfortable with one another.

Jack stood. "I'll check his vitals and start his IV. Then you can begin again if he stirs."

Kelsey remembered the old man's last words, about covering their tracks.

"Jack, have you called the hospital?"

He grimaced. "No, maybe I'd better do that first."

He disappeared with his cell phone. When he returned to the kitchen, he was visibly shaken.

"Something has happened," he said. "After we left, two men came looking for our John Doe, they were detectives. The floor super said that she's sure that only one of them left his room. Later, the room was sealed off, apparently, by government agents. When they left, they took a body bag with them. Everyone there assumed it was Arthur."

Kelsey's eyes widened. "You think it was one of the detectives?"

"It sure as hell wasn't Arthur.

"Shit."

"It gets worse. Our friend, the crazy nurse . . ."

"Yeah?"

"They found her in Arthur's room, dead. Apparent heart attack."

Kelsey shook her head. "Another one . . . my God!"

Jack nodded.

"They're getting closer," Kelsey said. "What did you tell the hospital?"

"I told them I had a family thing. I think I'm okay for now. What about you, did you call the Post?"

"Yes, earlier, but I only got his voice mail. I'll call him again, later."

As she walked away to place her call, Jack quietly wondered how this day, and this old man would change their lives. As he stood staring into space at the place Kelsey had been standing, without warning, a chill proceeded up his spine.

64

Washington, D.C. Near The Post
12:56p.m.

Eric was amazingly adept at walking in lock step with his captive, while holding the gun on him. Nelson was no super hero, but for now, he was more curious than frightened. His deepest concern was for Kelsey's safety.

He allowed the tall man to lead him to his destiny, outwardly displaying only malicious acceptance. This was not lost on Eric.

"I guess you are supposedly the Arnot person who called me earlier?" Nelson asked.

Eric loved these moments, the prey caught in the spider web. He was in complete control once again.

"Yes, but that's not my real name. My real name would not be of any interest to you." He smiled at Nelson, a cold calculating grin.

Nelson was annoyed enough to antagonize him. "I could scream," he said. "You'd shoot me, but then you'd have nothing."

Eric was amused and intrigued by the possibilities of a public execution. "I'd say that's your decision."

"I'm dead either way. Why should I tell you anything?"

Eric thought about the many philosophies and cultures that he had studied and smiled again. "Mr. O'Bryan, the overwhelming instinct of all living creatures—and certainly most of those from the Western culture—is to survive as long as possible. I don't really think you're different. Turn left up here," he added matter-of-factly.

For the first time, Nelson felt a twinge of real fear. This man was cold as ice. "What is it you want?" he asked.

"What I need, Mr. O'Bryan, is information, and I need it fast. You're just one resource, so if you don't give me what I need, I'll simply move to my next option." They arrived at the car.

As he opened Nelson's door, Eric spoke, "The decision is yours, so, for now, please, just get in the car and don't try anything. If you do, you're dead, and I'm only forced to become more creative." Nelson was chilled by the man's completely detached attitude, and understood his futile position clearly. But, once inside the car, he found himself beginning to feel an entirely different emotion, anger. Eric had no intention of moving until the information started to flow. He hummed tunelessly and watched the rear and side mirrors. He finally spoke after several moments of uneasy silence.

"You should really call Ms. Richmond now, and find out where she is. She solves my most pressing problem."

Nelson needed to know what this was all about, even as he stared death in the face—some lingering instinct—a curiosity fostered by years of reporting, or the understanding that his death deserved an explanation.

"Why do you need her?"

Eric understood the editor's resolve and tossed him the crumbs necessary to gain a response. "I need to find a man, and only she knows where he is. Though, no doubt, others are now involved on her end, but I don't know who they are."

"Who is he, who's the man you're looking for?"

Eric's plan had begun to crystallize. He reached into his pocket for the small needle that contained "instant death."

"His name is unimportant, Mr. O'Bryan, so please just make the call and let's just get this over with."

Nelson knew that the end was near and that he had nothing to lose. Any one of his next thoughts could be his very last. He thought for a moment, desperately hoping he could create a diversion, no matter how small. All he needed was that split second of edge.

Suddenly, he faked a loud cough, and in the middle of his body movement, and in a blur of speed, he smashed an elbow into Eric's face and grabbed the door handle. All hell had officially broken loose.

Unfortunately for Nelson, Eric was more surprised and shocked than hurt, so he managed to squeeze off two rounds from the 9 mm. The gun made a terrible spitting noise.

One of the projectiles smashed into Nelson's left arm, breaking the large bone. The other entered the chest precisely under his left nipple. Nelson's quick reaction and inertia allowed him to tumble out the opened car door and onto the sidewalk.

Lunchtime traffic made this a surreal spectacle on the crowded streets of Washington—a spectacle that Eric was not prepared to deal with. He started the engine and sped into traffic, barely avoiding the car in front of him, and an oncoming van.

As he made his escape, he visualized the shooting. Based on the angle of the shots, he concluded that at least one shot had made its way through the editor's heart.

Nelson's body jerked involuntarily, and a low gurgling sound escaped his lips as he lay in the gutter. In the distance, he heard a woman scream.

65

Baypointe 1:03

Arthur had begun to stir long before Jack inserted the needle for the IV. He eyed Jack with some admiration. *This doctor is vastly underrated*, Arthur thought, *intelligent and efficient*. Arthur realized that he and Kelsey made a formidable team.

"Would you grant an old man a favor?"

Jack looked at him, thinking Arthur was truly not himself.

"May I see out . . . that beautiful view . . . the ocean?"

Jack opened the heavily lined privacy drapes. The day had turned brighter.

"Better?"

"Much."

Arthur lay for a long time, not wishing to speak, but needing to tell his story. "Is Kelsey ready to proceed?"

"I'm the only thing she's waiting on, Arthur. I told her she could come in as soon as you were prepped."

"Good heavens, I'm not drugged, am I?"

"Nothing that would impair your thought process."

Kelsey appeared in the doorway, as if on cue.

"Come here," Arthur urged. "The time has come for me to tell you about the darkest time in all my years as

Director of the Committee. What was it Dickens' Scrooge said to the ghost of Christmas future, 'I dread you most of all'?"

He lay back, remembering endless decades of ruling the free world. When he began again, he was visibly shaken.

"There was such hope," he said. "A feeling that wondrous things were about to happen, or at least that they could happen during the first few years that the Kid took office."

"You mean Kennedy," Kelsey said.

Arthur looked at her. "Yes, but let me start earlier. As I told you in the ambulance, the fifties were tragically predictable, nevertheless wonderfully prosperous for the Committee. With the building of an interstate highway system, we were able to earn billions. The early years of the Cold War were mostly saber rattling. The 'Eagle' wasn't about to do anything to create or escalate conflict. His status as a war hero could have been revoked. The man became almost a dove in his later years. Even though he was credited with initiating assassination attempts on Chou En Lai and Castro . . . none of that actually happened on his watch. Maybe he had lost the stomach for it after World War II and Korea. He was much too soft on the Russians, but that is entirely another story. He served our purposes, and that was our concern.

"But, back to the point, there was a feeling that change was in the air. Our post-war euphoria and industrial successes were tempered by recession and about to be displaced by an indefinable, socio-political interlude that even I can't adequately describe."

Kelsey looked in amazement at Arthur, glad that she was both recording him *and* taking notes.

"It was during the '56 convention that he threw his

hat into the ring for the Vice Presidency –his father was aghast—and old Joe was a holy terror. He frightened even me sometimes. But the 'Kid' couldn't help himself; he was a natural leader and a consummate politician. Stevenson, while brilliant, frankly was not good theater and had become the Party's political albatross. He was so dry and uninspiring. Knowing the 'Kid' I can now see his move in '56 as simply a ploy to steal the convention and gain a following, which was exactly what he did. It was a masterful tactic, even beyond our comprehension."

Kelsey interrupted impatiently. "So you wanted Kennedy. . ."

"Joe was practically a committee member . . . practically, as he was only several hundred million dollars short of being a charter member. But, to answer your question, yes, the Committee saw Mr. Nixon as brilliant, but politically unsteady, and for want of a better description, unlikable with some very obvious personality defects. Plus, we felt that he lacked the political appeal to sustain two terms, moreover, not as controllable as the 'Kid.' After all, most of the money that came through the Committee was touched at some time or another by the . . . shall we say, underworld?"

Kelsey blinked, "The mafia?"

"Don't get naive on me, Kelsey. Those words you use are just labels with negative connotations. The words I chose described a group. The 'underworld' was heavily in favor of our young candidate and supported him with all their resources. They weren't joined at the hip. There were no nefarious schemes beyond that which I am sure you already have read in your Sunday Supplement. But the history was there with Joe, amassing a fortune during the early years of the Depression. Unknown to most, the Stock Market was his bread and butter—just not glamorous sounding. And, he had made good friends who had similar financial goals in the underworld.

"He groomed young Jack from the time Joe Jr. died, a defining moment in history for both Joe and the country as it turned out. He never recovered from his elder son's death. So, Jack became the focus of all his attention as he had become the heir to the legacy, but that's only history."

Arthur waited to collect his thoughts and to separate emotions from actual events.

"Toward the end of the fifties, the country was asleep. We wanted to revitalize the economy and change direction with a handpicked candidate who would do our bidding. By late 1958, it was apparent that of the two front-runners, young Kennedy seemed most electable. We committed to him and backed him with all we had. Even with our unlimited resources and influence . . . in the end, it came down to Chicago's Mayor Daley having to 'steal' Cook County. No one was more shocked than I when our boy only won by a little over a hundred thousand votes."

Kelsey wanted more of the human side. "What about the arranged marriage, and all those rumors about women?"

Arthur was annoyed and openly glared at her. "You're not one of those tabloid thinkers are you?" He looked directly into Kelsey's eyes, challenging her. She looked down at her notepad.

"The man was exactly what you think he was. He definitely liked women and pursued them aggressively, and often. And . . . my God, did they love him.

Of course, Joe realized that to be politically successful the young candidate needed to be stable, have a family and a good wife with a broad background, one who could help him politically. It was all true, if you're looking for the background dirt . . . but it simply doesn't affect the basic story. We were primed to do great things."

Jack had been watching, his arms folded over his chest. "A dream that you stopped prematurely . . ."

"You're thinking we ended Camelot. Well, there was no Camelot in Washington at that time. The mere thought that it existed in the contemporary sense is a classic case in point of revisionist history. We simply had a chance to do some wonderful things and along the way, he made some tactical mistakes. The beginning of the end, oddly enough, was the appointment of Bobby as Attorney General. Stubborn and . . . driven doesn't begin to describe young Bobby. The man would not listen to reason. He pursued the underworld with a vengeance, escalating the prosecution of mobsters in one year from twenty indictments to more than two thousand. I sometimes think Bobby had a Don Quixote complex. Needless to say, the benefactors of the young President were not impressed. These actions by our new Attorney General caused problems within the financial arenas we were very interested in. For example, there were plans to develop Cuba for gambling and resorts, before Castro took over. But the President failed to follow through and rid the island of that guerilla who replaced Batista. That only compounded Jack's problems, of course. His enemies were everywhere and the inevitable happened."

He paused. Kelsey wanted the whole picture, not the overview, and Arthur seemed reluctant to go on.

"Arthur, this is the story that the entire world has waited to hear. I need the details."

The old man hesitated again. "It was a committee decision, and I did not stop it. The financial side was so obvious I couldn't argue the logic. The Texas oilmen—as much as anyone else, had everything to lose. Kennedy was going to cut the oil depletion allowance. He was also going to pull out of Vietnam, and insofar as The Committee was concerned, Vietnam had incredible monetary potential, which the president did not really understand. And, with the Bay of Pigs, the Missile Crisis, Kennedy simply acquired so much . . . baggage. He had managed to alienate the Joint Chiefs with his heavy-handed intrusion into their authority in handling the Cuban blockade. He was fragmenting the CIA. The powers that had backed him could not believe that so much had gone so terribly wrong in such a short period of time. He had, as I said, enemies in the military and CIA, and God knows that Hoover did not approve of him; so our domestic and international intelligence communities both held him in low esteem, and unfortunately felt threatened by him.

Arthur pursed his lips. He recalled a different time—a simpler time when people, he thought, were different. He wanted to return to that moment, but he knew it was not to be.

Kelsey waited, knowing how difficult this was. Finally, she prodded the old man gently. "Tell us about the events leading up to . . ."

For the first time since she had met Arthur, he looked at her with confusion, and suddenly, she realized that the old man had never before shared this information.

"Yes. . . .yes. . . I understand. It began—the plan that is in late 1962. The topic of conversation at our committee meeting was the financial interests of our associates, but the unavoidable topic of the 'missile crisis' kept coming up. It had just ended in October, and while it ended well, most members felt that the escalation of the event was unnecessary from the onset. It was, in their minds, avoidable. They concluded that all too many of the events of young Kennedy's administration were marked by youthful inexperience or simple miscalculation." He paused and reflected again. "Their distaste for his actions had begun a year earlier with the Vienna Conference, where they felt that Khrushchev had set the tone for our future Soviet relations. There was an interesting quote from one member: 'we had to go to the brink of war, just to prove we weren't afraid of the Soviets. Kennedy let that fat Russian peasant push him around.' The Cuban patriots were already livid and hated Kennedy for his 'betrayal' at the Bay of Pigs . . . and as I said, the military was unsure of his intentions, ironic I thought in light of his military record. And he had frightened the intelligence agencies with his memo which detailed his desire to 'fracture the CIA'."

Arthur stopped abruptly and asked for a drink of water. His face was a somber mask, as if the truth were intolerable and painful for him. "I'm repeating myself, I know, partly because these elements are the key to the answer that everyone wants to know." He stopped again and thought for several moments. Then, reluctantly, he continued.

"The focus was put on the man who wanted the job more than life itself, Lyndon Johnson. The Committee had decided that not only were we in political jeopardy internationally, but we were at the precipice of becoming stifled economically. We were at a moment in time when a military conflict would inject billions into a reasonably healthy economy, and obviously the monetary potential of Vietnam was enormous for many of our 'investors'."

"The Committee decided to move Johnson into power. Lord knows he was crude, but he was also compliant and willing, with incredible internal political clout."

The reporter could not help interrupting. "If he was so perfect, why didn't you support him in the election?"

Arthur looked at her the way a parent looks at a

child. "Johnson was considered, and correctly so, un-electable on his own. And if you look at his numbers, even in his home state in the 1960 election, you'll see this to be true."

She nodded, which forced the old man to go on. "The meetings of the Committee had degenerated into discussions about people, rather than issues, always a bad indicator. Nonetheless, we continued these discussions into the early days of 1963.

"As was always the case, we never discussed details, only scenarios and outcomes. The message, however, was clear; the 'Kid' was to be out before the end of '63. Then we would have a President that would be re-electable, but more importantly, one who was tractable. It was no more, or no less, than removing the head of a company, and then replacing him.

As far as the actual assassination of Kennedy, that has never been important insofar as I was concerned. The actual "hit", if that's what we want to call it, was carried out through an international alignment with the Corsican Mafia. Their American counterparts brought them into this. You see, by using several go-betweens, the trail of evidence runs colder with each step. And during those days, getting these unsavory characters into the United States was a shamefully simple process.

We knew that this would have to be clean, no trails leading back to them or us. Therefore, false leads had to be generated. This was undoubtedly the most complex plan we had ever concocted; with an ongoing campaign of misdirection which will last for generations to come . . . forever."

Arthur closed his eyes and began to recount the past, as accurately as if it had happened moments before.

"And so it began. In the late fall of '62, the pieces

were put in place. We actually had three false plots going simultaneously. None of the players had a clue as to the existence, or motives, of the others. Conspirators existed within the CIA, the mob, the Cubans, and they were all so egomaniacal, that they thought they alone were pulling the strings. To a degree they were. All that nonsense about Oswald and Ruby was simple window dressing. It was obvious to the Committee that bits of truth had to be woven into the main plot.

Jack watched Kelsey as she hung on Arthur's every word. She was spellbound.

"The basics were simple. We had the hit squad, unknown to everyone, even us actually, and assurances from key insiders that the Secret Service would be . . . 'slow to react.' We had the FBI to ensure that the follow-up would be painfully slow, with careful misdirection. The autopsy, sloppy and incomplete and key elements secreted in the name of 'family privacy'. Real, verifiable, hard evidence was discarded, while great care was taken to promote a high profile witness who sounded . . . let's say, less than credible.

"Of course, we underestimated two things really. The first was the absolute disdain of the Warren Commission, the second, the ongoing fascination of the public for the assassination. Like most good mysteries, there was a fiber of truth woven in all the lies, and a boldly calculated lie hidden in the truth. And then, there was the damnable Zapruder film, which has kept this thing alive for almost forty years. Without the controversy which was started because of that, the trail could have stopped with the Warren Report."

Arthur stopped short of revealing his last thoughts on the subject, and the reason was unclear to both Kelsey and Jack. Kelsey was not rude, but she knew Arthur was dancing around the finer details of the actual event.

"We can finish this another time, if you prefer, Arthur."

"Nonsense. Now may be the only time," he said, rising to her challenge.

"There existed in the United States, in those days, zealots who considered themselves patriots. That fact is not extraordinary . . . only one factor. We were living in a time of bomb shelters—fringe crazies abounded, and inevitably, many of the more suspicious of them were positioned within our government. We had illegal operations running rampant, especially in the south, where many were unhappy with Kennedy. There were groups, counter-groups, all flag-waving patriots, and militant types. The Committee was not involved with any of these perfidious activities. It was all so unimportant insofar as we were concerned. Yet, when the time came for the decision, we decided that this chaos offered a shield. We set out on a six-month plan to plant false leads and trails, all leading to fringe groups and the underworld—or more important, anywhere but back to our own government." Arthur paused meaningfully. "And then there was 'the truth'—Lyndon Baines Johnson wanted to be president."

66

Washington, D. C. 1963

The Vice President was being briefed by a man whom he had not met before. The reality was, that the man was a messenger testing the waters. His information for the standard, daily briefing, was accurate and timely to the Vice President's requirements, but his true purpose was to set the wheels in motion for the Committee's plan, or to look for other options.

The briefing lasted beyond the Vice President's attention span, and was now winding down. The "messenger" gauged that it was time to begin the series of carefully crafted questions that would allow the Committee to measure the man's intentions, without revealing its own.

"Mr. Vice President, I think that's all we have."

"Good, I have enough horseshit on my plate as it is."

Johnson stood, large, powerful and intimidating. Unlike the President, he lacked any trace of polish. It was a dismissal, but the messenger did not budge. The Vice President eyed him with curiosity. The question was simple, incisive and direct, sure to get a telling response from the Texan.

"Sir, how are you and Bobby getting along these

days?"

The Vice President sneered loudly at the man. "Goddamn, you are new here, aren't you, son?"

The messenger did not move a muscle, but sat with his briefcase on his lap, his legs together, his hands placed on top of the case.

The Vice President knew there was more and enjoyed the intrigue. He looked at the clock on his desk. "It's already 8:00 in London, time for a cocktail as far as I'm concerned. Too early for you?"

The messenger did not move a muscle. He did not drink, but to refuse would break the moment. "Yes, sir," he said. "It would be my pleasure, Bourbon and water I believe."

He still didn't move a muscle, or change his expression. To allow the Vice President to make him a drink would put him in control, or at least give the illusion of collegiality.

Johnson poured the liquid into the glasses, adding a baptism of water. "Son," he said, "the good Lord created Kentucky bourbon for moments such as this." He handed the drink over with a mawkish bow. He was thinking that this man was different from most of the young Ivy League pricks who talked down to him. Yet, he still trusted no one. The rumors of being dropped from the ticket by the Kennedys were legion, and Johnson thought them to be true.

The Vice President downed half his drink with a loud belch and a full body shiver. "Now that's a 'by god' tongue orgasm." He laughed uproariously at his own humor. Then his expression darkened immediately, as he leaned forward, squinting at the messenger, like a mongoose assessing a snake.

The messenger had expected this kind of behavior, and sat silently, sipping the brown liquid. It burned his throat. Finally, he set the glass on the table, and only then, did he stare at the Vice President.

Johnson reacted just as calculated.

"Now, just why would you give a flying fuck—you little Ivy League cocksucker—how I'm getting along with Young Bobby?"

He smiled the most blood-curdling smile the messenger had ever seen. The private Johnson was very different than the public could ever imagine, he thought. As he sat, unmoving, with their faces only inches apart, the messenger remained calm. He could take his time working the Vice President. He opened his briefcase and pretended to search for something. Johnson's expression changed from contempt and domination, to a furrowed brow and curiosity.

"Because, Mr. Vice President, we see him as the root of all of our problems."

With that, he handed Johnson a file folder with more than fifty pages of documents detailing points of disagreement between the two. It was a carefully prepared chronicle, which served to infuriate an already sensitive and ego-driven man, and it worked. The Vice President skimmed the pages with a questioning look, stopping along the way to read unsavory presidential comments about himself.

The Vice President eyed his visitor carefully. "If you think I don't already know most of this . . ."

"No, sir, that's precisely the point. You *and* all of Washington know it. It's common knowledge that you are not in the inner circle, principally because of the President's brother. Bobby's presence is salt in the wounds . . . your wounds."

Johnson drained his glass and held it up to the messenger, who shook his head. Then, the Vice President poured himself another, this time dispensing with the water. The liquor seemed to have little effect on him, except to make him even less tolerant.

"Get to the point," he said.

The speech had been rehearsed several hundred times. "Mr. Vice President," the messenger began, "you may be the only hope that true patriots have. You can see that we are floundering. In October, we avoided nuclear war by the slightest of moments. Economic policies are not moving." The emissary was only hitting the highlights of each element, knowing that details would be lost on the big Texan. "Mr. Vice President, what if a group existed that could effect immediate change? Change that would put this country back on track, eliminate embarrassing problems that we see continuing."

"Who's this 'we'?"

"Patriots, Sir. Patriots who want our country back and think you're the man to do it."

Words like death and assassination were never used, but the Texan understood immediately. He looked off into space and did not speak, reflecting back to the Democratic Convention, when the Vice Presidency was offered, then almost yanked from him. All the ridicule, the nicknames, "Landslide Lyndon," the laughing behind his back, the calculated exclusion from key meetings. It all flooded back. God, how he hated those arrogant Boston bastards and their friends, the Ivy League pricks.

Often underrated intellectually, he had more political savvy than the young Kennedy brothers. He knew exactly how to deal with this man sitting across from him. He knew that these people who were approaching him were serious, and they were dangerous. He knew that he had to send the right message.

"What do you suggest?" he asked, squinting over his wire-rimmed glasses.

The messenger hesitated, and then spoke the word. "Change."

Johnson thought before speaking. "The presidency is very dangerous. I'm only a patriot trying to do the job that this great country elected me to do. If that requires me to step forward and do more . . ." He stopped short, having said enough.

White House the July 31ˢᵗ, 1963
2:03p.m. Oval Office

Arthur was seated in the red leather wing-backed chair in the Oval Office as the young president arrived, his hair still wet from his daily swim. He walked over to Arthur and shook his hand—somewhat tentatively, as he was, and made no bones about it, 'wary of that man'. For all of his polish in photo ops as well as his persona in front of the television cameras, President Kennedy, privately was, though self-assured, an introverted personality. He kept his private thoughts close, and tried not to tip his hand on any subject until he was good and ready.

He found Arthur, though roughly his age, a source of tremendous intimidation. "I don't know that I've ever been cowed by anyone quite like this," he told his brother, "everyone talks about intellectuals, and God knows we have them here, hell, we stole half of Harvard's best when we moved in, but this guy really, really unnerves me. Plus the secrecy of our meetings, I hate how he doesn't want to have anyone else in the room during our chats." Bobby nodded.

Kennedy was correct to be suspicious of Arthur, and, unknown to him, that today's meeting was designed to elicit a change of attitude, if not policy, regarding Viet Nam. The Committee had decided that there was an enormous amount of money to be had once again, as they had done in the late 1930's and early 1940's, and this time, with the onset of a controlled war. Unlike WWII, there was almost no threat to national security, not in the sense of the German, Japanese conflict.

"Arthur, it's good to see you again." The president eased into his chair, then fidgeted slowly, looking at Arthur with a pained expression. "Do you mind if we switch to the couch and rocking chair, my, ahh, damn back . . .", in his thick Boston brogue.

"Of course not, Mr. President, so it's not good these days still, I take it?"

The president rose slowly and with obvious discomfort and moved carefully to his rocking chair, motioning for Arthur to have a seat.

"No, and the swimming is supposed to help, the cortisone is supposed to help, the surgeries were supposed to help . . ." He looked right through Arthur, not seeing him, and remained in deep thought momentarily.

Such a young, beautiful and bright man, Arthur thought. Such promise, why can't I get him in line?

The president leaned slightly and carefully, toward Evelyn Lincoln's door, just outside the room, and spoke a little more loudly, "Evelyn?" In less than a second, a small woman with horn rimmed glasses opened the door.

"Mr. President?"

"Do you have any of my, uhh, medication, out there?" He looked at Arthur, gauging the man's reaction. Arthur, ever so slightly raised the fingers on his left hand, and barely shook his head, to imply his understanding completely, the need for pharmacological relief.

"Why, yes Mr. President, I do." She looked at Arthur, and hesitated. "Mr. Jacobson, do you need anything yet?"

"Why, sure, Evie", I'll take a tea if our President will join me." From Arthur, it wasn't a question, as much as a command—they all understood.

The president, who was in hopes of a short meeting, sighed internally and tried for an out. "Mrs. Lincoln, is my schedule . . . ?" Bailing out on her beloved boss, she simply said, "Cleared for as long as you two need, Mr. President."

It's a Goddamn conspiracy, he thought. "Good, good. Should we ask Bobby or Mac, to join us, Arthur?"

Arthur, barely moved his head, left to right, but it was definite. We are to be alone, and you know it, Mr. President, the unspoken words were deafening.

As they settled in with tea for both and a 'blue pill' for the president, Arthur opened the meeting, set the agenda, and made no bones about who was in charge.

"Mr. President, we've given a great deal of thought, as you know, to the Southeast Asian issue, and think that it's time for you to publicly embrace an escalation of on the ground 'advisors' there, followed by additional personnel, with a subsequent buildup of carriers and other sea going vessels into the Gulf area. My meeting with Max and Mac yesterday . . ."

"You met with my Joint Chief and my Secretary of Defense, without . . ."

Arthur ignored the interruption, as one would a child interrupting during a free for all dinner conversation. "And they agreed the time is right to go to the next levels of action to insure the area, the southeast Asian territory doesn't fall to communism—you know the 'domino theory' as our Chiefs call it."

The president was shocked, and it showed. He had known from the first day in office that he would be dealing with Jacobson and his people. What he didn't know was, his power as president was so fragile. On the strength of Jacobson's words, he would simply have to 'cave' in to anything as dramatic as a regional or perhaps even larger war. He felt, and correctly so, helpless.

"No . . . ."

Arthur sat, watching the young president. "No? No to what, Mr. President?"

The seminal moment had arrived—no president had ever openly defied the wishes of the Committee, and certainly not openly challenged their authority on a matter of such magnitude as this.

"Arthur, I am not, ahh, convinced, regardless of what you and Mac, Max, and whoever, whichever Joint Chiefs concur, that we should escalate in Viet Nam. We're only, what eight or nine months out of our most dangerous conflict ever, with Mr. Khrushchev. Now you want me to rattle the sabers and jump headlong into Viet Nam. Arthur, you're a historian, you know the French were there for years—and it is now and has always been a mess. We can't solve this, it's a regional, internal, and endemic societal and cancerous problem, one we're best avoiding, like the plague." The last part was punctuated with an index finger, as JFK so often did.

Arthur was impressed, Kennedy was right. Actually, he was spot on. *God, his instincts are good*, he thought—*right about all the issues, as usual, but missing out on one, the most important global perspective, the monetary potentials that a conflict such as this could create.*

"Mr. President, there are other considerations here, ones that transcend the issue of so-called creeping communism and Viet Nam. There are, for want of a more in depth explanation, financial considerations, and they've all been gamed out. We've decided that Viet Nam has the potential for enormous financial and political gain for our country, and frankly for your administration. We are only a year out from your next convention, and if we're to . . ."

President Kennedy did the unthinkable; he interrupted Arthur for the second time, and with a passion yet unseen by Arthur.

"Arthur, I know my role in this government, or I suppose I should say, I know what it **is**, not defined by the Constitution, but by a letter from President Eisenhower. But I swore an oath to 'preserve, protect and defend' that constitution—now, I'm here justifying my position to who, you, and your Committee? Whose bidding am I supposed to do—yours, Arthur or the American people? How do I know where to draw the line, Arthur? You're in here wanting me to commit American lives to a swamp in Southeast Asia, and to intercede into a conflict that's generations old, and spend millions or billions of dollars for what?" Kennedy shifted in the rocker, and winced as he moved.

"Now let me tell you something that you don't know, I went to see McArthur, General McArthur—he wouldn't even come to the White House, I know because I invited him—who turns down an invitation to the White House from the president—him, that's who. I talked to him in his little Georgetown apartment for a couple of hours. He liked me, and I liked him, and I understood him. He knows I took a hit from the Japanese during WWII, and in his own way, and more so than Truman, he has a touch of respect for those of us who have actually felt those 'hits' personally, Arthur. He told me in no uncertain terms, possibly the greatest military mind in all of history, 'We can't win a conflict in Viet Nam. We can place a million land troops in the region, and still cannot win. We'll lose thousands of troops, it'll drag on for months and years, and in the final analysis, we'll come home poorer and with a lot of dead, brave young men'—his words. I believe him, Arthur. I believed him then and I believe him now, and I refuse to commit to a lost cause in Viet Nam just so some very wealthy people can put more money in their coffers."

Arthur sat—stared at the president. It was an impassioned speech—was it rehearsed? It didn't matter. There was obviously no swaying him. He'd done his homework, and he was right. Arthur had debated people his entire life—he had taken either side of any question and could invariably win . . . but not this time. The president was right, and even Arthur didn't have the stomach to debate that which he knew to be so very wrong.

The strong belief of the man's certitude and intractability didn't, however, keep Arthur from setting the wheels in motion for the thirty-fifth president's rendezvous with destiny—in Dallas, Texas, some one hundred and fourteen days later, a rendezvous set forth by the greatest planners in the world. The Committee would plan, execute and hide yet another cesarean moment in history. Not with twenty-eight stab wounds as had happened two millennia earlier, but with some pieces of lead, propelled by gunpowder. During a fusillade lasting less than six seconds, one presidency would end, another would begin—and within the new administration, a compliance, a willingness to compromise, a malleable attitude, and while not visible at that moment, the opening of a murderous door, making possible the deaths of 57,969 American lives, which happens to be an exacting number on the black walls of a gigantic tombstone, along a rolling mall in Washington, D. C.

The Committee, yet again, had survived and conquered—no matter the price.

67

Baypointe 1:32

Kelsey watched Arthur as his mind sifted through the file that had not been opened for several decades. "How can you be so sure, so exact in your details?" she asked.

"There is no interpretation of that conversation. I was the emissary. This job was simply too important to send just anyone. Johnson was not really familiar with me, he had only seen me about, and it's not likely that he even remembered my face. Kennedy's inner circle and Johnson's did not really intermingle."

Kelsey looked at the old man, and waited. "What about Dallas?"

The question was ominous. The air in the room had become heavy. This was the day that Arthur kept in the cloudy recesses of his mind. He allowed himself the luxury of remaining the spectator and not a participant, as his regrets ran deep, but the day lived on in his subconscious mind.

"The stage had been set for some eight months. And as I said, there were so many false leads, so much so, that tracing the actual players was highly unlikely. I had personally begun to have second thoughts about the plan—young Jack had seemed to grow into the job. He had covered light years in his presidency, even since the Cuban Missile Crisis. While he publicly exuded charm and charisma, he was somewhat confused by the depth of his popularity. He even once said, 'the worse I do, the more they like me. I feel like Eisenhower'."

Kelsey waited for the detailing of the day, the essence of the story. But Arthur continued to talk about peripheral issues, as if to avoid the details.

"Arthur," she prompted, ending his rambling discourse.

"Yes . . . of course, Dallas, the city of choice. The Democratic Party was split, and Kennedy thought Johnson to be woefully inadequate in handling *his* own people, so Jack decided to make a swing into the state—an important state that had only been won by forty odd thousand votes in 1960."

Arthur lay back and took a deep breath.

68

Dallas, Texas
November 22, 1963

"The last day in the life of John F. Kennedy was his biggest political success . . . other than Berlin—and that was tragic and ironic. The morning in Fort Worth turned out rainy, but the President addressed the crowd with enthusiasm. Jackie stayed away piddling, as was her custom, back in the hotel, choosing the suit she would wear. The advance people had incorrectly predicted cool weather. As they reached Dallas, she complained to the Secret Service that she was sweltering in that pink suit.

"The parade route had been published in the paper, in violation of security protocol. Given the reception that Adlai Stevenson had received just a week or so earlier—being hit by a placard and spat upon—it seemed a warning.

"The names of the conspirators were buried, and remained that way. They were anonymous to one another. Each person knew his or her role only. The plan was meticulous. The actual shooters had worked on similar, ah . . . projects in the past. In all, there were four of them—and for the record, this wasn't their first payout. We paid a total of five million dollars for the job—a tremendous amount of money in the early sixties. And as is by now well documented, the ideal location, based on the parade route was Dealy Plaza, which by the way was not on the original route. The planners had figured and correctly so that the street crowds would be thinner and that access to the area was nearly perfect, so we made the final adjustment to their route, one extra turn, one simple yet fateful turn. If you can visualize the Plaza area, you know that the Texas School Book Depository was on the corner of Elm Street. Oswald had brought a mysterious package to work that day. Of course, the contents of the package have been debated for the past three decades. Whether it did, or did not contain that gun that you've seen from the black-and-white newsreels is of no matter. He was at the window yet he did not fire the weapon. 'That boy couldn't hit a bear in the ass with a bass fiddle,' I remember someone saying later.

"No, Oswald was the perfect dupe. He thought of himself as a revolutionary and an intellectual. Of course, the strategy was to eliminate him as soon as it was practical.

"One of the marksmen was in front of the Presidential car, hiding in the gully at the side of the overpass. Another was on the grassy knoll, the third behind the fence, and the fourth, in the DalTex Building. That was a prime location, behind the motorcade after its turn in front of the Depository. As the car turned onto Elm Street, Oswald was where he was told to stand, in the open sixth floor window. The hail of bullets, when they burst, as you might imagine, created hysteria in the crowd. Fragments of one bullet hit a man standing near the triple overpass. Two hit the President, one of which went on to hit Governor Connelly. And it would have been foolproof, virtually untraceable, had it not been for that 'inconvenient' Zapruder film. That, more than any other piece of evidence, did us in, clearly demonstrating that there was more than one bullet that hit the President . . . therefore more than one gunman."

Arthur paused and sipped the water.

"The killing shot came from the grassy area to the right and slightly in front of the Presidential car. Ironically it happened, fatefully, at the same moment the marksman in the rear, hit the president's head. This caused the front versus rear 'head shot' debate to flourish for half a century; though it was blind luck.

"The real test of our success came in the days and years that followed. We had enough people on the inside to ensure that the investigation and the dissemination of information would just serve to confuse the overall event. It was truly a master plot. We left nothing to chance.

"The original plan led the police to Oswald's house, where he would be confronted and shot, allowing the actual shooters to scatter. But it was decided to kill him on the street instead. Officer J. D. Tippitt's death was a red herring. And Oswald was arrested at the Alamo Theater. He had begun to realize that he was also on the hit list, and was simply trying to disappear. The police in Dallas made sure that none of Oswald's testimony was taped, and that only a few people had access to him while he was in custody.

"When Oswald started using words such as 'patsy' and 'victim,' we were forced into a damage control mode. He had to be eliminated, no matter the cost, and we turned to our mob acquaintance.

"Jack Ruby was a small time hood who owned a strip club. He was well known to the police, so he would have easy access to the police station. He was also from Chicago, and connected to the underworld, which made the mob hit scenario of endless fascination to conspiracy buffs.

"That night, on the way back to Washington, we realized that the official version of the assassination demanded a very special autopsy. The President's wounds had to be mysterious and debatable. You see, some fragments of the bullets found in the President's brain did not come from the Mannlicher Carcano rifle that was supposed to be the murder weapon. So, it became necessary to disguise the wounds in such a way as to make these conflicting details impossible to prove—more important, disprove.

"The autopsy conducted at the Bethesda Hospital was designed to obfuscate the truth, or create official confusion. Dire warnings were issued to everyone present. They were not to discuss what they had witnessed. Since various people, who had seen the body, first in the emergency room at Parkland Hospital, and then at Bethesda, saw things differently, the public would simply discredit all information that didn't flow from official sources. Or so we thought.

"In recent years, more and more people have ventured forth to offer some fairly accurate information. Apparently, they felt the need to speak out."

Kelsey was pulling away from the old man. He repulsed her with his completely dispassionate discourse on the death of the thirty-fifth President.

"What about the Kennedy family? Did they have any idea of what actually happened?"

Arthur looked at Kelsey for several moments. "Let's say the family accepted the President's death for what it was. Perhaps they recognized the danger and the futility in pursuing the truth since lead upon lead would bring them back inexplicably to their own government. It was fortunate for us that Bobby was paralyzed with a phenomenon known as 'survivor's guilt' and felt that he was at least, in part, responsible for the President's death."

"What about the Warren Commission?"

Arthur again looked at Kelsey before responding.

"The Commission was not connected to the Committee. They were, however, limited by our efforts to quietly obstruct the investigation."

Kelsey was indignant, and Arthur could see it. He waited until she appeared to gain control of herself.

"There is so much more, that I can't continue without mentioning names and places. I see no advantage there. My confession alone would give you the story of a lifetime. And more importantly, it gives me the leverage I need to regain control of the Committee.

Kelsey balked. "You've not confirmed much, Arthur. I'm not expert on this, but even with my limited knowledge of the assassination, I know that most of this has been kicked around for years."

Arthur looked pleased with himself, which annoyed Kelsey even more.

"Notice, you said confirmed," he replied. "That is the operative phrase. For the past forty years, we've strived for a story that the public would accept. Something between an absolute conspiracy and a crazed lunatic as the sole assassin. It must be said that we did have the President killed. We are the group that sought change, and I as the leader of that group, admit that we were the responsible parties. Even though I now consider that it was a mistake."

Kelsey continued to resist. "This proves nothing, Arthur. Your version is no more believable, or provable, than Oliver Stone's movie."

The old man had heard enough. "There's more," he said, looking into her eyes with a frightening intensity. She looked over at Jack, wondering if he somehow knew what the old man was about to say. She started to speak, but Jack shook his head gently.

"If I am to do this, I suppose that we must take it to the next level and actually point the finger at the responsible parties. And, yes, you were right to question me about the Warren Commission. They were carefully selected to help with the damage control. And those at the top, in the years since their report, have been rewarded in various ways. Not all of them were deeply involved in the cover-up, just the select few who unwittingly impacted the investigative process and the final report."

"Proof, Arthur, we need a smoking gun, something that will support your story. Hell, even I know that Caesar was stabbed twenty-eight times, that's not news, and neither is this . . . this, shit that you just gave me." Kelsey was in her element. The hard-nosed reporter in her that had been dormant for the last few years had reawakened.

Arthur hesitated, as if by continuing he would betray a trust that he had vowed never to break. He motioned for Kelsey and Jack to move closer. "We must be careful, because Phillip would never understand what I am about to share with you. He's not capable of shouldering the burden of this information."

Jack moved to the bed and sat on the edge. Kelsey looked out the window.

"Once I tell you this, your lives will change forever. Because at this moment there are only three people who know the truth. All the others are dead."

They both looked at Arthur with alarm.

"Oh, that's not as it sounded," he reassured. "They died naturally. In any case, there is more substantial evidence to prove my story. Two additional films taken by unfortunate witnesses who just happened to be in the wrong place at the wrong time. These amateur films show, in great detail, exactly what happened that day. The films are clearer than the Zapruder film, and they show better angles, proving precisely what I have said. My copies of those films are the only ones in existence. They are hidden away in a safe deposit box in Zurich, under an assumed name that I used only once. And, the unfortunate souls who made these films are no longer among us.

"At the time of the assassination, the films surfaced immediately. Those who had been privy to them included various FBI agents, the new President, three Commission members, and myself. To the agents, who were aware of their existence, we discredited the films as worthless, but nonetheless top secret. And, the people who filmed the incident, as I said, have disappeared."

Kelsey was once again the consummate, dispassionate reporter, searching for the list of conspirators.

"Did Hoover know? Was he a part of this?"

Arthur sniffed, "Peripherally, although I was against it. He was not trustworthy and had a very unsavory lifestyle." He waited, his thoughts turned inward for a moment. "There's more," he said at last. "In that same safety deposit box I have documents that contain more descriptive autopsy information, proving beyond a shadow of a doubt that there was a conspiracy. And further, that the Committee was behind the entire affair. I might also add that there is a very well kept journal detailing the affairs of the Committee in that same box as well. It is enough information to bring our government to its knees."

He stopped without elaborating. The last sentence had the tone of a deathbed confession, but it did not soften its effect on the audience. At that moment, Kelsey hated Arthur. Even though she was not a part of those years, she understood the magnitude of Kennedy's death, and felt that the world had changed forever after his passing.

"I need a break," she said, putting down her pencil.

Arthur knew how she felt. It was one of his rare

gifts.

"If you don't have the stomach for this, we can stop now," he told her. He was not bluffing. The story had to be made complete, and time was growing short.

"You bastard. How could you do this? You killed a part of America that day." She was close to tears, but her control was amazing.

Jack looked away—out the window across the Atlantic, wishing he could be anywhere else. As a child growing up during the 60's, he had no real memory of the day itself, just snippets of his mother crying and watching television. But he did know from the years that followed, the assassination shaped the country's attitude, therefore, history. He, too, looked at the old man with new eyes. How could he have saved this man who was responsible for the death of John Kennedy?

"I told you I dreaded this most of all," Arthur told Kelsey.

"You're sorry?" she exclaimed, angrier than she had ever been.

"Sorry doesn't apply, Kelsey. As I told you, I did not agree, but the vote was, other than me, unanimous. The times were different, the world was different . . ."

"And it was all about money," she said with disgust.

"What in life is not about money?" Arthur replied evenly. "Everything we do revolves around money. I won't justify the existence of the Committee to you. I told you going in, that we were a cold lot. Tell me, why are you so angry about Kennedy and not about the Chair?"

"Roosevelt, Goddamnit!" she spit. "At least call them by their real names. Do you think that if you use cute made-up names, they aren't real and it's just a parlor game?"

Kelsey was livid. Jack watched without interceding. He could not have added anything anyway. Philosophically, he agreed with *her*.

Arthur had expected emotion, but he had not expected complete rejection. Somehow, he had struck a chord that could end his all-essential plan. He looked out over the Atlantic again, as if waiting for some divine guidance. "I find this to be one of life's ironies," he said finally.

Kelsey was contemptuous. "Oh really? And how would that be?"

"You are both in the same position I was in some forty years ago. You can act to save the world by assisting in a plan, which you find personally, distasteful—perhaps even reprehensible—or you can stand by and do nothing and watch your country self-destruct. And let me take it even further—you have only two choices, both unpleasant."

Kelsey was not easily moved, "I sure as hell wouldn't have killed somebody."

"Really? Really now. How simple life is for those who lack the ability to calculate the implications of their actions," Arthur said. He would try to put it in perspective for her, in a way that she could understand.

"How many people do you think are already dead as a result of the attempt on my life?"

Jack was surprised. Did the old man know about the hospital? And if so, how? He began to calculate what he knew of the casualties—the ambulance driver, the nurse, possibly a detective. When he looked up, Kelsey was looking at him, imploring him. She wanted and needed an ally, and he was her only hope.

"Let's focus on the real issues," he said. "And be honest with each other. I think we both feel betrayed to think that you were part of the 'evil' that resulted in Kennedy's death, and for that matter, all the people who have died at the hands of this bloodthirsty lot. The real issue here, however, is getting everything back where we were before you were poisoned, Arthur." He looked at Kelsey, "That is, if we both agree that the Committee with its 'evil', is really the best for all concerned. Frankly, right now . . ." He held his last thought in check.

Kelsey, arms folded across her chest, said, "I'm not sure I support this anymore."

Arthur knew he was at risk of losing the only friends he had and any hope for his future.

"I see the world as a different place," Kelsey continued. "A worse place than before Kennedy's death. And I don't think that that is a Pollyanna view of history. The whole world went nuts in the sixties after he died; Martin Luther King, Bobby. So that tells me that if you supported or 'assisted' that plan in the name of some greedy bastards, and now have convinced yourself that it was in order to save the world, then we have nothing to talk about."

"Kelsey, at the risk of being brutally frank, I do not require your intellectual support," Arthur sniffed. "You are simply here to write the story. Whether you agree or not is of no concern of mine. Those in charge made a decision, to eliminate a problem. There was nothing I could do to prevent it. It was my job to see that the world continued. And, yes, I concur, things were and are worse. Something did die that day, and part of it was Arthur M. Jacobson. I lost something close to a son . . . I became cynical and unhappy. It was a mistake. Even the Committee has admitted as much. We underestimated the man, the times, and the results of the assassination. I tried for weeks to find another way . . . to stop this thing before it had a life of its own."

Arthur could not continue. He lay for several minutes, his eyes closed, a single tear trickling down the side of his weathered face. The emotion embarrassed him.

Jack and Kelsey looked at each other, and without speaking, left the room.

69

Washington, D. C. F.B.I. Headquarters 1:44

The President had actually been civil to him for the first time in recent memory. While it shifted his thinking somewhat, it did not dilute his distaste for the man. The Director would now give his men more latitude, he decided. There would be no more dead agents.

His assistant watched as he looked through the list of his top people, having decided to put ten agents into the field. That should show the President the level of importance he personally attached to Jacobson's disappearance.

He was reminded of his "special operative" and the request for $10 million, and he decided to withhold a response for five hours—that would be his backup.

For now, he would keep the investigation in-house. Based on the events at the hospital, their hope for success had improved dramatically. Still, he needed to know the real truth behind the Jacobson disappearance. This whole incident smelled, and he was just curious enough to look for answers at the highest levels. If the President couldn't tell him, maybe somebody else could.

While certainly not friends, he was well acquainted with the CIA Director, and knew that very little got past his office. The problem was how to approach him. Trust was the scarcest commodity in Washington. His only hope was to be as straight as possible, bargaining away some future favor, however outrageous.

He looked up at his assistant. "Do me a favor."

"Sure."

"Make sure the door is closed when you leave."

The FBI Director was already in motion for his meeting with the President. The mobile phone rang into a scrambled line, one that nobody could decode. The Director had made certain of that.

"Cole here."

"Cole, this is Taylor. We need to talk."

"OK, but I'm on my way to see the President, so you'll have to make it quick."

"Look, I'm gonna just drop the whole thing on you as it exists. It's classified in my files, so keep it tight."

"Sure."

Cole's curiosity was piqued. Taylor had never used him for anything or asked for any special favors. He listened to the entire story from the beginning—all the details, including Jacobson's 'John Doe' status, the dead detective and nurse. And, slowly he put the pieces together, realizing none of this could be attributed to anything less than a well conceived plan. The CIA Director deduced that Arthur M. Jacobson was the "Target" in his random scramble.

Then, his thoughts moved from the FBI Director's story to possible scenarios revolving around Jacobson. He was torn between sharing and just simply meeting the President to feel him out. To share his story might lead to charges of conspiracy, but, clearly, this was too big to go it alone. Reluctantly, he decided on an informal arrangement with his colleague.

"Look, Taylor, I'm meeting with the President on . . . something that may be related."

"No shit?"

"No shit."

"Jesus, what is it?"

"Look, I can't say yet, but I'll call you the minute I get out. We have to be careful on this . . . conspiracy is a dirty word."

"Hey, I'm not suggesting anything out of the ordinary, Cole. I just need some help, and it's getting pretty scary from my side of the fence."

"Mine, too. You got any idea what Jacobson might be doing . . . what's he involved with?"

"No . . . beats the shit out of me. All I know is that from over here it's pretty fucking scary, too."

70

Washington, D. C. Near the Post 1:46

Nelson lay half on the sidewalk, half in the gutter. He was in shock, but somehow still aware of the events around him. The pain was oddly minimal. He felt as if someone had punched his arm and chest, leaving him with a searing burning sensation.

One bullet had entered the fleshy part of his chest slightly in front of his ribs, and had ricocheted into the chest cavity, piercing the right lung. The other shattered his left arm. His breathing was shallow, and becoming laborious as the lung began to fill with fluid and blood. He was completely unaware of the extent of his injuries, other than the feeling that he could not move, and that his shirt was soaked with blood.

A crowd had gathered in the usual gawking fashion, and fortunately for Nelson, three people with cell phones had called 911. Exactly six minutes elapsed from the time he was struck with the 9mm shell, until the police and EMS were at his side. Witnesses were willing, but worthless, as none had seen the shooter, only the car. There were several versions of the incident, all similar, but with notable variations in critical details. Ironically, the accuracy of their accounts was not important, since the getaway car had been rented under a false name by a disguised man. The only true witness to this shooting was semi-conscious, his blood gushing onto the street.

The Emergency Medical Technicians were remarkably efficient, and had the editor on the gurney, and into the back of the ambulance within minutes. Nelson's sense of time had altered, so that everything seemed to be happening in slow motion. He remembered the moments leading up to the event—thinking he should call Kelsey on her mobile phone, but he couldn't understand why contacting her was important. His will was powerful, but his injured body was betraying him.

Inside the ambulance, he spoke to the EMT. "I need to make a call."

"Not now, pal, we're on our way to the hospital."

Nelson mustered all his strength for one run at the man, knowing that he could lose consciousness any moment.

"Look, asshole, first of all I'm not your pal, and second, I happen to have a phone in my back pocket. All I need is for you to dial." His grimace looked curiously like a smile to the technician.

The assistant was shocked by the man's lucidity. He complied. Moments later, the phone rang at the beach house in Baypointe, startling an already jumpy Kelsey Richmond.

"Yes?"

Kelsey could hear the sound of a siren wailing in the background, mixed with the radio transmission of loud agitated voices.

"Kelsey . . ."

His voice was weak, but it was Nelson. She could hear him wheezing. "What's wrong?" She had jumped out of her chair and was almost screaming into the phone. Jack ran to her, as if he could somehow help.

"They're close. . ." The words were gasps. "Arnot . . . you were right . . . shot me."

"Where are you?" she cried, her heart pounding in her chest.

"In a truck . . ." With that, Nelson lost consciousness, and the young EMT took over.

"Ma'am, I'm with County Medical Ambulance. It's not my intention to alarm you, but since the gentleman phoned you, I can only assume that you are family."

Time did not allow for Kelsey to tell the whole truth. "Yes, he's Nelson O'Bryan, editor of the Post. What's happened to him?"

She was now past emotion, into adrenaline mixed with anger. The young assistant was remarkably articulate, calm and thorough.

"Ma'am, Mr. O'Bryan appears to have been shot at least twice, once in the arm and one time, the chest. He's critical but stable. He has not been examined by a physician yet. We're proceeding to Washington General, and should be there in less than five minutes."

"Listen to me . . . please listen closely," Kelsey implored. "Nelson O'Bryan is in danger. Have hospital security alerted immediately, and, do not, under any circumstances, leave him alone."

71

Washington , D. C.
Oval Office

The President had changed shirts for the third time today, and it was just past noon. *Jesus, who would want this job,* he wondered? The Director was due shortly, with a recorded transcript of the conversation he had with the Committee. The President wondered what the hell he could do to muddy the waters. He looked out over the lawn, immaculately groomed and tended, and thought it was the only thing about the Presidency that approached perfection.

When he turned from the window, the office door was opening to admit the Director.

"Cole, it's good to see you."

"Mr. President," the Director acknowledged.

"Please sit down. Can I get you anything?" The offer was sincere; the President was a good and gracious host.

"Water. I'm dry as hell today, must be the stress." He laughed, and the president joined him. Then Cole began in a way that he knew would make it easy.

"I have the transcript here," he said, handing it over almost apologetically.

The president took the document and began to read

his own words with great interest, dissecting the dialogue for content. There was nothing here, other than the "code" name that tied him to the conversation. Still, the Director was not likely to let it die quietly.

"Cole, do you know who this . . . this, 'Trotter' is?"

The Director's expression remained the same. "Should I, Sir?"

The President stood at the brink of commitment, not knowing whether he should trust this man with part of the secret that *was* the Committee. Not the real parts, the peripheral outer layers—the conspiracy, for instance.

72

Washington, D. C.

Eric had never been so upset or confused. The discipline gained from years of training as a Navy Seal, and from pre-med, was crumbling. He was running on empty, and for the first time in his life, he imagined walking away from a contract. His instincts told him to leave this one behind. But to do so would signal the end of his career. It could even mean the end of his life.

He drove instinctively, unaware of the drive home. He needed to regroup and calculate the next moves.

Desperation, a new experience in his cold-blooded, loveless life, crept into his being, infecting his consciousness. Everything can't go wrong, he had always told himself. But it had, and it was totally illogical to him.

Eric found himself at a dead end. The implications of leaving a live witness were devastating. He had no way of knowing whether Nelson O'Bryan survived the attack. But he did know that his victim had seen enough of him so that identification would be easy. He would have to follow up . . . eliminate him. There was no other option.

No doubt, the hospital would be crawling with security, government agents as well. There were hundreds of pitfalls, unanswered questions, but Eric never burdened himself with thoughts that sapped his basic energy. He was focused on the editor, how to gain access before the man could talk. The choice now was born of necessity—kill or be killed.

73

Baypointe

Kelsey looked at Jack for help, but he could only stare back at her. From just beyond the doorway, Arthur called out to her.

"They have us firmly in their sights, child. It's as I said, only a matter of time until they're outside our door."

Until now, Kelsey had viewed her involvement as a remarkable developing story—one that would win her national acclaim. She knew that Arthur represented evil, but the evil was abstract until he began to deal with the Kennedy assassination. Then, the evil became real and very ugly.

She was no longer angry. Sometimes events took on a life of their own. She understood his predicament—leadership was often the most fragile of positions—but at the moment, her focus had shifted to Nelson. She folded her arms across her chest, and said, "I have to go to him."

Again, Arthur spoke from the bedroom. "Other than moral support, Kelsey, what can you do for him?"

He was right . . . always right. But that fact only served to annoy Kelsey. "Shut up, Arthur," she said coldly.

Arthur was not easily put off, even under the grimmest of circumstances. "Kelsey, Jack, please. Come in. Talk to me."

Kelsey shook her head, leaving Jack in the middle of a classic triangle. He had unwittingly become the rescuer, with Kelsey the victim, and Arthur the villain. To his credit, he recognized it immediately, and refused to play the game. He walked into the old man's bedroom, knowing that Kelsey would follow him.

Jack approached Arthur with a look of righteous indignation. Kelsey watched in much the same way that a young child watches her older brother take on the neighborhood bully.

"I've watched both of you sparring and debating one another," Jack said. "And I've had enough of it."

He turned first on Kelsey.

"You came into this thinking that you could spend a few minutes and have the story of a lifetime. You thought Arthur's governmental dealings were okay, as long as they were second-hand stories about dead people. You thought you wouldn't get dirty—that it would be easy."

Kelsey glared at Jack, but did not disagree.

"Arthur, I don't judge people . . . generally, that is . . . but if everything you've told me is true, I'm speechless. At this very moment, I'm wondering if I would have saved you if I knew all of this. As a doctor, that's a question I never thought I'd ask myself."

The room grew very still.

"Here we are now, dead bodies all over the city, and Kelsey's ready to jump ship. What's our mission folks? Saving our Republic, which is to say Arthur's ass, but at the cost of our own?"

"Jack, your tone belies your previous statements," Arthur said reasonably. "You really do have options beyond helping me."

Jack bristled. "I'm not quite finished, sir. You say I have options—well, what are they? Earlier today, you said,

'Suspend all your political beliefs,' and I was so naive, I thought you were talking about partisan politics. I had no idea that you were responsible for the death of God knows how many people."

"Jack, apparently you missed the entire meaning of my discourse, particularly about World War II. The entire process was inevitable. We only capitalized . . ."

"Quit intellectualizing it, Arthur. Everything may be black and white to you, but it's not to me, and I refuse to debate this."

Jack had flexed his muscles for the first time, and both Kelsey and Arthur were surprised at the depth of his position.

"Well, well," Kelsey said. "Still waters run deep."

"Jack, your speech and your ardor are wonderful, but where are you going with this?" Arthur smiled smugly.

"Don't patronize me, you old bastard. It's time we all bared our souls. We all have a different agenda, and there's no way to make progress until we come clean with each other." He looked at Kelsey and Arthur for a reaction, but they were not forthcoming.

"Kelsey, you're here for the glory. A comeback, perhaps."

It was abrupt and painfully accurate. She began to protest, but Jack held up his hand.

"God, you are naive if you believe this man *casually* chose you to be a part of this?"

She furrowed her brow.

"I would suggest to you that this contemptible old bastard hasn't made a move in his entire life that wasn't calculated. If you don't already know that, you really are in way over your head."

Kelsey looked at Arthur, gauging his reaction. The old man was non-committal, which meant that Jack had hit the mark.

Arthur was in control of his emotions, but he knew he was in danger of losing his allies.

"One doesn't rule a democracy for sixty plus years by having the intelligence of a goat," he said, with British flair. The humor broke the tension in the room, at least for the moment.

"We have to decide, and now, if we agree on a direction," Jack said more gently.

"First, I must concede that you're correct about me, Jack . . . to be fair. You have both been part of a larger plan, but not just because of your availability. You are both worthy."

The word hung in the air too long. It became an evaluation, and they both bristled.

Kelsey broke the silence. "Fuck you, Arthur. Who are you to deem me worthy? If you really think about it, you represent a fraction of thinking in America, and I do mean a fraction. You may be irrelevant to *us* . . . unworthy."

The old man was impressed with his young friends. They were performing on-cue.

"Bravo," he said. "You've just stated my case better than I. In the absence of real leadership, the masses prevail, at least theoretically. Given the performance of the human race, wouldn't you find that somewhat unpredictable?" Again, the last word became a challenge.

Jack was up to the task. "You know, Arthur, I'd say that if a democracy were run by regular dumbasses like us, it could probably still survive evil old bastards like you."

74

Washington D.C.

The Director of the CIA was indeed perplexed. Not since he had come to this godforsaken town had he had this much excitement. He felt alive for the first time in many years. There was obvious guilt that he should enjoy such a mystery, but that was human nature. Back in his limo, he replayed the conversation over in his mind. The President had been straightforward, but there were still no answers. He was good, this president. But the Director was not so easily dissuaded. The name Trotter meant something to someone.

Perhaps the only source of that information was the F.B.I. Director. He placed the call; the phone only rang once.

"Taylor here."

"This is Cole. Are we clear?"

"Just a minute."

Taylor could hear the muffled noises of the Director dismissing someone.

"Go ahead."

"Who the hell is Trotter?

Ironically, had either of these super sleuths called the agent in charge for Secret Service, he could have instantly told them that the president's code name had been changed without notification. Not policy, but life's reality.

75

Eric had become a different person. The qualities that had allowed him to remain anonymous had all but disappeared. His thinking had become reactionary instead of calculated, with a quiet desperation working its way to the fore of his consciousness. He realized that he was about to embark on a course that could easily place him squarely in the sights of the CIA, the FBI, the office of the president, and more importantly, the Committee.

Nelson's female guest had intrigued him. He had seen her before. She enjoyed celebrity status in this town but stress blocked the clues he normally would have remembered. Within minutes, though, he had figured out both her name and her likely whereabouts. He considered pursuing her instead of Nelson, but he was no longer sure of why. The primal instincts had replaced the logical processes in his mind.

He glanced at his watch. It was exactly 1:49, more than thirteen hours since his aborted attempt on Arthur's life. He wondered how different it would be now if he had succeeded at the Senator's cocktail party.

He knew that Nelson would soon arrive at Washington Medical. Security would be very tight, but he still did not see this as a real problem. Only average people see limitations imposed by others. And then, there was the young ambulance driver who spilled his guts to the reporter. Perhaps he offered a lead.

As his mind raced in all available circles, Eric failed to note his own spiraling descent into confusion. He was spinning out of control.

76

George Washington Medical Center Trauma Room 2 2:23

Nelson fought for his life. The damage to his right lung was extensive and would require a protracted surgical procedure. Even a person in reasonably good health made a difficult candidate for this type of wound. But given Nelson's lifestyle and physical condition, the surgery was very high-risk.

Jack took control of Nelson's care from Baypointe, forty miles away, notifying the trauma team of the incoming patient, and calling the best cardio-thoracic team in the city. Within twenty-five minutes, Nelson was on the operating table, prepped and ready to go.

By using his cell phone, Jack received a running commentary from the surgical suite. He heard the surgeon grunt, as he moved around to assess Nelson's gray body.

"How'd you know this guy?" the surgeon asked him.

Jack was not ready to explain. "I'll fill you in later. But there's something you need to know. This guy's the editor of the Post and the shooting isn't the end of it. They'll be back for him if he makes it." He eyed Kelsey; he hadn't meant to be so blunt. "He'll need top-notch security."

"Sorry, pal. I'm a doctor not a cop. I'll do the cutting, you call out the troops."

77

Washington, D. C.

After waiting twenty minutes for Nelson to return, then searching, she simply assumed that some Post emergency had pulled him away—and, since Nelson was not known for his social skills—to simply disappear was not in her mind a red flag.

Jan learned about the attack on Nelson while she was on her way back to the White House. She asked the taxi driver to turn his radio up for the late-breaking story.

"To repeat, though details are sketchy, it appears that the man found outside the Washington Post—shot several times—we have no accurate information on that as of yet—has been identified as Nelson O'Bryan, Editor of the Post.

"Details available from eyewitnesses are, as to be expected, sketchy. The seemingly executed victim fell or was pushed from a late model Ford Taurus that was parked adjacent to the Post building. The car sped away into traffic as horrified bystanders watched."

Execution . . . my God, was Nelson dead? Jan thought she was a seasoned veteran. She had been outside the hotel the day President Reagan was shot, but this was vastly different. Nelson was her personal friend and she had just come from his office. My God, what the hell was he involved in? She tried to remember everything he had said to her. Finally, she dialed the White House.

"Marge, is the chief in?"

"Yes, but he's . . ."

"Put me through, now!"

The woman did not hesitate. She had known Jan for twenty years and had never heard her bark an order.

"Jan?" The President had already been alerted to the urgent tone in her voice.

"Did you hear about Nelson at the Post? He's been shot!."

She was frantic—not her style—the President could only speculate. He sat slowly, and began to consider whether this too had something to do with Arthur. Agents shot, the Director in possession of his taped conversation, now the Post editor shot . . . how the hell could this all happen at the same time? And if it did, how could it not be somehow related?

"Sit tight," he told Jan. " I'll be back to you."

Before she could respond, he was gone. Within thirty seconds, he had both Directors on a conference call. Wrapped in the cloak of national security, he demanded to know everything.

Two minutes later, he had what he needed, including the name and cell number of the doctor operating on Nelson.

At Washington Medical, the President was patched through to Nelson's surgeon. The nurse who answered the phone, with a puzzled look said, "It's the President, for you."

The surgeon, blinked. "President of what?"

"The United States." She said it almost as a question.

He motioned to the nurse who held the phone to his ear.

"Mr. President?"

"Doctor, this is the President. That man you have in front of you, Nelson O'Bryan, is he going to live?" he asked.

"He's extremely critical, sir. So far we have things under control, but it's too early. If I hadn't been alerted by Doctor Ryan that O'Bryan was on the way, we would have lost five minutes and the patient. It was that close."

The President was not a man who missed details. He committed Dr. Ryan's name to memory.

"Here's my personal number, would you please keep me advised."

"Certainly, Mr. President."

The president hung up.

As the nurse took the phone away from the doctor the staff looked at the physician quizzically.

The surgeon couldn't help himself.

"Me and the President, we're tight."

78

Washington, D.C. The Oval Office 2:25

The President took stock. The events of the day, particularly the past six hours, were mind-boggling. He was now the true leader of the free world, thanks to the power wielded by the Committee. He reasoned that he should seize the moment to cement his control of the electorate, and decided that the only course of action was to put the entire investigation into the hands of his Directors.

The President was privy to all the information, and therefore had the advantage. Until an hour ago, the FBI Director only knew about Arthur's disappearance, and the resulting investigation that had cost him an agent. The CIA Director knew that someone in the city was the target of an ongoing assassination plot.

Both Directors were curious about the true victim of an assassination attempt. Privately, each arrived at the same conclusion. Arthur. Why then was the President playing out a bizarre charade that included a search for the man. They were confused. If the President wanted a man dead, it could be done quite efficiently. Why the pretense? That was the question.

"Arthur is the target. Why is he concealing this from us?" The CIA Director asked his FBI counterpoint.

"Yes, but *why* is he a target?" the FBI Director replied. "He's an old . . . war horse diplomat."

This was the essence of the Committee's success. It existed in plain sight, but operated out of view.

79

Baypointe 2:31

Kelsey looked at Jack. Having heard the ominous conversation between the doctors, she was shaken. Predictable recriminations crept into her mind. For several years, she had taken Nelson for granted. As her boss and friend, she accepted his favors without keeping the unspoken score card that is wrapped around all relationships, realizing, with guilt that the score was heavily weighted in her favor. Now, for the first time, she realized the depth of her feelings for the man.

She tried to hold herself in check, but the day had taken its toll. She awaited Jack's reaction, but he was not forthcoming.

"Well. . . is he going to live or what?" Her eyes brimmed with tears.

"I think so, he's got a good doctor. But if we hadn't called . . ." He shrugged.

"It was that close?"

Jack nodded. Kelsey put her hands to her face, and began to sob silently. "What have we done?" she said at last.

The question was rhetorical, but meaningful. Jack walked toward her and hesitated. She sensed his approach and turned to the doors leading to the deck. Outside, she leaned against the railing. Jack followed her.

The afternoon was windy, the smell of the ocean overpowering. At this moment, all of Kelsey's senses seemed to be heightened.

"Poor Nelson," she said helplessly, biting her lip and trying to stop the tears. Her face was aglow with the afternoon sun.

They stood silently for several moments before she spoke.

"You know, Jack, the man who represents all this evil is lying in your bedroom. And now, that evil has claimed another victim." With that, she broke down again, her shoulders heaving.

Jack let her cry as he watched the ocean with its endless, restless churning. He began to reflect on how insignificant he was, while, at the same time, recognizing that he and Kelsey were possibly the only links to the "truth." The moment was overwhelming. He wanted to console her, but he was incapable. So, they both watched the ocean, smelling the fresh salt air, alone together.

At the hospital, a curious thing happened. Within moments of the surgeon's conversation with the President, several men appeared outside the operating room. Each man non-descript, no identifying facial marks or facial characteristics, and dressed identically in khaki pants and navy sport coats. Had anyone bothered to check, each man packed a semi-automatic weapon concealed beneath the coats.

The perimeter of George Washington Medical Center had been sealed by order of the President of the United States—the new Director of the Committee.

80

Washington, D. C. 2:36

Eric's life, by his own estimation, was the least valued commodity in the nation's capital. He was compelled to pursue the only lead he had, but Nelson O'Bryan of the Post had just become the second most protected man on the planet. He decided that honor and duty transcended all else. To him, the ultimate sacrifice was an acceptable option.

He had changed vehicles, in anticipation of his mission, navigating through the traffic as if on autopilot. His mind, which once operated solely on cold logic, now wandered. Cars are curious things, he thought—so easy to acquire, then ditch.

He knew that George Washington Medical was the hospital closest to the Post. And given the severity of O'Bryan's wounds, he would have been taken there.

When he approached the hospital, it was with calm resolve. This was the defining moment of his life.

He was fully aware of hospital protocol, the location of the operating suites, critical details that would serve him. And he knew that O'Bryan, if he survived, would require hours of surgery to stop the bleeding and to close the gaping hole in his chest. It would be his window of opportunity.

As he pulled into a secluded section of Washington Medical Center's visitor lot, the nondescript men on the surgery floor waited patiently his arrival.

81

Baypointe 2:38

Kelsey studied Jack's face. "What do I do now? Nelson is probably dying because of me."

Jack was the perfect foil for her guilt.

"Let me see if I have this right. You're somehow convinced that this whole thing, including Nelson, is your fault. Get a grip; Nelson was shot because of Arthur." He watched her. She was not buying his appraisal. Her guilt was greater than his attempt to describe the reality of their situation.

"This thing with Nelson is nothing more than random bad luck. I see it all the time in the emergency room. Freak accidents. The kids that get hurt are the worst to me, Kelsey. I've asked myself a million times, who controls these events?"

She looked through him, to the ocean beyond. "You still didn't answer me. What do I do now?"

Jack gave it serious consideration. "You write the story, become a reporter again, and forget the personal side."

She gave him a hard look.

"Could you interview a murderer on death row?" he asked.

"Could and have," she admitted.

"Then you have your answer."

She grudgingly agreed that the truth and the story were more important than her view of Arthur's universal guilt. Besides, any story emanating from him would be a tribute to Nelson.

"You're right. Nelson lived by the rule, 'Get the story.' So, I guess we'd better get the rest of it."

82

*Washington, D. C. George Washington Medical Center
2:40*

Anticipating several hours of surgery was correct—yet the surgeon had elected to stop the bleeding, and do as much temporary work—then allow the patient to stabilize before performing a lengthy surgical procedure.

He had phoned, inquiring as to the 'condition' of Mr. O'Bryan. The staff, only doing their job indicated to him that the patient was 'out of surgery and stable.'

Eric was prepared. He entered the hospital's employee entrance, which, as he had calculated, lacked any semblance of security. Most of the workers knew one another, yet, the occasional laborer who cleaned floors and emptied trash, went unnoticed. Eric also knew human nature. In his vast experience, the best way to avoid a confrontation was to ask questions being supplicant. He promptly collared the first authoritative looking nurse.

"I'm here for housekeeping, but my service didn't tell me where to go."

This incarnation of Eric was a simpleton. He looked at the floor, avoided eye contact, and used a practiced stutter.

The nurse loved to help the hopelessly incompetent.

"Those people should really give better instructions. The custodial dressing room and supplies are in the West wing basement."

He looked blankly at the floor.

"That way," she said, pointing, and shaking her head in disgust.

Five minutes later, Eric the custodian was carrying a mop and pail to the fifth floor, in the general direction of the surgery suites. He had chosen a jumpsuit that was one size too large for him, adding to his gaunt and simple look. Plus, no one questioned anyone carrying a mop and a pail. The nurses generally looked the other way. He hummed a simple tune as he stepped off the elevator. The timing for his visit was optimal; cleanup crews worked during slow times.

He had brought several wet floor signs with him, one of which he placed at the end of the hall. He then proceeded to mop. He was meticulous in his work, stopping to scrape non-existent matter from the floor. This completed the picture of a straightforward, hard-working janitor. He pulled a rag from his back pocket and polished a chrome handrail.

A curious nurse questioned the slight variation in the daily cleanup routine. But Eric simply lowered his head in absolute submission, satisfying her. She clucked and returned to her own duties, content that the simpleton was only doing his job.

At the end of the hall, Eric could see government agents. They watched him as he knelt and began polishing individual tiles. His realistic portrayal, coupled with the nurse's tacit acceptance, allowed them to quickly lose interest in the hard working custodian.

He mopped patiently, to the door of the recovery room. The agent on duty was careful to accept nothing at face value, so he approached him. Eric had anticipated this, so he fetched a wet floor sign and looked questioningly at the man. The agent eyed him with confusion, judging him to be either retarded or a deaf mute.

"You got ID.?" The question was a formality, Eric sensed it from the tone, and knew that he had been convincing. He stared blankly at the agent and tried to hand him the wet floor sign.

"Never mind," the agent muttered. He then pointed at the floor, and said, "Go ahead." Eric wrinkled his forehead and nodded slowly. The agent smiled, then turned his back and walked away. Eric saw him speak quietly into the microphone hidden in his left cuff.

The assassin entered the recovery room, mopping backwards. He quickly surveyed the room, finding Nelson attached to a host of tubes and monitors. He continued mopping the floor; the cautious agent peered into the room. All he saw was the janitor carefully swaying with his mop.

As the door closed, Eric realized he only had a few moments. He eyed the room carefully. In the corner, there was a plastic bag containing the blood-soaked clothes that had been cut from Nelson's body. He searched the pockets for any information that might be useful. Then he saw it—a black object on the windowsill—Nelson's cell phone.

Eric's mind raced. He walked to the door and dragged a chair into the hallway. When the agent looked up, all he saw was the janitor polishing chrome arm piece. A moment later, Eric reentered the chamber. He knew he had another two or three minutes, no longer. He eyed the cell phone, knowing that it held the clue to Arthur's whereabouts. Intuitively, he punched redial.

At Baypointe, the telephone startled Kelsey. She grabbed her phone. "Richmond."

The line was silent for a moment. Then she could

hear the sound of monitors in the background.

Eric whispered into the phone, the effect was terrifying. "So . . . Ms. Richmond . . . time is short and I need answers."

Kelsey knew it was the assassin but was able to stifle a scream. Jack moved to her side.

"What is it?" Jack asked.

"I'm with a friend of yours," the telephone voice continued. "Frankly, he looks bad."

"You bastard, leave him alone," Kelsey spit angrily.

She regretted her comment immediately. Attackers were stimulated by a victim's willingness to beg.

But Eric was not interested in begging, only success. "You have thirty seconds to decide," he told her. "I will finish my job now unless you agree to lead me to Jacobson. It's your choice. The clock is ticking. You have thirty seconds. If you alert the hospital by using another phone, I'll simply trade my life for his. Again, it's your choice."

Kelsey froze for several seconds, but there was no other way. "We're at Baypointe, on the beach," she said.

Jack grabbed for the phone and she slapped his hand away. "We're in the salmon-colored house, there's a fountain . . ." she added quickly.

Eric was surprised at her compliance, then suspicious. "You wouldn't lie to me, would you, Ms. Richmond?"

"I'm not lying," she replied, continuing to hold Jack at bay. "Nelson's too important to me."

"I'll be there at four o'clock."

Eric disconnected, letting the phone drop into the pocket of his jumpsuit. When the agent opened the door a second time, he saw the simple janitor mopping the corner of the room adjacent to the bed.

83

Baypointe 2:45

Jack waited for an explanation, but Kelsey offered none.

"Well," he said finally, "we have three hours or so."

From the bedroom, a baritone voice called out to them.

"If you really believe that our 'friend' will come when he said, you're both delusional. The man is the most skilled assassin in the world. He's killed several people already today. And, at the risk of breaking your heart, Kelsey, your friend Nelson was probably dead the moment you gave him our location."

Arthur's voice was steady and clear as he offered his dispassionate analysis. Kelsey looked at Jack for verification, but he only shrugged and said.

"I can check."

"Do it!"

Jack disappeared into the kitchen, leaving Kelsey standing in the doorway of the master bedroom. The old man was waiting for her to attack. He had heard the blame, the tears earlier.

"Arthur, whatever I think of you and the things you've done . . . none of that matters now. I'm a reporter on a story and you're it. I want the rest, before this assassin shows up. And by the way, you'd best have a plan that will save our asses."

Arthur was pleased at her recuperative powers. He had thought her lost, but she'd proved once again that he possessed great instinct in his estimation of human nature.

She sat in the chair by the bed, her pad and paper ready. But before the old man began, Jack appeared in the doorway.

"He's alive, stable but critical condition. That's all I could get, except that the room is surrounded by men in navy blazers, what would that suggest, Arthur?"

The old man looked puzzled. "It must be the Secret Service, but why they'd be there at all, and so quickly, is beyond me." He closed his eyes as the true import hit him. "The President ordered it. Only he would have done this! Jack, your surgeon friend, can you call him again?"

Less than a minute later, they were through to the hospital. The surgeon had just sat down, pulled off his glasses and propped up his feet. Jack could hear him as he tried to make a temporary recliner out of two chairs. "Why didn't you tell me I was working on a VIP? The President called me while I was operating."

"The President called *you* . . . why?"

"He said he was pretty worried about his friend, that probably explains a lot about their editorials. Oh, and then a little while ago, a bunch of men—Feds I think, you know, khakis blue oxford cloth shirts, navy blazers—anyway, they showed up and sealed off the recovery room, pronto."

The surgeon hesitated, but Jack offered him nothing, so he continued to speculate.

"Lots of weird shit here today. You heard that the old nurse, Nurse Rachet died? Well, hospital rumor has it that some government men, or detectives, whatever, were poking around when it happened. That was about the same time you left." The realities of the day hit like a thunderbolt. "Hey, what are you into here?"

"I can't tell you, not yet. But I need a favor . . . a big favor."

"You're running up one hell of a tab, old buddy—you already owe me for this guy O'Bryan's lung."

Jack implored. "I don't have much time to explain—what if I send you a package and maybe this package contains, I don't know, some information that nobody would believe . . . and, if I'm not around anymore, would you see to it that it makes its way to the press?"

The surgeon did not answer.

"The man you worked on today," Jack continued, "the editor of the Post. We think the government may have had something to do with his attack."

"But *they've* got him covered . . . *they're* protecting him!"

"They are now . . . look, this goes all the way to the top. Why else would the President call you in the operating room, for Christ's sake? Hell, you were inside Nelson's chest within twenty minutes from the time he was shot. How the hell did the President of the United States know where this guy was and who was working on him?"

"Look, this is tough to explain without sounding nuts, but I don't have an alternative. Right now, we're sitting here at my beach house, waiting for the guy that shot Nelson to show up, a paid assassin, supposedly the best there is. And, there's a reporter with me who has the most incredible story you've ever heard. If I send you her tape and notes, will you listen to it or read it, then get it to the press?"

"Sure, then I can go hide out like you, and call my friends and tell them crazed government killers are looking for me . . . yeah, that's a plan old buddy."

Jack played his last card. "You know how we used to sit in political science and argue about the government and conspiracies, and I used to laugh at you because you thought there was a spook behind every tree?"

"Sure I remember man, but we were kids and that was school, right after Watergate. I was a wacko imagining all kinds of crazy bullshit. Hell, I was prepared to believe anything. This is the real world now man."

"You're not listening. What I'm trying to tell you is that most of that clandestine shit you came up with, dreamt up, whatever—spooks, black ops, government assassinations, right down to the Warren Commission—well, I don't exactly know how to break it to you, other than to tell you straight out. You were right. The answers to a lot of your questions and suspicions, even a lot that you don't even want to know, will be on the tapes."

The surgeon asked one last question. "Jack, are you fucked up—or having some kind of quiet nervous breakdown?"

"No, this is the real me. I'm in deep shit, and I need your help, and I've never been more serious."

Jack looked at Arthur for the first time. The old man was actually smiling at him. His young doctor friend had been as convincing as only he himself could have been.

84

Washington, D. C

Eric had successfully leveraged Kelsey's panic over Jack. He was amused that he could actually control someone over the phone some thirty miles away. The hospital setting with its platoon of secret service men did not lend itself to another killing, so he walked away from O'Bryan. He had no compunction about finishing him off; the man could conceivably identify him. But there were two reasons for allowing him to live. If he had killed him, the only avenue to Jacobson would be cut off, and it would be days before the man could identify him anyway.

Eric considered that this was to be his last official job. The moment in his life had come for him to buy a new identity, and to leave the United States forever.

His known problem was gaining access to the old man. He was certain that now that he knew the location of Jacobson an elaborate trap of some sort awaited him. He stopped at his second residence, to pick up his blue blazer, khaki pants, and counterfeit federal identification. The last person they would expect at the beach house would be a government agent.

85

Baypointe 2:52

Arthur was again holding court with his companions, and as usual, again able to exhibit his uncanny ability to spellbind them with his quick wit and insights.

"Our friend will come early and use a frontal attack," he warned. "Regardless of what you think, or what you think you see, unless we make other arrangements, the first person to come to our door will be the assassin."

Kelsey blinked, she could not grasp the meaning of the old man's words.

"That's crazy, Arthur. You really think he'll just show up and knock on the front door?"

"Thank you for making my case. You just said, 'That's crazy.' Therefore, it's the last thing we would expect. With all due respect, he thinks three dimensionally, and you only see two dimensions. Trust me on this. This man is brilliant."

"He walked into the hospital as a doctor," Jack agreed. "And for all intents and purposes, was one. How many people could pull that off?"

Kelsey was confused. "So now, since he kept his word and didn't kill Nelson we sit here and wait for him to show up?"

"I don't think so, " Arthur said with a wry smile. "I think it's time to call my friend."

From memory, Arthur dialed a fourteen-digit number, followed by another six digits. Unlike the others who had used secure lines, his was truly beyond being intercepted. He had written the program himself.

86

Washington, D.C. The Oval Office 3:16

The phone flashed the dreaded three light sequence that the President had hoped to never see again. He let it cycle three times, then answered, "Trotter here."

The rich baritone voice the President so feared began in an ingratiating tone.

"Mr. President, I hope I'm not disturbing you."

The President's jaw was clenched; he was moments away from yet another anxiety attack.

"Arthur," he said, "thank God you're all right! We've all been so worried."

"I really should have called, I suppose. But you know how I love my time alone, Mr. President."

"Is everything . . . all right?"

"What on earth could be wrong?"

The man in the Oval Office did not respond; there was nothing he could say. Arthur let him stew for several uncomfortable moments, until the President was forced to lead.

"What can I do for you, Arthur?"

"I hate to ask for special favors, but I have this annoying problem that has me at wit's end. I was hoping that you might be able to help."

"Arthur, you know that I'll do anything I can."

"I've taken ill, quite suddenly and unexpectedly."

"No, it's not serious, I hope," the president feigned shock and surprise.

"Oh, I'm afraid it's quite serious. Debilitating, in fact. So much so, that I was forced to bring in a private physician to see me through the worst of it, of course this puts me at risk with my other more pressing commitments"

It was a game of cat and mouse, and the president knew there was a point to it. "Arthur, there's nothing so pressing that it can't wait until you're up to speed," he said. Then it hit him.

"Arthur, did you say private physician?"

The old man was feisty with his prey. "Yes. I'm in his care as we speak."

"Do you think that's a good idea, Arthur? We have staff that's equipped to handle anything and they all have top security clearance. I can dispatch them to your side immediately."

"But, Mr. President, I feel so safe with this particular doctor. He's taken such an interest in my case. Plus the down time will allow me to work on my memoirs. It's fortunate that his good friend is the perfect person to help me write them; you may know her, a Ms. Richmond who works for the Post. Her editor is Nelson O'Bryan."

Thoughts spun in the president's head like the colors of a Rubric's Cube.

Jack and Kelsey had been enjoying the game Arthur was playing. But they both shuddered as they watched the frail old man transform into a jackal as he spoke to the President.

"Listen to me, you third rate parasite," Arthur said in a frighteningly depraved voice, "I would have called you a saprophyte, but since you didn't quite hit the mark,

I'm still alive. Your 'man,' no doubt our famous File Three code name Abraham . . . Yes, I already know your choice . . . has left human flesh lying all over Washington today. None of it was mine, however, and that presents some real problems for you."

The old man's voice while wicked was still rich and resonant, making him all the more frightening. Jack watched Kelsey's reaction. It was very obvious how Arthur had managed to survive the past sixty years as the world's most powerful man.

"Your people have given amateurs a bad name, Mr. President. I'm embarrassed to have been associated with you. As for *your* Committee, you may now file your report as you, alone, are finally in charge. It comes with a heavy price. Ironically, I'm the only reason you're sitting in that office."

The President paced as he spoke. "Arthur, you've been a part of this thing for sixty years. You of all people know these decisions weren't mine."

The old man let the President's words hang in the air. "Is that the truth or just a coward's denial?" he asked finally.

"I'm caught in the middle of this, Arthur."

The President's voice shook. Arthur knew the truth when he heard it. "Good," he told the man in the Oval Office. "Then, this is what you need to do *immediately* to save all of us."

87

The President mopped his face with a monogrammed handkerchief that was not sufficient to the task. He was drowning in perspiration from his conversation with Arthur—a dreaded voice from beyond the grave. Much to his surprise, Arthur had declared himself a willing ally.

"Christ," the President whispered. "I'm the fucking President and I feel lucky to have a friend like Arthur. The only problem is that everyone's trying to kill him."

And yet, he recognized the political reality. The old man had been in control for sixty years and was omnipotent. He would do whatever Arthur asked. He picked up the phone and dialed the coded number for the CIA Director.

"Yes, Mr. President."

"Cole, I have a job for your . . . uh. . . Special Team."

"Mr. President . . ."

"Don't even ask if this is 'need to know.' You don't! For that matter, everything that has happened in the past twenty-four hours remains deeply classified. As you and your people are so fond of saying, 'Either forget it, or be prepared to explain it.' My message to you is simple. Shut up and do what you're told!"

The Director sat back and listened. This had the earmarks of a valorous decision, the modest beginnings of courage from the President.

"I need a team of six blind deaf-mutes, all with amnesia, who can fly a chopper and then a jet—and it's domestic—outside your purview. You got anybody that fits that description, Cole?"

The Director smiled. "Sir, I'm proud to say that my Special Team prides itself in all specified areas."

"Good, then here's the plan . . ."

88

Baypointe 4:37

Eric glanced at his watch. The trip from the city had taken him exactly forty minutes. Of more importance, it had only been an hour and nine minutes since he had called the reporter. And though it was just past three o'clock, the day had turned dismal again.

He sat near the entrance of the well cared for development, and watched the salmon-colored house for anything unusual. Other than a lack of the manicured lawn as was typical for the 3-acre tracts, the house was among the finest in the area.

There was no visible activity. Nothing suspicious. In fact, it was ungodly quiet, leaving him without a feel for his next move. He sensed that something was wrong, but couldn't quite put his hands around it. Uncharacteristically, he was perspiring. He dabbed at his face with a towel.

He looked at the salmon-colored stucco house and tried to imagine its occupants. The house was well lit, but there were no shadows moving within. He would wait another minute or so, and then approach.

His plan was the essence of simplicity. He would present himself as a federal officer proffering assistance, claiming that the agency had intercepted calls that led him to them. Unless they had laid a master trap, he could easily handle anything they threw at him.

He started the engine, and covered the short distance to the drive. He noticed the name on the mailbox, remembered seeing a Doctor Jack Ryan, on the physician register at the hospital.

He knew his prey. He knew the old man's cunning, but was wary of the other two—with no profiles, he felt unprepared. He was aware of how Arthur could have persuaded the doctor to help him; but how he managed to involve the reporter in his escape was a mystery. Plus, they had to have used an ambulance to transport the old man, and that meant that there was at least one additional person. Too many unknowns, but with his skill level he held little fear. These were considerations, not problems. The adrenaline was beginning to flow.

Eric's movements had now become instinctive, reflexive. He knew they would be watching, so he tried to appear as casual as possible. He even imitated the look of the agents at the hospital—aware and in control, but not menacing.

As he stepped from the car, a gust of wind swirled through the front yard from the ocean. It caught the car door and pushed it into his leg. The pain only served to heighten his awareness. Stepping onto the pebbles Jack and Sarah had carefully chosen for the drive, he looked at the windows on either side of the door, checking for motion. But there was still nothing. This was, he decided, a well-conceived trap, or no trap at all.

As he neared the door, he took a deep breath. The salt air was strong. The wind was misting the incoming tide. He stood on the porch, fingering the false I.D. in his pocket, ready to begin his deception. He rang the bell. As a precautionary measure, he stood to the side of the door. It was the best angle in the event of a quick attack by limiting the enemy's view. From inside, there was no response. He had not heard the bell ring, so he knocked hard. As he did, the door gently swung open.

He stepped back and reached into his coat for the 9 mm. He waited, then pressed forward, and called into the house.

"This is Special Agent Clarke, is anyone home?"

The house was silent. He assessed his options. They were most likely huddled in hiding, prepared to pounce.

He pushed the door completely open and stepped aside. He could now hear music in the background. Again, he called out.

"Hello, inside. This is Agent Clarke. Is anyone home?"

Nothing.

He felt no presence in the house. Nonetheless, he closed the door, cradled his weapon and began to stalk the house. He turned left and walked into the kitchen. It was well lit and perfectly clear of any clutter. He looked around the room, glancing at everything, his detailed eye, stopping at the counter top. Almost invisible to the naked eye were tiny droplets. He walked over and looked at the white surface. On it were rivulets of a dark stain that appeared to have dried then wiped. The droplets trailed onto the floor. They had been cleaned, but not well enough, giving the appearance of a hastily planned clean up.

Suddenly, he felt completely alone and very exposed. He crouched in the corner under the eat over bar, and listened to the soft music. There was no other sound other than the wind and surf in the distance. He slipped into the family room and addressed all angles with his weapon. Again nothing. Yet, near the large red and blue sofa, on the white carpet, he could see another stain. No doubt the same as the kitchen . . . blood.

He was now in frenzy. He entered the master bedroom. The bed was made—nothing to indicate that anyone had been there. He looked into the bathroom carefully. There was nothing out of the ordinary. He stood still and looked out across the ocean. His mind raced. Instinctively he gazed down at the bed—then felt it. There was something, he could sense it, as well as feel it—dampness, and an iron-like odor. He jerked the bed covers down. The sheets were soaked with blood, with no pretense of a cleanup. On the pillow, there was an envelope containing a neatly typed letter:

Mr. Arnot:

Congratulations. By finding this note, you have again proven your stealth. As you are doubtless aware, by now, we have walked away from this dreadful business. We sincerely recommend that you do the same. Don't tarry, however, as interested people have been alerted and will soon arrive. If you choose to pursue us further, you will become the hunted . . . A. M. J.

P.S. . . . By implication, your presence amongst all this blood simply doesn't look quite kosher, does it?

Eric cursed, and then slammed his fist against the wall—leaving a perfect imprint of his knuckles—yet feeling no pain. He screamed Arthur's name. *The hunt was over for now,* he thought as his rage abated. Whatever the consequences, they would wait . . . another time and place.

89

St. Maarten- The Caribbean Three Months Later

The sand clung to her long suntanned legs. As a fair skinned blonde, she had never been so dark. The young woman rolled over and looked at her companion. He had drifted off into a lazy sleep. She looked him over carefully—he was very different from the man she had known three months ago. Self-conscious of his scars, he wore an appropriately flowered shirt, open in the front. Kelsey leaned over and pulled it up gently, examining the scar on his left side. It looked more like a burn than a gunshot blast. She shook her head in amazement. The surgeon had done a remarkable job. The man lying on the beach was fitter than he had been at the time of the shooting. The daily swimming routine had increased his lung capacity, and served to trim his once pudgy body. He was at least thirty pounds lighter, and had a tan that did wonders for him.

Kelsey reached for the sun block. He had started to look burned. She carefully spread the white lotion over his knees, jumping at the sound of a voice behind her.

"I turn my back for a couple of days, and come back to find you with your hands on the knees of a half-naked man."

Except for much longer hair than when she'd met

him, and a day's growth of beard, he looked unchanged, although much healthier. He stood above her, blocking the sun's rays. She shaded her eyes and smiled up at him. He did not return her smile.

"Caught. It's all I can do to keep my hands off him. When you're gone, he fills in. You don't mind terribly, do you?" He ignored her banter.

"Kelsey, have you looked in the mirror lately?"

"Well, you know how vain I am, Ryan."

"No, I'm serious. Your blonde roots are showing."

She couldn't help but smile. "Jack, do you know how many women would love to hear someone say that to them?" Self-consciously, she clutched at her short, brunette hair.

"Will you ever get used to it?"

"Will I have to?"

"Do you always answer a question with a question?"

"You always ask so many questions."

"People in love make me sick. Why don't you two get a room?" Nelson turned his head away from them and closed his eyes again.

Jack looked at Kelsey, but didn't speak. She stood and they began walking down the beach. She knew Jack had something to say that even her best friend should not hear.

"You look like the little kid that dropped his ice cream cone, Jack. What's up with you?"

"My surgeon friend who worked on our buddy there, left on a two-week vacation three weeks ago, and isn't back yet."

He picked up a sand dollar and threw it into the breaking surf. He dusted the sand from his hands and stood quietly.

"He never took a two week vacation in his life. Never. He always said that if his patients could do without him for two weeks, they didn't need him." He shook his head. "There's more. Fuck it, there's always more, isn't there? I spoke to Arthur yesterday. He says he's coming down to see us on Friday. But that's a two hour story."

"Jack, you're going to have to give me more than all this unconnected bullshit."

Jack continued to look out over the ocean. She was a tough audience. This time too tough, he thought.

"You think he's missing, don't you?" she said.

He looked at her and shrugged. Then, he turned and walked down the beach, farther away from Nelson. Kelsey followed a step behind.

"How much money would you say we have in our accounts?"

"I don't know," Kelsey replied. "Arthur was generous."

"Five million is what I'm thinking," Jack said. "Of course, it was worth a lot more in the sixties when the Committee paid it out to kill Kennedy." He shook his head and clenched his jaw.

"What are you saying?"

"How much of it is ours to use as we want?"

"What kind of question is that?" She looked directly at Jack, her forehead wrinkled. He seemed to have become unglued in the past two days. There had to be more that he hadn't shared with her.

"What is it Jack—or is this twenty questions?"

"Two days ago I left here, not to visit my parents in Colorado, as I told you. I left to make plans for our escape."

"Escape. . .escape from what?" She flailed her arms wildly.

A wave broke around them, soaking Jack's pant legs. He ignored it, and looked at her.

"Don't interrupt," he said. "Just please listen."

90

Jack entered the bank wearing his Ermenegildo Zegna suit. It was hand crafted, and had been virtually sewn onto his body by an octogenarian tailor. The suit was made of superfine merino wool, and was perfect for summer weather. The material was navy blue, and offered micro pinstripes of deep burgundy. He completed the look with a white silk shirt, adorned with solid gold cufflinks bearing the initial's WB. The final touch was a Prince Philippe, hand-painted silk tie. On his feet were alligator shoes, which felt very much like Indian moccasins—moreover, nothing at all.

As a surgeon Jack had never indulged himself with clothing so auspicious, but as an 'associate' of The Committee he felt that one day he might have a need for such an outfit. His instincts were correct, and today was that day.

He had called the branch manager to set the appointment for 11:00 a.m. He had not shared the reason for his visit, but had given the manager his new name, William Brereton. During their conversation, the manager indexed Brereton's account, noted the mid-seven figure balance and became very accommodating. The new name and a suitcase full of cash had been a portion of the parting gifts from Arthur Jacobson.

That morning, Jack had camped out at a fast food restaurant across from the bank, watching the comings and goings. He had become suspicious of everyone and everything over the months since their run-in with the Committee. Moreover, Jack had become even more suspicious about their special arrangement with Arthur.

This morning's two-hour wait produced nothing except beads of sweat on his forehead. It was, apparently a typical Tuesday, an unspectacular day at most banks.

At precisely 10:56, he left his car, walked behind the McDonald's and made his way through the alley across from the bank. The bank was quiet, as late morning office action was winding down, and everyone prepared for the lunch hour rush.

Mr. Brereton was welcomed by the branch manager, who shook his hand vigorously, while making a mental note of Jack's twenty thousand dollar attire. As he took a seat, Jack surveyed the whole office, family photos, awards and certificates of merit, so far, so good.

"What can we do for you today, Mr. Brereton?"

Outwardly calm, Jack's heart was racing. He was a horrible liar. "Lately I've had an urge to go on a first class gambling junket," he said. "Hit Europe, visit Rome and Paris, go to the Bordeaux Region, see the vineyards, then maybe a stop in Monte Carlo. So . . . I'd like to make a cash withdrawal." He smiled to help sell the lie. "Probably one fifty-maybe two hundred thousand. Then, as I'll be staying in Europe for an extended period of time, I'll need to transfer three million to an account in Zurich."

The branch manager stifled his disappointment at the loss of such significant funds. "I can make the transfer to Zurich," he said, "but it's not really necessary. For a customer such as you, Mr. Brereton, I would gladly waive wire charges, and we can transfer into your account as needed."

Jack's mind raced well ahead of the banker. "Well, that won't do, since I may be gone for several months. One must plant roots, you know." Again he smiled. The finality of Jack's statement made the banker realize that he had lost his bid to keep the funds, so he pressed on.

"The two hundred thousand will take an hour or so. We may need to call for additional funds." He then gave Jack a paternal smile. "But I must say that I have some reservations about your carrying that much cash, Mr. Brereton."

"No problem, I've done it many times . . .Vegas, Monte Carlo."

The manager shrugged. "Certainly, sir. It's just that we have to consider our customer's safety. I'm sure you understand."

Jack backpedaled just slightly, "Well, I'm sure Travelers Checks would do nicely." With that the manager relaxed, but silently wondered whether the bank had enough checks on hand to cover such a large request.

Jack didn't speak, he only smiled, allowing the banker to realize that a prized customer was waiting patiently. The manager regrouped and called for his assistant to bring him the Brereton "hard file." Moments later, a young woman entered the room with a folder. She stared openly at Jack. She smelled money, and liked it. Today, he was an odd mix of, uncharacteristically long and somewhat unkempt hair, and a five o'clock shadow, far too early in the day. He looked to her like the bored and pampered rich that she had seen many times before in the bank. Jack tried to ignore her.

The manager opened the file, assayed the contents carefully, and stood abruptly.

"Mr. Brereton, I only need your identification, and

we can begin the process."

The manager ushered the assistant from the room, leaving Jack to wait alone, impatiently.

Jack shifted nervously, looking around for hidden cameras. *Jesus, I've become a paranoid freak.* He raised the cuff of his shirt and checked his watch, it was 11:18. Four minutes had passed since their departure. Jack's cell phone rang breaking the silence of the room, and startling him.

The voice on the line began before Jack could speak. The caller used his pseudonym.

"William, how are you?" It was a rich recognizable baritone.

Jack's heart raced. "Fine, and you?" he said.

"Things are well here." The man paused.

Jack was curt. "You called me, Arthur. Chit chat isn't your style."

"I understand that you're planning a trip," the old man said.

Jack stood. His heart was pounding wildly.

91

St. Maarten

Kelsey did not speak. The ninety-degree heat did not stop the chill that enveloped her body. "My God, it's starting again." She said it aloud, but it was meant to be a private thought, only spoken in her mind. Jack watched her, understanding her confusion.

"Look, I need to call Phillip. I'm sure he has no idea . . . If we're in jeopardy, so is he."

Kelsey began to recover from her initial shock. "We need money," she said. "We can't use the bank account."

Jack interrupted her with a small smile. "Not to worry. After the call from Arthur, I told my banker that I had changed my mind and wanted two hundred thousand in cash, straight up. I also wrangled two million in cashier's checks.

"I don't get it, why do that?"

"Look, Kelsey, as of now we are officially on the run. I should have known that Arthur would follow our every move. Hell, he was the one who suggested we bring Nelson down here."

She shook her head. "No, I was the one . . ."

"No, Kelsey, you said, 'God, I miss Nelson,' and Arthur had him down here on the next plane."

She nodded. "You remember Phillip's cell number?"

"I do, indeed."

92

Florida The Keys

The phone hummed. The sound was barely audible above the noise of the dual diesel engines of the boat. Phillip looked like a surf bum. He wore baggy shorts in a Hawaiian print and no shirt. His thinning hair was dried from the sun, and he had a two-day beard. *The Kelsey* was a beautiful example of what Committee money could buy. Phillip justified it as a new career. *The Kelsey* was a charter craft, and he was a more than adequate skipper. But with his generous endowment from the Committee, he rarely took on passengers. Usually, wealthy college girls who liked to sun bathe topless and swim off the back of the boat. Phillip had never been happier.

"Yeah," he answered the phone breathlessly.

"Skipper man," Jack said, "we need to talk right away."

"Hey, Doc, we are talkin'." Phillip lifted a long neck to his mouth and took a deep pull. Nothing tasted better than cold beer, out on the salty ocean.

"This is serious, Phillip. Our friends may have turned. Where are you now?"

"Well, I'm in dock, engines hot, ready to cast off."

Jack smiled, "Paying guests or tits?"

Phillip laughed. "Paying guests, a guy and his wife. They came aboard an hour ago."

It sounded all right, but Jack wanted more. "What do they look like?"

Phillip spoke softly into the receiver. "Well, he looks like a rich chubby nerd, accountant maybe, or a stock broker, with a trophy wife. Why?"

Jack was relieved. "Look, as soon as you get back, call me. This is life and death. Do you understand what I'm saying, Phillip?"

"Sure, man." He thought about it and was chilled by the news.

"Look, I get back at five, unless they want to do an all-nighter. I'll call you then." Phillip disconnected and felt a slow shiver run up his back. He loved his new life, and somehow felt unworthy, quietly knowing that it could not last. He looked around the craft; it was indeed beautiful. A woman's voice broke into his consciousness.

"Hey, Captain."

The woman had come up from below deck, wearing a silver bathing suit that covered very little of her ample figure. She was completely brown from the sun, with jet black hair. Spanish, Phillip thought absently. The guy must be loaded to keep a woman like this.

"Ma'am?"

"That looks delicious, you got any more beer up here?"

Phillip pointed to the port side. "Under the seat cushion. It's a hidden cooler, built in, more convenient that way." She smiled at him as she made a dramatic production of bending over to get the beer. Phillip took in the show, while watching the lower deck for signs of her husband.

"Where's Frank? I'm ready to cast off," he said.

"He's below. He's not much for the sun."

Ten minutes later, they were five miles out to sea,
heading due west. The woman had taken a position on the
upper deck directly in front of Phillip, and unabashedly
pulled off her top. There were no tan lines around her large
breasts. He shook his head slightly. *Life sure is strange*, he
mused. He used to make twelve dollars an hour, driving
around D.C., rain, snow, dying people. Now he lived like
a millionaire, charging some guy a thousand bucks for a
five-hour boat trip while his wife showed him her tits.

The man came to the hatch. "How far out are we?"

Phillip calculated the time and speed. "Five, maybe
six miles."

The man nodded.

Phillip tried to avoid the appearance of gawking at
the man's wife.

"Great body, huh?" he said, motioning toward the
woman. She smiled and Phillip shrugged.

"I try to keep to myself, Mister. I get lots of people
on this boat." Phillip changed the pace of the conversation.
"Say, how about a beer? I've got a full cooler under the
cushion."

"Sure." The man walked to the cushion and pulled
out a long neck. Rivulets of sweat were running down his
face as he opened the beer.

"Say, Mister, you might want to lose that shirt. It
gets pretty hot out here."

"Great idea." The man pulled the shirt off his pudgy
body. Underneath, he wore a large, molded body vest.

Phillip squinted at the man. "What the hell is that?"

"That, my young friend, is a heavy bulk suit. I wear
it when I want to look different. You know . . . it's a disguise." Eric laughed cruelly.

Phillip looked confused.

In one lightning quick motion, the man pulled a silver object from his pocket and fired three rounds into the woman. There was almost no noise as she collapsed, blood appearing at her chest and abdomen.

He turned to Phillip.

"Well, that takes care of that." He smiled at the young captain. " Are the others still in St. Maarten?"

At first, Phillip couldn't speak, then a stubborn un-yielding look appeared on his face. He knew that he had seen too much.

"No matter. I'll find them with or without your help. By the way, if you run into your dead partner, give him my regards." The man squeezed the trigger. Four quick pops. Phillip didn't have time to contemplate his death. Four rounds entered his chest, but he did not feel them. He fell backward, and was dead before he hit the deck.

Eric went to work, first removing his stiflingly hot body suit. He surveyed the boat, knowing the exact location of everything he may have touched, carefully wiping it down. Then he filled the bait bucket with salt water, and rinsed the rear of the boat where he had stood and spoken to young Phillip. No DNA would be found from the assassin. He then washed the blood from the boat, knowing that it could be discovered with a careful forensics analysis, but he did not care. His only concern for now was the color red, and it had disappeared. By the time any crime scene investigators became curious, he would be on the other side of the world, and untraceable.

He carefully weighted both the bodies, tying them securely enough that they would not resurface any time soon. Dead bodies, he mused have a nasty habit of coming to the surface as the gasses build, and that would lead to questions. After checking the ropes for the third time, he dropped them overboard. He watched impassively as they disappeared beneath the surface. He knew that very soon, the sharks would circle. Nature's own food chain would rid the world of any evidence, long before the bodies could fill with enough gas, which could cause them to surface. He stepped back, and admired his work. It was very neat.

He turned the ship about, pointing the craft due east for a leisurely trip back to dock. Then, he picked up his cell phone and dialed the fourteen-digit number. He whistled softly, while waiting for the call to connect.

93

Arlington, Virginia

The old man sat uncomfortably in his wheel chair. His limbs would never work as they once had; yet, he had made remarkable progress in the three months since the attempt on his life. He could move most of his body. Walking, however, was not yet an option, and he continued to require a private nurse.

His first Committee meeting since the attempt on his life had gone well. Uncomfortable silences were kept to a minimum by his well-orchestrated good-natured banter. Everyone played their roles, as concerned friends and colleagues, all pretending that nothing had happened.

The group accepted his return to power as inevitable. He had expressed his willingness to bring the Committee's existence to the attention of the world. He had done it through the President, his new champion. Arthur had also agreed to an amended version of their military options. Even so, he had clandestinely begun to move behind the scenes, so that the short term impact and long-term results would mesh with his more moderate thinking. All was well—all that is, except for the three people who knew too much.

Dreadful business this, he thought. In his own limited way, he truly liked and admired both Kelsey and Jack, and, he regretted the action that had to be taken. Jack had saved his life, and Kelsey had brought him back to power with her well-crafted documentation.

But he now saw them as simple tools, necessary for his success. They would be casualties in his battle to regain control. He had not shared their existence with the Committee.

Of course, he had not counted on Jack's trip to Florida, which had thrown his plans into a tailspin. To Arthur, that action on their part had not been logical. He had been warm and generous with them. Insofar as they knew, they were set for life. Why would they become suspicious?

His phone rang, a short and then a long burst. It was a coded message. He lifted the receiver. A computer generated voice, flat and lifeless, reconfigured Eric's words.

"The business in the Florida Keys has sunk. Our losses were four million. Will advise you on the Caribbean investments no later than tomorrow. We need to invest at least ten million for assurance of maximum return."

Arthur understood. "Proceed with the investment," was his instruction. And again he was impressed. File number three was indeed the essence of efficiency. Arthur outwardly held no grudge, or for that matter any telltale emotional response toward Eric's actions. The man had simply attempted to do his job. Arthur took great pride in the fact that he had become the assassin's only failure. He frowned to himself. One down, three to go. He was fairly certain that he had placated Jack. The offer to visit and "catch up on the past three months" had been a little melodramatic for Arthur—but he had taken care to convince them that he had all but retired from geopolitics. Instinctively, he knew it was unwise to underestimate Jack. It would be best to act quickly. He leaned back, and let his mind work through all the possible scenarios.

By Thursday, it would be over. Everything would be as it once was.

In a completely rare fit of pique, the dark side of the old man surfaced—a ghastly look on his face—"They're dead, they just don't know it." He smiled a chilling smile.

94

St. Maarten
2:27am

Eric navigated the small boat along the shoreline. He knew that the condo was roughly one mile from the point. He pulled to shore.

There was no beach activity, but the terrain made him vulnerable. He had scouted well, and knew that he would have reasonably easy access to his targets, and limited, if any witnesses. Concealed in a black wet suit, with hood, blackened face, and matching gloves, he felt invisible. He swam gentle strokes, watching the shoreline for lights he had committed to memory.

First, he would sedate the victims with a drug that would not show up in an autopsy. He would then set, what would ultimately be diagnosed as an electrical fire, leaving obvious clues that the St. Maarten police would accept as plausible. The anesthetized bodies would be placed so that they would appear to have failed in their attempt to escape the flames. Smoke inhalation would be the coroner's determination. He had done this several times, with great success.

He swam to a depth where he could stand, floated carefully on his back, and opened his stomach pouch. He pulled out Government Issue night vision binoculars and scanned the shoreline carefully. It was clear, no activity. He then trained them on the house. The kitchen light above the sink was on, serving as a night light, he thought. The room to the left showed the flicker of a television set, and the outline of bodies sleeping peacefully in the beachfront bedroom. There was no obvious movement and Eric guessed that they had fallen asleep watching television. The living room drapes were open, but the sheers were closed. He could see clothes lying on the sofa. He continued to watch for several minutes. This would be an easy in and out. He floated again, replacing the binoculars in the waterproof pouch. He swam into the breakers and once more scouted up and down the beach. Conditions were perfect.

He crouched at the edge of the water, and then sprinted to the foliage at the property line. He checked to the rear once more. He sat listening for any sign of activity. The only sound was the low drone of the television.

Moving gracefully, he reached the door and gave it a gentle push. Yes! Just as he had known, it was unlocked. Only a screen separated him from his prey. He gently cut the screen and entered.

From the bedroom, the sound of the television droned on. He pulled his mask down to listen for night sounds, or any activity. All of his senses must operate to the maximum. He was patient. Speed offered no advantage in this assignment. He scanned his surroundings while pulling the syringe from his stomach pouch.

He remained crouched as he moved toward the doorway. The dresser hid him from view. He duck-walked to the edge of the bed. The syringe was ready; a small dose would do the job. He reckoned that if he injected the small needle carefully, it would not awaken them. He rose slightly and positioned the needle. He carefully plunged the needle through the bed sheets, but did not hit human flesh.

He jerked the covers back, exposing a collection of feather pillows.

"Shit," he swore hoarsely. Recklessly, he ran to the second bedroom. It was empty. He opened the closet; it was still full of clothes. He walked back into the master bedroom. Hairbrush, clothes, all remained. But they were gone . . . gone again.

Eric fell to his knees in despair.

95

Arlington, Va.

The coded triple bursts of the telephone awakened the old man. He looked at the clock . . . 4:15 a.m. The construct of Eric's words, played back as a computer's lifeless voice reconfiguring him into a disguised electronic monotone for those who might chose to be eavesdropping, even though the actual message was benign.

"No investment possible. The three necessary in-gredients for success missing. Please advise as to next op-portunity."

The line went dead. Eric had not waited for a response.

Arthur cursed aloud. He had judged his past associates to be more predictable—more important he underestimated them. He lay for a long time, thinking of Jack and Kelsey, wondering where they would go from here.

A grimace crossed his lips as he remembered the doctor who had saved his life, and the idealistic young reporter who had helped him regain his throne. They were quite something, he thought—but since they were not part of the financially social elite known as Committee members, he could only envision them dead. Frustration overtook his cool exterior—he threw his tableside glass across the room and uncharacteristically swore.

"God damn it!" He swore again.

At that very moment he made final plans regarding the taking of several lives—just as he had so many times in the past. He knew from past experience that there had to be a careful sequence to these killings, so as not to alarm nor alert the survivors, arousing suspicions which couldn't be easily explained away.

Now, in his wheel chair, he motored to his computer and searched his 'files' for an assassin other than File 3.

96

The violent death of Eric was shocking to the select few who knew of his work—though not to Arthur who had skillfully planned each detail of his demise with typical precision.

As only one of handful of people who knew of the Committee and its actions, he had to be silenced. That, plus the reality that he had failed in his three recent assassination attempts, made for evidence that he had perhaps lost his edge over the years. In his profession, this ratio of failing to perform was a De Facto death sentence.

With two months to watch the patterns of Eric's comings and goings, the 'pair' trailing him as their target knew that he lived a reclusive life, even to the point of having groceries or take out delivered to one of two residences.

Generally at night he worked out while listening to his cherished music. Not the life of a normal person, they thought, but then they killed for a living—atypical also.

Tuesday night was chosen as it coincided with his order from a local health food store in the neighborhood. Since the delivery boys were transient Eric would not be suspicious of a new face at his door with his order. This was fundamental to their plan. What they didn't know was that Eric always carried a weapon beneath a towel, to the door, part of his work outlook. Arthur took no chances and knew that this job would require two men instead of just one very talented man.

As the doorbell rang, twenty minutes later, Eric, while not suspicious, was merely compulsively careful.

His hair and sweats were wet with perspiration, and the music was loud, as he answered the door as he had so many times before—cash in one hand and a towel draped over a silenced 9mm Glock, in the other.

"NatureCare delivery sir," said the man. "That's $16.48."

Eric handed him a $20 bill, and said, "keep . . ." but before he could finish, another heretofore unseen man crashed through the door. Shocked only for a moment, Eric fired into the chest of the intruder killing him instantly— then turned to the other man; his distraction gave the other man just enough time. The other 'delivery man' lifted his left hand and fired point blank into Eric. The tumbling shell tore all the way through his body, yet missed vital, 'killing' organs.

While falling backward, Eric fired back, but his stumble caused him to miss his target—the shell barely grazing the man's right arm.

As Eric hit the floor the deliveryman was on him instantly, kicking at the weapon—taking no chances—having been forewarned of the incredible danger that this man represented. His kick missed the gun, and Eric fired again, only to hit the man's leg—the fleshy outer part of his thigh, passing through, yet missing the femoral artery—and though it hurt like hell, he stood his ground. This time the aim with his foot was better, pinning the weapon to the ground, smashing Eric's wrist and hand onto the floor.

The man knew nothing of the Committee or Arthur, but had been given a succinct message to deliver.

"Your benefactor sends his greetings."

With that he placed the gun four inches from Eric's forehead, and hesitated only long enough to see if there was a reply. Surprisingly, Eric only smiled.

In the background Ella sang "I'll Be Seeing You".

The silencer let loose with a spit.

Eric saw only darkness.

* * *

During his lifetime—after the age of 25 years, Eric Suskind became invisible. The building he lived in was bought in the name of a trust, as were his cars—with no connection back to him, as the trusts, which handled these items, were handled in the financial sanctuary known as the banks of the Grand Caymans.

He had nothing shown with his correct name—no checking account, no credit cards, and no cars registered. Insofar as the world was concerned, he had dropped off the face of the planet.

Even private communications were done electronically and in code, therefore untraceable. He was able to do this through the help of one person—someone from many years ago.

No one knew of Eric except Arthur and a now obscure attorney operating under a false name, who lived in Sundance, Wyoming, located in Crook County, the north east region of that state.

This particular attorney had enjoyed enormous power and status in New York—and was, before Eric became the Committee's File #3, a target for Eric Suskind—Eric's first target.

Through the years, as his reputation for trial litigation grew, the attorney became embroiled quite by accident, defending mobsters—and had successfully done so for eleven years. Each successive case brought yet another—he was a legend in his profession. He didn't lose and he was their 'go to' man—no matter how guilty. Because of his enormous clout with judges, every one of the defendants asked for a trial by judge, not by jury.

Year number 12 became very unlucky for him. As his fame and wealth grew, his work and trial prep had become sloppy—he was drinking daily and whoring at night—so much so that judges would privately admonish him—and even allow for his 'failings' as he was a magnetic and charming character. He had won his last sixteen cases through the graces of their benevolence and former respect.

Judge Michael Nichols' Chamber

The judge walked into his chamber, and in total disgust, threw his papers in the air. The attorney, John Brickham, knew what was coming—even though he had 'drunk' his lunch, and was unsteady on his feet.

"John, I've given you a pass on your last three cases that you've brought before me—but you're not even close to a real defense for this man. He had motive and opportunity—most important, no alibi. If I 'walk' this guy, I'll be thrown off the bench."

John was in no position to defend himself—it was true.

"What'll they do to you if I send this guy up for 15 years, the minimum, by the way?"

The thought of a mob boss going to jail because of

his failure sobered John in moments.

"They'll probably kill me, Mike."

"You know, John, we've played poker enough that I know you're not bluffing—this is most likely true—but sure enough, and you know I love you like a brother, but my hands are tied—you've done this to yourself. Maybe we can get you some protection."

Those were the last words John remembered until he heard the verdict of the trial, pronounced: 'Guilty as charged.'

The gavel sounded very much like a guillotine falling onto his neck to the attorney—and he was right.

A younger Eric, with the promise of $50,000 for his first hit, appeared in the attorney's home three weeks later, to the day. Even though it was his first job, he decided that this job, especially given the circumstances, called for misdirection. He had decided to stage a robbery. The attorney lived very well, and in an incredibly swank neighborhood.

Eric, who had scouted the job for three weeks, parked about a mile away with the knowledge that there was access through enormous unfenced back yards, sporting heavy ground cover and trees—making the getaway an easy chore. A quick in, hit the victim with poorly placed shots, making it look like a panic shooting, after having been walked in on—and then a ransack—the job would be finished.

He had not counted on one thing—a sober, charismatic, highly intelligent attorney sitting in his den with two glasses and a bottle of Scotch on the table.

John heard the door open—it was done without a 'latter day' Eric's expertise. In his defense, he expected a drunken John to be sprawled on the couch or lying across the bed—a soft touch.

"Come on in," came the call from the wood paneled

den. "What's your pleasure?"

Eric was young, unprepared and frankly stunned.

John smiled at him—a 100-watt smile that had won over several dozens of juries in days gone by, and Eric, though cautious, was no match for a man like John, at this point in his career. "John Brickham Esquire, as we 'barristers' like to say." Again with the smile.

"You're here to make me account for Scorchenso . . . yes?"

Not knowing what to do with such a straightforward approach, Eric admitted it.

"Yes", he said, holding the gun more casually than the modern day Eric. "You failed the family, and they think . . ."

"I should pay."

Eric hesitated. "Yes . . . yeah."

"You know, I've been waiting up all night, sleeping days since the last trial . . . expecting you each night . . . frankly, I'm surprised they waited three weeks."

Eric was completely frank with his 'hit'. "Well, it's my first job and I told them it would take a month—they didn't like it, especially Lucco—he was . . . ."

"Lucco's a hothead. But you know what? I deserve it. I've been skating for two years now—living off a reputation that was both earned and deserved—then I started with the women and booze, and trust me, either one will do it."

Eric just stood—fascinated by the guts and honesty of the man—as well as his complete candor.

"Sit, really, it's not a trick, relax before you do your job—have a farewell drink with me. You know, I've lost my wife to a golf instructor who makes less than one tenth what I make, but looks like that actor from, uh, what was it . . . Butch Cassidy?" The attorney looked almost pathetically sad at this memory.

Eric didn't answer.

"Yeah, Redford I guess. Lucky bastard. He gets my wife AND money. But, the house is worth two million, it's paid for and a life insurance policy for ten times that. He'll be fucking my wife and spending my money while bugs are eating my flesh. That doesn't seem right does it?"

Eric, young and more malleable, nodded in full agreement—he, as did the attorney, believed that life offers empirical truths and fairness.

John, the world-class negotiator, picked up a bottle of very old Scotch, poured Eric three fingers, then the same for himself, and began to bargain for his life, in a slow and cleverly calculated 'build', much the same technique as he would use in a 'closing' statement, in court.

Eric, wise beyond his years, knew that there was something special here—maybe it was the naiveté of a first job—but more likely it was John's brilliance that turned the events into a deal that would last beyond Eric's life.

In the end John moved to Sundance, Wyoming— was ultimately financed partially by Eric's successes— while a very toasty body with the 'correct' dental work, found in a flaming Mercedes was passed off to all concerned as John—satisfying the 'family' and endowing Eric with a lifetime colleague—one who would guide and counsel him—where to put his money, how to invest—all the pieces necessary to complete Eric the Assassin's virtually perfect persona.

Now, at the moment of Eric's death—John had one trip to make—to deliver some very important paperwork to two people whom he had never met—but gave more meaning to Eric's existence.

None of the previous preparations would have made any difference had Eric not only been compulsive about the who, what and where, and employers of each of his contracts. All this damning and important information verified each of Eric's actions with enormous clarity—details of each 'hit' that only the assassin could possibly know. It also chronicled the funds paid, and how—something harder to hide than most other items, in spite of the fact that most Caribbean banks do not exchange information or divulge any data to the U. S. Government.

This journal could help to serve as the 'only possible shield from the Committee' to the people who had avoided Eric's expertise—and this sharing of information was homage to their cunning—this truly was, a final show of respect.

John, in his own clever way and after much research, located the two through the trail of check cashing—in what became a cross continent chase, finding them in the foothills of the Smokey Mountains of Tennessee—Gatlinburg.

* * *

Jack and Kelsey sat in the hot tub, oblivious to everything but the beautiful spring weather. It was clear though somewhat cool—the tub was hot and bubbly. They laughed about the body politic, the world in general, and the local news—all was fair game in their transient world—cause for moving each month. To Jack, even though they had a great deal of money, it was, in many ways similar to his existence with Sarah—though he would never say that to Kelsey.

Behind them, they heard footsteps coming from the road. It was the attorney, John Brickham.

At first they were alarmed, as John approached silently.

"Jack?" John asked in a more than gentle voice.

He had been Blanchard so long, his real first name sounded frightening.

"Who is it?" he asked suspiciously.

"I am a friend and representative of someone who is recently deceased."

Kelsey's ears immediately pricked. "Nelson?" she asked.

"No, Eric Suskind."

Jack balked, "I'd hardly consider Eric . . ."

"There's more to know about Eric, sir."

Jack stood his ground. "There'd have to be for me to be considered someone that he'd want to communicate with."

"Well, to get directly to the point, Eric died about two weeks ago, and forwarded this information to Jack and a Ms. Kelsey Richmond. "Now I am quoting him, 'for the purpose of freeing them from the shackles of The Committee'."

Kelsey simply looked at the envelope with unfettered hope, Jack with dread and suspicion.

After an updating, they both had a 'clearer' picture of Eric, the Assassin.

"He really is giving this to *us?*" Kelsey asked.

John smiled, realizing that her lack of trust was attributable to inexperience, though she had every right to be suspicious.

"Yes, it's in his records that he 'engaged you twice' and that neither time was successful."

Jack thought about it, "He tried to kill us twice and failed both times." Kelsey understood, and nodded.

John looked at Jack. "Well, Sir, I'd say that your statement is somewhat skewed from my client's perspective—yet useful for this private conversation."

After updating Eric's professional resume and the totality of his actions, and fairly intense discussions of his past, everyone agreed that accepting Eric's folder was in the 'best interest' of all concerned.

The irony that Eric's information indicted the Committee, just as Arthur's story had, allowing him to leverage his way back in as their, once again Director, was not lost on Jack or Kelsey.

For the first time since the day Jack and Kelsey met Arthur—they both felt relief.

97

Seattle Two Weeks Prior

Though not as dangerous to Arthur—Nelson represented the link that Jack and Kelsey had to the world, therefore, completed the trace back to the Committee, making his very existence unacceptable.

Arthur's plan was to eliminate all ties to the dreadful 'stroke' days, and though he held great respect for the two, he recognized that they would by necessity be next to meet a tragic end—very shortly after Nelson.

After moving back from the Caribbean Nelson had settled into his old habits of wine and pretzels for dinner while watching sports. Without the daily swimming routine, his body had changed somewhat from the rather trim figure in the Caribbean to something more akin to the previous look—plain and simple he was again, out of shape—not that it would have mattered. At his age and having had a gunshot wound through his chest, very little suspicion could be gleaned from a myocardial infarction—thereby virtually eliminating the likelihood of an autopsy. People in better shape than he died every day for lesser reasons than his medical history would portend.

The Mariner's game had just started and he had settled in for the night, his article as Editor Emeritus for the Post, finished sometime earlier—he could now afford the luxury of drinking his beloved Silver Oaks, enjoy the game, fall asleep on the couch, then stumble to bed at 4:00am. This was a well-rehearsed routine—except tonight there was one important variable.

Distracted by the game, he did not notice the tiny hole in the aluminum seal of the wine cork. This tiny hole allowed for the dispensing of a killing dose of 'Dead Man's Bells' also known as 'Witches Gloves'. This unusually beautiful flower, not unlike those that would surround his casket soon, was, ironically, the source for the deadly overdose of Digitalis. When ingested in proper doses it was helpful to stabilize the heart rate—in this instance, the 'additional' digitalis he would be taking in, multiplying his normal daily dose allowed the drug to become toxic to his system.

Two glasses into the bottle, he became nauseous, and thought incorrectly that he was coming down with a stomach virus. As he stood to walk into the bathroom, he stumbled dizzily—*wow, this is sudden.*

He walked slowly and carefully into his bathroom to sit near his toilet, 'just in case.' As he became more nauseated, he slumped to the floor at the commode.

This is where he was found, three days later.

The police pronounced it a heart attack instantly—depriving him of an autopsy, and the world, of the news that he had been murdered.

Arthur laughed maniacally at the news of the deaths of both Eric and Nelson—his targets, finally shrinking.

He paused and recounted his life's work. He had been, for many years, the most powerful man in the world—virtually unknown to the public, but nonetheless the most powerful.

Who could have guessed that a young man of his

background, his heritage, his *ethnicity*, could have ruled the planet—after all, he was born just 48 years and a few months after a momentous date in history. A date which forever changed the lives of many Americans—a date on which one of his own personal heroes—a man for whom he had patterned much of his life, *released Arthur's ancestors from slavery*. That man was the 16th president, Abraham Lincoln.

98

St. Augustine, Florida
Three Months Later

As Kelsey stood on the Lion's Head Bridge, which connected the old city to the beachfront, she drank in the sun as it cast a faded yellow onto the whole area. She gazed down on the restaurants along Matanzas Boulevard, the street that separated the beautiful old city from the inland bay. Horse drawn carriages lined up in front of the restaurants; ready to take the tourists on a scenic view of America's oldest city. She then looked out on the water, at the boats in the marina, thinking this to be the most beautiful city she had ever seen.

They had been here for three months, since having met John Brickham, and she had begun to adjust to the loss of Phillip. Nelson's loss though, left her despondent—her life now unthinkable—all that she had had just a few short months ago, the people she loved, the city she craved—were all part of her past now. Her vision of the world had changed from a richly colored Monet to a poorly conceived watercolor.

Her stomach rolled each time she thought of Nelson—sure that somehow Arthur was at the root of his death—but there was nothing she could hang her 'blame' on.

Jack was no help—he even sided with the 'heart at-tack' theory. He had told her, "Kelsey a man with Nelson's history—the gunshot, the medications—he was a prime candidate for a heart attack."

She would never accept that as fact—regardless. At night, as Jack would sleep, she lay awake recalling the times they spent together—the 'breaks' Nelson had given her in her darkest moments. It was as if she had lost her father. She cried endlessly, but was careful to not let Jack see or hear her.

And though he was inwardly suspicious of Nelson's death, Jack would never admit it to Kelsey. Given their status as 'fugitives from the Committee' they couldn't go to Seattle and 'press for an autopsy'. They were unable to seek justice. Again the omnipotent Committee prevailed. She knew though, that time would heal those wounds. If it weren't for her first true love, Jack, she could not have fought through this moment in her life.

During their months together, he had also been her life support to help her stop her addictions to the power-ful drugs—the Valium, the amphetamines—he was instru-mental in her well-being, in so many ways—she adored him for all of it. She was finally healing.

He approached from across the street. She watched him, smiling. He was fit and trim, had a newly acquired tan, and was looking terrific with his newfound taste in stylish clothing.

"Hey, Beautiful—how about a date?" he yelled.

"Fitty dollah—maka you so happy," she kidded.

He kissed her.

"I'm already happy."

"Me, too, baby."

"So . . . when do we use our information?" Jack

asked.

"Well, I don't know, it's so carefully documented—and so damning that we can send one copied page to John, then have him, quietly, secretly, send it to Arthur. That'll do the trick—especially when we explain the, 'in the event of our death' clause that it all goes public."

Jack, looking into the water, watching the catfish scurrying about for food, nodded. "Also, I am thinking we need a raise."

Kelsey looked at him questioningly. "A raise?"

"Sure, five million for what we did—and more important, what we *can do* . . . that makes us very valuable to Arthur—*alive*."

Kelsey nodded—then turned to watch at the fish as they searched for morsels—her shoulders drooped barely, as she truly and unequivocally relaxed for the first time since this all began.

She laid her head on his shoulder.

Author's Bio

L. R. Staples was born in Louisville, Kentucky, and now lives in Palm Coast, Florida with his significant other, Pat Scott. He has three children, girls, she has two boys.

The author enjoyed a diverse career in Sales and Marketing for more than thirty years, but is now retired writing full time. Hobbies include music, movies and reading, bicycling, walking and swimming.

He currently has two books published, 'In Plain Sight—The Committee' and 'Richard Dix Private Detective.'